streetlight people

ALSO BY
Charlene Thomas

Seton Girls

It's You Every Time

streetlight
people

CHARLENE THOMAS

DUTTON BOOKS

CONTENT NOTICE:

This book is a work of fiction, but it depicts many real issues, including addiction, classism, bullying, racism, and stalking.

THE LIBRARY OF CONGRESS HAS CATALOGED THE HARDCOVER EDITION AS FOLLOWS:

Names: Thomas, Charlene (Charlene Verdelle), author. | Title: Streetlight People / by Charlene Thomas. | Description: New York: Dutton Books, 2024. | Audience: Ages 14 and up. | Audience: Grades 10-12. | Summary: When have-not teen Kady uses her newfound abilities to replicate a blissful summer with her have-lot boyfriend Nik, she unwittingly reveals her small town of Streetlight's biggest secret. | Identifiers: LCCN 2023043793 (print) | LCCN 2023043794 (ebook) | ISBN 9780593618868 (hardcover) | ISBN 9780593618875 (ebook) | Subjects: CYAC: Ability—Fiction. | Secrets—Fiction. | Social classes—Fiction. | Love—Fiction. | City and town life—Fiction. | African Americans—Fiction. | LCGFT: Novels. | Classification: LCC PZ7.1.T4483 Pe 2024 (print) | LCC PZ7.1.T4483 (ebook) | DDC [Fic]—dc23

LC record available at https://lccn.loc.gov/2023043793
LC ebook record available at https://lccn.loc.gov/2023043794

First published by Dutton Books, 2024
First paperback edition published 2025

Manufactured in the United States of America
LSCC

ISBN 9780593618882
1st Printing

The authorized representative in the EU for product safety and compliance is Penguin Random House Ireland, Morrison Chambers, 32 Nassau Street, Dublin D02 YH68, Ireland, https://eu-contact.penguin.ie.

For anyone who's ever felt like time was moving faster
    Or slower
        Or backward
            Or not at all . . .

                    Maybe you were right.

streetlight people

November 1968

The Boys sat in the chapel with cold beers in their hands.

The chapel stood on the other side of campus, gray stone with stained glass windows. There was nothing around it but trees and the path that would lead back to Iverson's main campus. Vast like a college, even though it wasn't.

The setting sun cast beams of light onto the altar where Davey, Mike, and James sat with their beers. Brian lounged in the pulpit. Others kicked back in the pews. A bunch of high school boys who looked identical in their khakis, sweater vests, and navy blazers. Classmates, yes. Best friends, even more so. But brothers, most importantly, whether they liked it or not. A pact they'd made like their fathers before them: that even in Iverson's tiny world, they'd create a world that was smaller. One that only belonged to them. The IV Boys.

"How can you say that with a straight face?" Greg Jack-Laurence didn't have to speak up to be loud. His heavy voice carried to every corner of the chapel. Preacher-like.

The other Boys sucked from their beers, waiting for someone to answer.

They'd been arguing for days now, about what the IVs would become. For decades, it hadn't been a question. They were the most exclusive social club in Streetlight. They threw the best parties, had the best connections, owned every square inch of this town. An oasis they'd created for themselves—generation after generation.

And, in this moment, they were more powerful than they'd ever been. They all believed that. Their eyes twinkled when they thought about what that meant for tomorrow, and the next day, and the next year, and forever. Their big plans for their tiny town. All the Boys except one.

They waited in the old chapel, full of wood that creaked and popped, for someone to answer Greg's question: *How can you say that with a straight face?*

It was James Hendricks who finally said something. Lately, it always was. He swigged from his bottle and stared down at Greg in the pews from his place at the altar. "Which part?" he asked dryly.

Greg leaned forward on his knees, his beer on the floor next to his feet. He clasped his hands in a giant fist, the same stance he took in debates over football or movies or anything he was sure he'd win. James hated it. He'd hated it for years.

Slowly, Greg said, "You really think the entire point of having this kind of power is to just . . . keep it all here?" He frowned and kicked the cooler in front of him, looking around their little chapel like that's all it ever was—a little chapel filled with little Boys. "Just . . . keep on being kings exactly where we are?"

James shrugged, smirked, swigged. "Yeah." The others chuckled.

Greg stayed in position, hunched over his knees. "You know there's an entire world out there, right?"

"It's not my job to save the world," James insisted, daring Greg to blink first. "I've got family right here. I've got brothers in this room. *That's* my job. It's supposed to be yours, too."

"It's a bullshit job," Greg muttered.

"Come again?" James's eyes narrowed.

"*It's a bullshit job,*" Greg repeated. "I mean, how can you think that this is actually what life is all about? Fighting for a bunch of guys who don't even need saving? There's a movement going on out there, man." Greg held his arm out to the heavy wooden door. "And we've got power dripping from our fingertips right now. What's the point if we don't use it to change something? What the hell are we doing, otherwise?"

"*We're doing exactly what we were meant to do,*" James snapped. "We're doing what the guys before us did for us. The IVs were never created to save the world, and I'm not gonna sit here trying to explain that shit to you for the fiftieth time. Join the Peace Corps if that's what you want. We're here to protect what *we've* built, exactly where we are. And that's what we're gonna do."

A supportive murmur rippled through the chapel, Boys who agreed with James or were too afraid to admit they didn't. It was safer that way, keeping things how they'd always been. Their small town, their small school, their small club. Everything they could ever want, in the palms of their hands. IVs protecting IVs, since 1923.

Greg had argued with them for days. He showed them headlines. He regurgitated facts. He called upon their egos—did they want the world to know the IVs, or just the same old people in the same old place? But none of it worked; none of them cared. And the anger—that had once been loud, fiery, boiling—had settled in now. Into something that just existed, that Greg accepted.

"Well, I'm not gonna do what you guys are gonna do," Greg answered.

But it didn't work that way, not in groups like theirs.

James squinted. "What'd you say?"

"I'm not doing it," Greg repeated. "I'm not gonna close my eyes and pretend like we need each other more than the world needs what we have. You guys have at it, but I'm not doing that."

The air thickened as the Boys watched Greg stand and walk up the aisle. They nudged each other, sat up straighter. Should somebody say something? But there was nothing to say. They wouldn't change, and neither would he.

James called after him, eyes glaring and hands just barely shaking. "This doesn't get to be all about you, Jack-Laurence."

"Tell me about it," Greg answered.

"Hey." James's voice was sharp as he stood and walked over to where Greg had been sitting.

Greg stopped at the end of the aisle, but he didn't turn around. So James kicked the cooler just enough to make the ice slosh, enough to make Greg flinch. "You don't get to choose when you're with us or against us. Do what you want, but there's no in-between. Either you always are, or you never were."

James walked back to the altar and sat, and the room relaxed, because they knew Greg would turn around, go back to his pew, finish his beer. Nothing was better than the IVs. No one left. No one quit.

Until the day Greg Jack-Laurence slid his hands into his pockets, pressed his shoulder against the chapel door, and let it swing shut behind him.

TODAY

Life starts all over again when it gets crisp in the fall.
—F. SCOTT FITZGERALD, *THE GREAT GATSBY*

Kady
Sunday, October 25

Someone's following me.

I don't turn around, but I feel them there, watching. Stepping when I do and breathing the same crisp air. From the corner of my eye, I see a shadow slant with mine—stretched extra tall under the morning sun.

A car taps its horn, and I veer from the middle of the road to the right side, the way we've been trained in the neighborhoods with no sidewalks. The car is an old Volvo, and the driver waves as she passes. I don't actually know her, but Streetlight is small. She wouldn't just drive off if some guy behind me had an axe. I don't think.

I walk a little faster.

The shopping bag on my shoulder starts to sound like a pony trotting, stuffed with all this empty Tupperware that Owen stole from Mom. I wish I'd been at his apartment picking up something sharper, like knives.

Knives?

The shadow speeds up, too, steps landing a half second later than mine, every time. Owen has me by sixty pounds, but if I get a kick in behind his knees, I can still bring him down. *I'll do it with this perv, too. Easy.* My skin gets hot.

I reach the busy cross street, where there's a stop sign for people going north and south but not for the ones going east and west. I have to wait for a break in the traffic, but the shadow keeps coming.

Over my head, birds sing, flitting from one tree to the next. The branches shake, and the leaves fall to the ground in a blinding gust of oranges and yellows and reds.

I wonder if anything else looks prettiest just before it dies.

The shadow stops so close behind me that it's not a shadow anymore, it's real. Real breaths. Real warmth. My heart's beating so hard that I'm trembling. Bad things don't usually happen in Streetlight. But when they do, they happen here—on our side.

I start to slide out my right leg. Ready to leave this monster on the ground like roadkill.

But before I can, arms are around my waist, and just as quickly as I tense, I let them hug me.

Nik.

I smile as I watch the passing traffic, and every muscle in my body melts. "I hate you."

His strong arms slide from my hips to around my neck. He brushes my waist-length braids away from my face and kisses my cheek. I feel the smile on his lips, and I hear it in his voice. "That's kind of harsh."

I spin around and face him, his smooth, brown skin beaming in the sunlight; the dimple on the side of his mouth is even deeper now that he's chuckling. He pushes his fingers through his jet-black hair, perfect like a Ken doll.

I stomp on his foot, and he yanks it back and laughs.

"You scared me!"

"What are you scared about?" He pulls me in again.

I don't know, to be honest, why my blood is ice and my heart still hasn't slowed down. Nik and I have been sharing our locations since we started dating three years ago. We've been surprising each other our entire relationship. But he left for college at the end of August, and, for the next four years, he doesn't live here anymore. So maybe that's what it is. It's weird, all of a sudden. Being followed.

"You didn't tell me you were coming home," I argue. "*And* you never walk anywhere."

He makes a face. "I walk, Kades."

I laugh and say, "*You do not,*" as he spins me back around now that it's safe to cross. His parents gave him a Range Rover for graduation, and he's barely taken four steps since. I've seen him roll down the driveway just to get the mail.

He rests his hands on my shoulders as he guides me across the street.

"Really? I didn't walk this summer?" he asks when we reach the other side. He stays behind me as he slips his fingers into the front pockets of my jeans, and he rests his chin on my shoulder, and his breath smells like Colgate. "With you? As far as we could go? All night? Too many times to count?"

The memory makes me warm and cracks my heart at the same time. That was different. He was leaving. We had to make every day last.

But I tell him, "Yeah, you did walk this summer."

The time goes by so fast now.

We locked ourselves in his room for as long as we could when we got to his house, tucked under blankets while his twin little sisters lurked mischievously in the hallway. I crawled on top of him and squeezed his cheeks while I called him a freaking loser for coming home just for laundry. For handing a whole basket of linens to their housekeeper because "washing bedding isn't like normal clothes."

"No one knows how to do that," he insisted. "Do you know how to do that?"

"I've been washing all my own stuff since I was ten."

At first, he sucked his teeth and waited for me to tell him the truth. But when he realized that *was* the truth, he slid his hands onto my thighs and said through mushed-up cheeks, "Well, you're everything."

But now the sun is setting, and we've been sitting on his brick front steps for the past five minutes, trying to say goodbye. His friends already texted. They'll be here to pick him up any minute.

Nik kisses me anyway. Slow and deep until I feel it in my stomach. I always knew he'd leave me here one day—the curse of dating a boy who's one year older and lives on this side of town—but I never knew I could want him more than I already did. That that feeling could somehow get even bigger, until it wasn't just a part of me but it *was* me.

He tugs me closer. "I'm gonna miss you."

"I'm gonna miss you, too," I tell him. And while he kisses my ear, and I can feel how much he means it, I ask, "Have you thought any more about the ball?"

His lips go still, and so does my breath. *The ball* is never a casual conversation. It hovers over our relationship like a cloud—sometimes light and wispy, sometimes dark and brooding, but always, always there.

He runs his thumbs along my cheeks. His brown eyes, like always, are so reasonable and calm. Amazing when I don't want to worry and *so annoying* when I want to be pissed.

I brace myself for the latter. Again.

"Yeah, I have." He nods and keeps my face in his hands. "Maybe this year."

I blink. He's never said "maybe." He's said, "You know we can only invite Iverson kids." He's said, "You know I can't change the rules." But he's never, ever said anything close to "maybe."

Before I can kiss him all over and demand to see the birthmark next to his armpit so I know it's really him, an all-black BMW pulls up to the bottom of the driveway. And now it really is time to say goodbye.

Nik hugs me one more time. It only takes a second, but Hendricks is already calling at us in his typical unimpressed voice. "Wrap it up, chief."

He's standing on the driver's side, his arm resting on the roof. It's Sunday, and all they did today was come back to Streetlight for fresh underwear, but he's still in a pullover with a lime-green polo underneath like he's about to have lunch at the golf course they own. They used to own way more, generations ago, but they sold a bunch of land to their other rich friends and only kept the big stuff for themselves. Like the apartments and the car dealership and the bank.

He used to make me cringe, the way he so effectively doesn't give a shit about anything, and how the stench of his family's money oozes from his pores. But he and Nik have been friends for so long that I'm used to the smell now.

Nik stands up, swinging his laundry over his shoulder while I grab my bag of Tupperware. He offers me his hand, and I take it as we walk through the grass to the car. Hendricks raps his knuckles on the roof at the same time that the passenger's-side window rolls down.

Saige Alexander. It's never a surprise when she's around—it's been the three of them forever. The kind of forever that's equipped with baby-picture proof and Instagram feeds that date back to eighth grade. She was the first girl Nik ever kissed. And even though they swear *it doesn't matter*, stuff like that always kind of matters.

Saige smiles and slides her sunglasses onto her head, pushing back her long brown hair.

"Hey, Kady," she says sweetly.

"Hi," I answer.

Nik tells Hendricks, "We pit-stop at her place and then get on the road?"

"No room," he answers, just as I start to tell Nik I'll walk.

I glance at Hendricks as he shrugs like *It is what it is*. Impressively dickish behavior. Even for him.

Nik insists, "You can make room."

"What do you mean there's no room?" Saige asks on top of him.

"All that shit he has? And I've got your whole closet in the trunk." The words are meant for Saige but Hendricks watches me as he says them, a stare that leaves my throat dry.

Saige smiles like he's such a baby. "It's a five-minute ride."

"No room," Hendricks concludes, sitting back in the driver's seat.

Nik frowns. "Are you kidding?" he asks through Saige's open window. "What's the matter with you?"

But I brush it off like I always do, so Hendricks can't point at my reaction, nudge Nik when I'm not around, and say, *See?*

"It's fine, really. I'll walk. I want to."

Nik's annoyed, but he's also not gonna start a fight, so he kisses me a final time, whispers that he'll call me, and throws his stuff in the back seat. Barnes College is only an hour away, and he'll be fine by the time they get back. They never stay mad at each other, no matter who started it or what it's about.

Saige waves at me as they pull off. Nik presses his fingers against the back window, and I blow him a sad kiss as Hendricks takes him away.

It sucks. But he'll come back. He always does. Whenever he has sheets to wash, or he misses me, or the IVs need him back in town.

Kady
Friday, October 30

"Shouldn't all these people just . . . get off the plane?" Shawn argues, studying the giant screen as he analyzes *Final Destination*. "Like, if some dude started completely losing his shit and saying the plane was gonna blow up, wouldn't you just . . ." He frowns. "Risk the change fee and get off?"

I smile to myself as the world around us screams, covers their eyes, laughs in the aftermath of another jump scare. "Yeah, but that's the point. Whether you stay on or you get off, you're still screwed." I grab another handful of popcorn from the bucket between us.

Under the night sky, the movie flickers on Shawn's pale skin. Whites and blues and the occasional red, whenever there's blood. "In a movie, yeah." He stares at the screen, hating this premise for the millionth time.

"You don't believe they pissed off fate?" I pop a kernel into my mouth.

His Coke fizzes as he twists the cap. "I *believe* that if we're on a plane and someone starts yelling about a bomb, our asses are getting off."

"So we can get mutilated by a garbage disposal or electrocuted by a garage door instead?"

He turns to me in his backward white baseball cap, a twist of brown hair licking his forehead. He's squinting like I just asked him where babies come from. "You think we won't make it, but *these kids* make it?" He holds his arm out to the movie and starts laughing now that I am. "We'll be fine."

The Drive-In is packed for day six of our annual Halloween movie marathon. People like Shawn and me are on the lawn, stretched out on blankets. And people like the Iverson kids are in the gravel lot behind us, in their fancy cars. It's not mandated separation, or like Mom and Dad meant for it to be that way when they started leasing this land from the Wilshires and opened The Drive-In back when Owen was a baby. But that's Streetlight. Two populations, close but not touching. Friendly but not friends. The Have-Lots and the Have-Nots.

Except for when it comes to Nik and me.

That's my favorite thing about how we met—that it was *here*. That Nik had lived in Streetlight his whole life, too, and he knew what it was to like a girl on the lawn. To see her from the front seat of his friend's car and decide he had to talk to her. To get out before we'd even gotten to the college scenes in *Love & Basketball* and walk over to her blanket to ask if he could sit. He knew what I was, and what he was, and where we were. But he sat down anyway.

My phone vibrates next to me, and the whole blanket trembles. "Em?" Shawn assumes, eyes on the movie.

"Yes," I tell him, and put my phone to my ear. "Hi."

"Hi," she chirps. "I'm here. Can I have a light?"

"Yes, ma'am." I hang up and tell Shawn, "She's here."

He nods and pulls his phone out of his pocket, turns on his flashlight, and holds it in the air a moment after I do the same with mine.

Em's heading toward us now, hopping over stretched-out legs and blankets. I kiss in her direction. Her hands are full, so she catches it in her mouth and swallows.

When she reaches us, she sets two giant paper bags on the blanket like payment. "Thanks for lighting my way."

"Always," I promise.

"Wow," Shawn says. "You came stacked."

"Did you walk with all this?" I reach for one of the bags. They're from The Spot, Em's family's fast-casual restaurant designed to be the food representation of their own heritage: Filipino, Mexican, and American.

"No," she says lightly, as the three of us start to unpack dinner. "Milo picked me up on his way home from the library."

"We stan an academic boyfriend," Shawn declares.

"He said to tell you guys hi. He also says he and Owen are really struggling without their Tupperware."

"Because they literally use it like dishes," I insist. "They eat cereal out of it."

"Really?" Shawn frowns as he considers it. "Huh."

"That's gonna be us one day." Em smiles as she folds up the empty bags. "In our first apartment. Broke. Stealing from Kady and O's parents."

For a second, we admire our free feast. Peanut chicken quesadillas, garlic deep-fried rice balls, sticky adobo wings, spiced fries, Shawn's boba tea. The kind of food that fixes problems that you never knew you had.

Em hands us each a napkin and declares, "Bon appétit."

We dig in, our first bites sticky and greasy and warm. I lick adobo sauce off my thumb.

"Em, we have a question," I tell her.

Shawn's busy chewing, but he looks at me like, *We do?*

"Yes?" Em sweetly answers.

I reach over her lap to grab a fry. "Can you break fate?"

She smiles. "Because Shawn wants to get off the plane?"

"*Who wouldn't get off the plane?*" he insists, a garlic fried rice ball stuffed into one cheek.

Em giggles and scoops her long, dark hair from the hood of her sweatshirt as she pulls her knees to her chest. "For what it's worth, I really don't think getting off the plane breaks fate." Shawn smirks and nudges me victoriously as she goes on. "Because I actually think you have two fates. The life you'll live if you do one thing and the life you'll live if you do another. I don't think it's this forced existence that happens no matter what. I think you have to choose it. Like . . . fate is the decision." Her big, brown eyes gleam at us in the light from the movie screen. "*The* decision. This predestined moment when you're gonna have to make a choice, no matter what. Because someone stands up and insists there's a bomb on a plane, or . . . I don't know . . . because you choose to believe in yourself or not. And then there's two paths from there. Yes or no. Two fates."

Something about Em glows when she talks about stuff like this, even when the moon isn't full and the stars aren't twinkling like they are tonight. And that's why I always want to ask her about the things that can't be proven. Because even when she's just thinking out loud, wondering and speaking in *maybes*, I know she's right.

"We've got to get you a booth at Spooks," Shawn declares, sipping through his straw. "You're better than every fortune teller act they've got, and you're not even trying."

Em smiles like she always does when he tells her she's good enough for Spooks. Honored, like being highlighted at our little Halloween carnival is the equivalent of being told you sing like Mariah Carey.

"Is Nik coming tomorrow?" To Spooks, she means.

"No." I take a break from stuffing my face. "He has midterms next week, so he's trying to cram." It's sad, when I think about it too much: the way that night was magic for us for the past three years, and now it's just another day I'll do without him.

Em pouts. "I had a dress I wanted to show him."

I smile as she pulls out her phone. She's been searching for a dress for me ever since she heard the update on my walk home from Nik's. That *maybe* I'm going to the ball this year. I'll need something to wear so I can look like them. In the outfits we've never seen but we've imagined for years—midnight-blue tuxedos and gowns dripping in crystals.

She holds her phone out for Shawn and me to see. It's this spaghetti strap, backless, floor-length dress. Silver and glistening. It's stunning, and I swipe through the carousel while Em and Shawn watch over my shoulder, pretending like the angles and the close zooms actually matter. But it's just fantasy, really. A fun one, but still. No way I'd be able to buy this dress, and we all know it. But when we go to the thrift shop instead, the one in the old row house that smells like books, we'll at least have inspiration.

"I can't believe you may finally get to go," Em whispers.

"Yeah," Shawn agrees as I hand Em back her phone. "Are we sure Nik isn't dying?"

"If he is, he better not die before he takes me."

Shawn's cup is in his hand, and I hold his gaze as I lean over and sip from his straw. Shawn hates the ball and The IV Boys and all the made-up rules that keep us spinning right where we are. *The Poison IVs*, he calls them, every now and then. But tonight, he laughs.

"What day is the ball again?" Em asks.

I stop drinking from Shawn's tea. "December nineteenth."

She nods—remembering the date that I can't ever recall telling her—and covers her ears at the same time. I turn to the movie even though I already know why she's doing it. There's a kiss on-screen, and the entire lawn braces for what's coming. The IVs always blare their horns whenever there's a kiss in a movie at The Drive-In.

But tonight, it stays quiet. And the absence of their chaos makes me notice how still it suddenly is. The crickets aren't chirping. There isn't a breeze. It starts to creep me out, and I take a deep breath just to prove I still can.

People on the lawn turn around curiously, but Em turns to me. "Is there an IV meeting tonight?"

I glance at the quiet lot. "I don't know."

"Well, if there is"—Shawn lies back on his elbows—"they should have meetings while we're here more often."

We barely watch the rest of the movie; we've seen it so many times. We eat, and we laugh, and we talk instead—about fate and ball gowns and tomorrow. And even in our tiny town, the three of us on our blanket create a world that's even smaller.

My phone vibrates. A text message from Aaron Johnson. He's our age and is Nik's "blood brother"—the honor that a veteran IV gives to a new one. It basically means he's Nik's butler.

He's also one of the only IV Boys Shawn actually likes.

I open the message, intrigued. I haven't heard from Aaron in weeks.

Hey. Can we talk?

"What's wrong?" Em asks.

I shake my head and fix my face. I write back:

Yeah . . . what's up?

A few seconds later, my phone buzzes again.

Getting out of a meeting in a min. Can we meet here?

If he's getting out of a meeting, then "here" means Iverson. A fifteen-minute walk on the good side of town. I respond:

Yep! See you soon

The movie will be over in five more minutes, and, when it ends, I'll tell Shawn and Em where I'm going. That I can walk by myself, it's fine.

And that the IVs did have a meeting tonight, after all.

When I walk onto Iverson's campus, the Boys are too far away to see but still close enough to hear. Their big laughs ricochet off all the brick and money like a pinball. It's tunnel-y here, especially at night, every path unnecessarily skinny because it's lined with trees and low stone walls. It makes it so sounds bounce, all the time. Birds singing. Rain falling. Even when you whisper, it feels like everyone is listening.

God, I used to spend so much time here with Nik before he graduated. Hanging out with him after IV meetings. Watching his home soccer games against Billingsley, Anderson Prep, and Seton. Hiding under the stone bridge when we were supposed to be in class, but he'd text, begging for a kiss, and that was all the convincing I needed to ditch. That's where the ball always is—on the same side of campus as the stone bridge. It's this event hall they have, a stand-alone building with pillars and a peaked roof. It's not gaudy or anything, just brick with an impressive number of steps out front. But I want to know more than anything what it's like on the inside. What it looks like. What it smells like.

Aaron is waiting where he said he'd be, on the bench next to the campus's main entrance. He smiles, that smirk that always gets me to smirk back. He seems normal, at least. A relief, since that text didn't.

"Yo, KD," he says, standing up and slinging his backpack over his shoulder. It's the very specific way that *he* says it: KD. My initials—Kady Dixon—which also happen to be *my name*. Aaron's brain blew up the first time he realized. "Still stalking the grounds, I see."

I walk his way, down the path that's flanked with two giant stone lions. Iverson's mascot, with eyes that seem to follow you as you pass. "Shut up. You literally begged me to come here."

"I mean, *begged* is a little strong . . ."

"*Pleaded* . . ."

"Asked?" He twists his mouth, gray eyes twinkling. "Pretty sure I just . . . asked. But I know how much you love to listen to those voices in your head." He squeezes me around my shoulders and lets me go.

"How was battle today?" I ask, hugging myself against a breeze that sends leaves scattering across our feet. I've called a school day at Iverson a "battle" for years. It's the intense uniforms: perfectly ironed khakis, polished dark brown shoes, a white button-down, and a blue-and-gray argyle sweater vest. Even when it's a hundred degrees outside. And if you're IV, on top of all that, there's the navy blazer with a patch on the chest—this family-crest-looking thing, like it came straight out of medieval England.

They remind me of soldiers, not because you'd fight a war looking like that, but because it's intimidating as hell.

I only say "battle" to Aaron, though. The other Boys won't think it's funny.

Aaron yawns as he sets down his backpack and shrugs off his blazer. He hands it to me instinctively, now that I've shivered. "Battle was long today," he tells me. "I need a fresh canteen. New socks."

I accept the blazer because I know he won't let me fight it. "Is that why you openly wept until I agreed to come see you?"

He laughs, swings his backpack back over his shoulder. "Yep. Exactly."

I slip my arms into the sleeves. "So, what happened?"

Aaron's smile fades as he slides his hands into his pockets. He glances around his campus, at everything and nothing at the same time. The full moon tints his skin—a little bluer now than brown. Mine, too.

He keeps a clean fade on the sides and around back, with a mini Afro on top. His ears are pierced, but he can't wear his studs while he's at school—dress code. So he stands here now, like himself but a different version. With no studs and no smile and skin that looks just a little bit bruised.

"There's a rumor going around here," he says, nodding at the Iverson buildings. "About us. That we kissed."

"I'm sorry, *what*?" My laugh bounces across campus. "That's ridiculous."

"Yeah." Aaron nods. But he doesn't say he's kidding. He only says, "I know."

His gaze holds mine, this thing he does sometimes. Not just with me, with everyone. Where he looks so closely that you wonder what he sees.

I squint. "Well, who's saying it?"

"Everyone." He takes a tired breath. "All the guys. Look, I told them it's bullshit. Hopefully it's squashed . . . I just wanted you to know. You know? Hear it from me, since stuff travels so fast around here."

"But they should know it's not true. They know I'd never do that to Nik—they know *we'd* never do that to Nik."

I want him to agree, to assure me that most of the Boys reacted like I just did. That they know me by now. Trust me. Are happy about me dating Nik. I want him to clarify that he's only telling me this because it was annoying, not because it's some kind of *problem*.

But he just slides his tongue across his front teeth and answers, "Yep."

I wrap myself tighter in his blazer. "And even though they know that, they're saying it anyway?"

He nods again. "Yep."

I roll my eyes. My braids are buried inside the back of his jacket. I reach my hand behind me and scoop them out. "You did have a long battle today."

Finally, he smiles again and slowly starts to walk. "I'll be alright. Come on, let's get out of here."

I fall into step next to him, down the path back to the road that will take us home. Leaving behind the main buildings that look like castles. Leaving behind the lawn that's so perfect, it could be Astroturf. Leaving behind the fountain with the naked stone boy peeing.

And the lions' eyes . . . I can feel them, watching us as we go.

Aaron
Friday, October 30

The moon. *Almost full but not all the way round. Like a sphere of ice someone took a blowtorch to.*

The road. *Cracked on the right. Enough of an incline to feel it in your ankles but not in your calves. An empty Coke bottle wedged in the drain.*

The air. *Breezy enough to move leaves but not that Coke bottle.*

KD. *Talking a bunch of smack in the middle of all of it.*

She was a few feet ahead of me, walking backward up the middle of the street as we headed to her house from Iverson. We always walked up the middle, especially once the lampposts turned on. They were at least fifty feet apart, bright enough for you to see the next one but not much else. That was why so many houses left their front lights on, but it never helped much. So you walked up the middle of the road, and the cars went slow, and that's how their headlights would find you in time to stop and let you move to the side.

For a town called Streetlight, it was the darkest damn place I'd ever been.

"Give me someone else," KD insisted.

"Impress me first," I answered.

"Are you joking?" she cried. "I sound more like you guys than you guys do."

I smiled. Messing around with KD felt more like being back home than anything else in Streetlight. Besides being with Pops—but he'd started to change, too. Started liking it here.

"Alright," I said with my hands in my pockets. "Hendricks."

She retched. And I laughed, because, around KD, I could. He *was* the kind of dude that made you feel nasty, but you didn't know why. One time, I sent a picture of him to the group chat with the guys back home. Because they'd get it. Because I'd left them back in the real world.

The first thing one of them texted back was: **Why's he gotta look like Rose's brother in Get Out, tho??** 🫣

KD shook off her disgust and got into character. Like the professional smack-talker that she was. She popped the collar on my blazer and finger-combed a few of her braids into her face. She gave her best Hendricks pout and said, "No disrespect to Ben Franklin, the Wright brothers, or Edison, but I'm pretty sure the fact that *my* family basically created the IVs makes us the greatest American inventors of all time."

I howled, and she bent over laughing, too, safe to shit-talk whoever we wanted as long as we were in her neighborhood instead of mine.

"Give me another." She said it right as we passed under one of the lampposts, and I could see on her face how proud she was. Like a little kid. Maybe happy about the impersonation she did, or maybe happy about how much I loved it.

"How about Nik?" I answered.

She drummed her fingertips together, plotting. "Our favorite." Then her eyes lit up, and she flattened the collar on my blazer, pushed her braids back out of her eyes. "Okay, you be me."

"So I can't find my keys?"

"Ha-ha. Come on, be cool." She rolled her shoulders and took a

deep breath before sauntering over. We stopped in the middle of the
street, facing each other. She ran her hand down my cheek, peered into
my eyes. "Oh, Kady . . ."

"*Yo* . . ." I laughed, breaking character already. But she laughed, too.

"You can't be me for *two seconds*? Come on. It'll be the best two
seconds of your life." She stretched her neck and got ready to start
again. "Okay." She stroked my cheek. "Oh, Kady . . ."

"*Oh, Nik,*" I answered, high-pitched and breathy.

"You're the best, prettiest, most perfect girl I've ever known."

"Yeah, of course I am."

A laugh popped out, but she caught it. "And I love you so much.
Do you wanna know how much?"

"I mean, you're gonna tell me anyway, *so* . . ."

"I love you *so much* . . ." She leaned in closer, so her face was an
inch from mine. "That *I'm* gonna take you to the ball this year."

Her eyes shined, black on these unlit roads but dark brown in the
sunlight. I couldn't tell if she was messing around or not, and that
meant I didn't know whether to smile or not. I think I did, halfway.
Enough to take it back if I needed to.

"For real?" I asked.

"Well . . ." She spun away from me and started walking again. I
followed a few steps behind. "He said *maybe* this year. But it was the
way he said maybe." She turned to me. "Like how he says *maybe* he'll
come home this weekend. And then he does."

He doesn't mean it—that's what I wanted to say. Protect her, because I knew how much that dumb ball meant to her. For every one
time I heard her talk about it, Nik probably heard her talk about it ten
times that. And I would have his back—a million percent—if he really
was ready to bring her. If he really had stopped caring about what KD
was—or really, what she wasn't, what she *couldn't be* in their eyes. If

he really didn't care anymore about what those guys had to say or what it would finally *mean*, I'd walk into that ball right next to them. Play third wheel all night.

If Nik was ready this time, I was right there with him.

But I knew he wasn't ready.

"I mean, don't you think I've earned it by now?" She was insisting just as much she was hoping. "I've been playing by your guys' rules for *years*. Always kept it cute at your awful parties. Made sure there were never any bad stories about me floating around Streetlight. Let you guys call me External Venture like it's my actual name. And never talked shit to anyone besides Shawn and Em. Well, and you. But you wouldn't snitch."

"No chance."

"So it's about time." She watched me while she wrung her fingers. "Don't you think?"

"Yeah, KD, no doubt," I promised. "You've been great—you *are* great—it's just . . ." She kept my pace while we walked, so synched up that I couldn't hear the difference between her steps and mine. "What if he just means maybe?"

She looked at me. "Do you say maybe when you mean maybe?"

"Yeah," I admitted.

She nodded to herself, considering the possibility of someone straight up saying what they mean. "Well, when Nik means maybe, he says no." She tugged my blazer tighter around her waist when another breeze blew by. Then she smiled, moving on. "Okay. Give me another one."

I tried to move on, too, while my hands stayed in my pockets, and my left one messed with a loose thread I'd found inside. "Do me."

She turned to me like I just gave her permission to swing a bat in a jewelry store. "You think I can't?"

"Never said that."

"Okay." She watched the road straight ahead, thinking. As we passed a light shining down on us, one popped on in her head. She shoved her hands in the pockets of my blazer. She glanced around her neighborhood, nodding to herself. Taking it in.

I guess I do do that.

"Yeah," she said, in character now. Taking a breath. Looking around. "I'm a Jack-Laurence." She curled her lip, shrugged. "But I'm not *that* kind of Jack-Laurence."

She waited for me to laugh first. It wasn't big, like the one she got for Hendricks, but it came.

"Bravo," I said, and she bowed.

Her house was on the corner, less than a minute away now, and she didn't ask me to give her any more names. We both quieted down, and maybe it was just because it was almost time to say goodbye, but it was still kind of weird. The thing about KD's jokes that made them so good was the same thing that made all good comedy good—that it was based on what she really saw, and what was really true.

Hendricks *was* trash. Nik *was* in love with her. And when Pops married Charlotte Jack-Laurence three and a half years ago, we *did* become part of one of the most powerful families on the East Coast. Like, *for real*. Her cousin, Phil, was such a big-deal investor he'd been featured in the *New York Times*. Twice.

So yeah. I was a Jack-Laurence. But I wasn't *that* kind of Jack-Laurence.

I wondered how KD had meant it. If it was the fact that I never really talked about them when everyone else around here wore their last name like it was their best accessory. Maybe because, on weekends, I still chose my Jordans over some fancy-ass boat shoes. Or maybe it was the fact that she was walking home right now in *my* IV blazer. And Jack-Laurences—the *real* ones—never, ever joined the IVs.

We reached her house—white siding with red shutters, and a front light that was always on. There was no car in the narrow driveway. Her parents were probably still at The Drive-In. It was only nine.

"Do you ever look at the stars and think about how there are a million wishes swirling around up there?" KD said, peering up at the sky. "Em said that to me once."

I'd been looking at the sky, too. It changed every night when you looked at it from the same place. And the change was never big enough to notice day to day, but I'd try to, anyway. It was a giant clock, really. Physical proof that the world was still spinning, even though we were too small to ever feel it.

"What do you think happens once a wish gets granted?" I asked. "You think it stays up there, or it comes back down to earth?"

KD thought about it, head tilted back. "I think it comes back down. Makes room for a new one."

She looked at me, my blazer hitting her mid-thigh, the gold threads in the IV Boys patch glinting in the light. It was the size of a coaster and crammed with so many secret details that not even the guys could point them all out. There were two lions facing each other. A sword and a helmet for the guys who claimed their ancestors were soldiers. Red poppies for the ones with ties to World War I. An *IV* embroidered in the middle and *1923* stitched under that. The year The IV Boys were founded—with Hendricks's family leading the charge.

There was a bunch of other stuff, too. The kind of details that belonged on the back of a dollar bill to make it too hard to pass a counterfeit. But those weren't the ones they quizzed us on before initiation.

"What do you think happens?" she asked me.

To granted wishes, she meant. And I had no idea. But ever since Pops was on his way home and got a flat right outside the Four Seasons in Philly, where Charlotte Jack-Laurence was doing a charity event, and she walked up to see if he was okay, and he asked her if he could buy her a drink, and seven months later we ended up here—I didn't question what was possible anymore.

"I think you could be right," I told her.

She smiled and slid out of my blazer, handing it over by the collar. "I know I've never met them," she said. "But, for the record, I'm willing to bet you're my preferred type of Jack-Laurence."

"Yeah, right." I shrugged my blazer back onto my shoulders. "Probably because I give you my coat whenever you want it."

"No offense," she leaned into my ear and whispered, "but we both know that coat kind of sucks."

I smirked to myself as she walked away, and pulled the collar off my neck so it didn't itch so much. I stayed there while she went to her front door, dug around for her keys, found them. She turned in the doorway and watched me as she said, "Thanks, Aaron."

"Have a good night, KD," I told her, and waited until the door was closed to walk away.

Most of the kids at Iverson would drive to school, but I usually only did that when there was a reason to—like snow or rain, or we needed ice to refill the coolers. Back home, I walked or took the bus or rode my bike everywhere. I only got a car last year because Charlotte insisted. She said my grades were too good and I was too old (sixteen) to not have my own wheels. And I thanked her on repeat and promised she didn't have to do that—but I knew she couldn't help herself. She'd adopt every boy back in Philly and give them a car, too, if she could.

Still. I mainly drove it on weekends. When the guys needed me to.

It'd take me about twenty minutes to get back to my neighborhood on foot, and I slid in my AirPods for the walk. I was in the middle of this podcast one of my boys had sent me—this thing about cryptocurrency. How it was really just this big conspiracy being run by a bunch of rich people so they could build a society that kept everyone else out of it.

Maybe.

Behind me, lights flashed. Twice—so the road ahead went dark and then bright again. A car that needed to pass, that'd probably tapped its horn like common courtesy around town said to do, but I was too into that podcast to hear it, too zoned out to feel it.

I veered to the curb, ready to wave as they passed.

Except they didn't pass.

They crept by slow, and I just looked ahead. Avoiding the eyes that I knew were watching. Curiously, probably. But sometimes suspiciously. *Who's the Black kid dressed like a royal?* they always wanted to know.

I was used to it by now, but my heart still sped up as I picked out the ways I could run if I needed to. Took note of where I was and how far away the nearest bright lights were—a gas station or a store or even a lamppost. Somewhere I could show myself and say *I'm just an IV. I know I don't look like it, but I am.*

I slowly slid my hands out of my pockets, just to make sure things stayed cool.

But then the car, a white Maxima, rolled past, and the shadow of a friendly hand waved at me through the rear window.

Streetlight was a strange fucking place.

I'd talked to Nik one time about how the cars would always take a little too long to pass me. Only when I was dressed like this. When I was walking the in-between—too far from KD's side and not close enough yet to mine. When I could feel them looking at me like they were imagining me, like they didn't get how I could be real.

But Nik had just laughed about it and slapped my shoulder. *So don't walk,* he'd said.

I used to wonder if that was the real reason why Charlotte wanted me to have the car.

I pulled out my AirPods. I needed to pay attention. I knew that by now.

I slid my hands back into my pockets. I played with that thread in the left one. I looked around.

Moon. *Blowtorched.*

Road. *Flat now.*

Air. *Suddenly a little too still.*

white shirt with an unbuttoned flannel on top of that, and an unzipped gray hoodie on top of that.

Behind him, the sky is purple and orange—the sun setting behind wispy clouds. And he's doing that thing again—where, even though he's smiling, he's looking at me so hard that I can't imagine what he sees.

"Okay . . ." I squint at him. "So, at first I thought I was joking, but now I'm not sure."

He laughs. "I slept at home. Just here to escort you to your weird-ass little carnival, that's all."

I cross my arms. "Because you want to, or because you're supposed to?" I get a whiff that he's on an errand. That Nik sent him.

"Can it be both?" Then he thumbs over his shoulder. "We picking up Shawn and Em, or they're meeting us here?" He waits for me to answer, eyebrows raised. Assuming we're all going together, because of course we are.

But I roll my eyes and brush past him instead. "You don't have to keep being such an IV Boy around me, you know." I hop down my steps, and he follows. "You can relax. I'm not gonna tattle to Nik if you don't"—I pluck at his sleeve—"wear fifteen shirts just so I can maybe borrow one."

We're quiet for the next few steps, and I'm pretty sure that's my choice—not his. But even though we aren't talking, it's not silent. It's busy right now—with people getting home from work, dogs on their walks, birds chirping about whatever it is they say to each other before the sun is officially gone. And people drifting to Spooks, just like we are.

Spooks!
Frightening Streetlight Since 1968

Kady

Saturday, October 31

---

49 DAYS BEFORE THE BALL

I stick my hand out my bedroom window one more time. It's forty-nine degrees outside, whatever that means. I wish they'd just tell you. Instead of talking about highs and lows and dew points, they should just be like, *You need a coat. And a hat.*

It's harder in Streetlight lately, too. Because some parts feel ten degrees colder for no good reason at all. Like you wandered into a completely different world, just long enough to notice it. Em says it's energy, what happened in a space before we were ever there. She heard somewhere that good energy feels warmer than bad. "Then why is the calculus classroom always so freaking hot?" Shawn answered at the time.

Regardless, I think forty-nine degrees means I can make it through Spooks in just a hoodie. I push my window shut and leave my bedroom

"Would it make you feel any better if I told you that me being here

There's something strange in the air tonight that makes my skin tingle. Maybe it's all the neon lights that turn this place into an entirely different world, or the new brand of oxygen that tastes like pizza and deep-fried everything. It really is gorgeous, even though there are murderers everywhere. Zombies stumbling through the crowd. Chain saw–wielding monsters lurking behind every other tree. I've never been sure which it is: if Spooks is deceivingly innocent or deceptively horrifying. But I think I've finally decided that it's a little of both.

We get split up at the basketball shoot-out game with the hoop that moves. IVs swooped in and pulled Aaron aside a few minutes ago, and they still have him—talking by a bench a few feet away. We're far enough apart that I can't keep a steady eye on them; people keep passing in the space in between. But whenever I do catch a glimpse, it never looks any better than it did before. Three of them standing on one side and Aaron alone on the other. The smirk Aaron gets when he's being a smart-ass and the sly smiles on their faces because they're *always* smart-asses. The way they haven't stopped looking at one another—Aaron at them and them at Aaron—except for the one time when the crowd clears just enough for me to get a perfect view. And like I have a string connected to the blond one's head, his gaze spins in my direction, and he stares until I don't.

External Venture. I feel their nickname for me like I'm wearing a branded sweatshirt. Nik swears it's a term of endearment, but I know it's really meant to be a reminder. That I'm not a girl like Saige, with a convertible and etiquette training. That I don't go to Iverson.

I gnaw my lip. Maybe they're talking about the rumor.

"Buckets!" Em cheers as the buzzer goes off on Shawn's game. The balls stop rolling toward him, and the hoop slides back to where it belongs. She squeezes his hips from behind. "You're so good at this."

Kady
Saturday, October 31

I stick my hand out my bedroom window one more time. It's forty-nine degrees outside, whatever that means. I wish they'd just tell you. Instead of talking about highs and lows and dew points, they should just be like, *You need a coat. And a hat.*

It's harder in Streetlight lately, too. Because some parts feel ten degrees colder for no good reason at all. Like you wandered into a completely different world, just long enough to notice it. Em says it's energy, what happened in a space before we were ever there. She heard somewhere that good energy feels warmer than bad. "Then why is the calculus classroom always so freaking hot?" Shawn answered at the time.

Regardless, I think forty-nine degrees means I can make it through Spooks in just a hoodie. I push my window shut and leave my bedroom door cracked behind me.

"Keys, phone, money," I mumble to myself as I jog down the steps. I pat myself down one more time on my way out the door, just to be sure that I have everything. I swear, my parents are gonna weld my keys to my forehead if I lock myself out again.

I slam the door behind me and practically face-plant. Aaron, just sitting on my front step.

But Nik had just laughed about it and slapped my shoulder. *So don't walk,* he'd said.

I used to wonder if that was the real reason why Charlotte wanted me to have the car.

I pulled out my AirPods. I needed to pay attention. I knew that by now.

I slid my hands back into my pockets. I played with that thread in the left one. I looked around.

Moon. *Blowtorched.*

Road. *Flat now.*

Air. *Suddenly a little too still.*

He smirks. "Walk much?"

"Did you sleep here last night?"

"Yeah, and can I just say that that patch of grass right there?" He nods to the right as he stands up. "Straight up memory foam."

His studs are back, glinting from each ear. He's in black jeans and a white shirt with an unbuttoned flannel on top of that, and an unzipped gray hoodie on top of that.

Behind him, the sky is purple and orange—the sun setting behind wispy clouds. And he's doing that thing again—where, even though he's smiling, he's looking at me so hard that I can't imagine what he sees.

"Okay . . ." I squint at him. "So, at first I thought I was joking, but now I'm not sure."

He laughs. "I slept at home. Just here to escort you to your weird-ass little carnival, that's all."

I cross my arms. "Because you want to, or because you're supposed to?" I get a whiff that he's on an errand. That Nik sent him.

"Can it be both?" Then he thumbs over his shoulder. "We picking up Shawn and Em, or they're meeting us here?" He waits for me to answer, eyebrows raised. Assuming we're all going together, because of course we are.

But I roll my eyes and brush past him instead. "You don't have to keep being such an IV Boy around me, you know." I hop down my steps, and he follows. "You can relax. I'm not gonna tattle to Nik if you don't"—I pluck at his sleeve—"wear fifteen shirts just so I can maybe borrow one."

We're quiet for the next few steps, and I'm pretty sure that's my choice—not his. But even though we aren't talking, it's not silent. It's busy right now—with people getting home from work, dogs on their walks, birds chirping about whatever it is they say to each other before the sun is officially gone. And people drifting to Spooks, just like we are.

"Would it make you feel any better if I told you that me being here isn't IV shit, just friend shit?" He's watching straight ahead as he asks. But he rocks his shoulder into mine when it takes me a second too long to answer. "Come on . . ."

It does make me feel better, even though I hadn't realized that I *needed* to feel better. Needed to make sure Aaron felt the same way as I did about all the rules we've been following over the past few years. That yeah, they exist. But *our* existence is bigger than that.

"Friend shit?" I repeat, offering him my fist. "Promise?"

And he bumps his fist against mine. "Friend shit. Promise."

We split apart so a car can pass between us. A Kia that lives at the end of the block. We wander back together.

"Hey." I nudge him. "What if *you* got a little blood brother? A baby minion to do all your dirty work for you?" Nik told me once that every IV gets a big blood brother, but not everyone has to take on a little.

He smirks. "I'm good."

"But he could get you cheese balls in a snowstorm."

"Oh, you planned this?"

"You're not feeling even a *little bit* ready to boss someone else around?"

He turns to me, and the last bit of sun shines behind his head like a halo. He smiles, sorry to disappoint. "I could never do that shit to somebody else." And it feels the way it feels sometimes—this heat that starts in my cheeks and grows—when I know he's only finished half a thought.

His gaze drifts back to everything besides me, and for a second, I'm not sure if he's being serious. If he thinks *I'm* being serious. He can't, though. *Duh,* he doesn't have a little blood brother. The same way he doesn't have polos in every color. Or *any* color. Because any of the above would look ridiculous on him.

He knows I get that, right?

"Get my own cheese balls," he defiantly mutters.

We both snort out laughs that start in our throats, watching the road ahead instead of each other. It's funny longer than it should be. But at least he knows it's funny.

"Shawn's at Em's," I tell him once we're breathing normally again. "So we're stopping by there."

He bows and holds his arm out, rolling his wrist. "Lead the way."

He says it like he'd follow me anywhere tonight.

It isn't weird for Shawn or Em when I show up with Aaron. It's like showing up in a dress or with pink nails instead of purple. Unexpected. Different. But still me. Em hugs him and makes plans to split a turkey leg. Shawn smirks and asks if he was too scared of the dark to go to Spooks on his own.

"Nope, not scared," Aaron answers, bear-hugging Shawn so hard that Shawn groans. "Just missed the shit out of you, that's all."

It's only a fifteen-minute walk to the fairgrounds. The closer we get, the busier it gets—the street's so packed with people that we don't even have to make room for cars anymore; everyone knows not to drive this way on Halloween.

There's no entrance fee to get through the front gates—just five dollars per attraction and any tip you might want to give on top of that. So the throng just flows as the pavement turns to gravel, and the giant arched sign over the main entrance—with dozens of light bulbs that hum even louder than the crowd—flashes the same welcome that it does every year.

Spooks!
Frightening Streetlight Since 1968

There's something strange in the air tonight that makes my skin tingle. Maybe it's all the neon lights that turn this place into an entirely different world, or the new brand of oxygen that tastes like pizza and deep-fried everything. It really is gorgeous, even though there are murderers everywhere. Zombies stumbling through the crowd. Chain saw–wielding monsters lurking behind every other tree. I've never been sure which it is: if Spooks is deceivingly innocent or deceptively horrifying. But I think I've finally decided that it's a little of both.

We get split up at the basketball shoot-out game with the hoop that moves. IVs swooped in and pulled Aaron aside a few minutes ago, and they still have him—talking by a bench a few feet away. We're far enough apart that I can't keep a steady eye on them; people keep passing in the space in between. But whenever I do catch a glimpse, it never looks any better than it did before. Three of them standing on one side and Aaron alone on the other. The smirk Aaron gets when he's being a smart-ass and the sly smiles on their faces because they're *always* smart-asses. The way they haven't stopped looking at one another—Aaron at them and them at Aaron—except for the one time when the crowd clears just enough for me to get a perfect view. And like I have a string connected to the blond one's head, his gaze spins in my direction, and he stares until I don't.

External Venture. I feel their nickname for me like I'm wearing a branded sweatshirt. Nik swears it's a term of endearment, but I know it's really meant to be a reminder. That I'm not a girl like Saige, with a convertible and etiquette training. That I don't go to Iverson.

I gnaw my lip. Maybe they're talking about the rumor.

"Buckets!" Em cheers as the buzzer goes off on Shawn's game. The balls stop rolling toward him, and the hoop slides back to where it belongs. She squeezes his hips from behind. "You're so good at this."

Shawn glances at his score: twenty-eight baskets in sixty seconds. He twists his mouth like he could have done better. "Yeah."

"Narcissist," I mumble, loudly enough for him to hear on purpose.

He puts his hand to his chest like it's a compliment. "So sweet."

I laugh, and so does he as the machine starts spitting out his tickets.

"Should we keep playing?" Em asks, and even though she says *we*, it's really just Shawn. He always kills this game. Sometimes he does it with his eyes shut, just to see what happens.

"Up to you guys," Shawn says, studying the prize wall. "Is there anything else you want?"

Em and I both already have a pile of prizes at our feet. Stuffed animals and plastic sunglasses and tacky T-shirts.

"I kind of want that crown . . ." Em admits.

"I want Nemo." I was eyeing him the whole last round, when I wasn't busy trying to eavesdrop on Aaron.

Shawn nods to himself, cracks his neck, and takes out five more dollars. "On it." He hands his money to one of the guys working this game, and, two seconds later, the balls start rolling and the hoop starts moving.

I take a deep breath of this air that's heavy enough to wrap myself up in. Em threads her arm through mine and rests her head on my shoulder.

"You know what else I kind of want tonight?" Em asks.

"Deep-fried brookies?" I assume. She pretty much lost it when we passed the booth by the entrance.

"Those. For sure. But also . . . I kind of want to be haunted." She says it like she's been thinking about it for a while, but she still can't decide if it's a cool idea.

Sometimes, I imagine Spooks as the kind of place where Em *always* lives. With us but not. Parallel universe kind of stuff. Walking among all the scary—believing in it, even—but never actually being scared.

"Because I've been thinking about it, you know?" she goes on, like we're talking about fairy tales and not ghosts. "How being haunted gets this awful rap. How people decide it's dark, and terrifying, and evil. But *why*? I mean, what's so bad about someone loving you *so much* that they never wanna leave you, not even once they're gone?"

"Well, if I die first"—I rest my head on hers—"I promise to haunt the shit out of you."

I hear her smile. "Romantic."

Shawn's game ends. Twenty-eight baskets again. His machine starts spitting out more tickets. "Alright, ladies." He rips them from the feeder. "Let's see what we can afford."

He counts his tickets five at a time. Ninety-eight. This game is packed like everything is, and one of the guys working the booth will be by eventually to see if we want to play some more or cash out. We have enough tickets for a crown, Nemo, and a key chain. So we decide to cash out.

It's not the boy who's been helping us so far who comes by this time to check on us, though—the one I recognize from the grocery store. It's someone different, about our age but not familiar.

He has the kind of smile that makes me instantly smile back.

"Don't tell me you're done," he says to Shawn, glancing at the wad of tickets in his hands. "What about the Streetlight puffer?"

Shawn squints. "The *what*?"

"The Streetlight puffer?" He laughs and tightens the strings of his red Spooks apron. "So, I'm not the only one who had no idea what that was? Because these guys tried to act like I'd never heard of Jesus. I figured it was because I'm new."

"To Streetlight?" Em asks interestedly. It's weird. For anyone to be new around here.

"Yes ma'am," he answers.

"I'm so sorry to hear that," Shawn tells him, like his goldfish just died.

He laughs. "Why? I like it here. I get to taste deep-fried pepperoni and also teach cute boys about the Streetlight puffer."

I'm only sure I heard what I heard because Em looked at me when she heard it, too. Is there really a cute new boy in Streetlight? And is that cute new boy really flirting with Shawn?

I can tell Shawn isn't even stunned. More like convinced this is a prank.

"So what is it?" I speak up, to make sure something happens. To make sure we don't blow this. "The Streetlight puffer?"

The new boy leans on the ledge separating his side from ours, folding his arms on the surface. "It's this puffer jacket you can win if you do well enough at a game. I've actually seen it; it's pretty nice. Black. Warm. Patagonia or something. Most of the booths have one as a secret top prize. Here, you need to make thirty-five shots." And then he tells Shawn, with all the confidence in the world, "You can do that."

Em nudges him, smiling. "Yeah, do that."

"I'll comp you this game if you try." He raises his eyebrows. "Stick around?"

I pinch Shawn's elbow. "Stick around."

"Thirty-five?" Shawn asks the boy, his vocal cords finally working again.

"That's all." He smiles.

Shawn cracks his knuckles. "Let me see what I can do."

And the lights from the hoops dance on this new boy's skin until he glows.

Kady
Saturday, October 31

"His name's Luka," I say.

Aaron leans next to me on the fence that separates us from the line for the Spinner. "Luka from LA, huh?" He watches the three of them—Shawn, Em, and This New Luka Person—at the shot clock. We have a pretty good view as long as people aren't walking by.

I bump his shoulder with mine. "Luka from LA who's stoked to be working at Spooks because he believes in ghosts just as much as Em does, *and* Luka from LA who apparently finds it nearly impossible to stop flirting with Shawn."

"Oh?" Aaron raises his eyebrows. I nod, and he looks at Luka closer this time. "He doesn't go to Iverson."

"Fairmont, either." My school. And those are the only two options for people our age in Streetlight. "His mom homeschools him."

"*Ohhh.*" Aaron nods. The impossible explained with an exception to the rule. He folds his arms and smiles. "So basically we're chillin' here for a while."

"Until Shawn hits thirty-five buckets," I agree.

Aaron's sneakers slide forward in the gravel, and he rests his hands behind him, along the top of the fence. Settling in for the wait. "Shawn's LeBron. He'll get it eventually." He glances at me, his gray eyes a disco ball under all these flashing lights. "What's it for again? Some Cocoa Puffs?"

I laugh, because I know he knows that's not what I said. "A puffer jacket."

"That's wild, man." Aaron shakes his head. "Who knew this place had a secret prize menu?"

"It's Streetlight," I remind him. The screams echo through the night. "Everyone's got secrets."

His mouth twists as he takes in our world. The games and the rides and the food. The zombies stumbling through the crowd. "Do you think you'll stick around?"

"Like, in town?" I smile, not sure if I'm the one joking or he is. "Doesn't everyone?"

"You don't get sick of it?" he asks. "The same people . . . *the same nights* . . . over and over and over again?"

He's squinting, and one of his feet scrapes the gravel on repeat. Aaron is fidgety when he gets serious. When he wants to talk about things that aren't meant to make me laugh. I guess that's the reason why I ask, "Do you?"

He takes a deep breath and glances at Shawn and Em and Luka again. But I don't think he's really looking, not at them. "I've been thinking I wanna go to Vanderbilt."

It's the weirdest thing I've ever heard. "Vanderbilt isn't Barnes, though."

But he shakes his head, hard. A little kid refusing cough medicine. "I don't want Barnes."

There are things around here that just are. You're either a Have-Not, and you'll go to the Street U community college, get a job nearby at the hospital or one of the restaurants or Fairmont, settle into the apartments or get one of the homes on the east side. Or you're a

Have-Lot, and you leave for a shiny degree but come back for your family's businesses or the homes you'll inherit one day or even just your legacy.

The IV Boys . . . they go to Barnes. All of them. And they come back on weekends and for the ball. And then they come back forever.

The way those Boys circled him earlier tonight flashes through my mind.

"Why Vanderbilt?"

His foot keeps scraping. Scratch, scratch, scratch. "It's a Jack-Laurence thing. They send most of their kids there. Six generations back now."

"Since when are you into Jack-Laurence things?" My voice tightens with a nervousness that shouldn't be there, and I swallow so I'm still again. But the thought of him leaving—like, *permanently*—spikes my blood pressure in a way that I never expected, and I know it isn't fair. So I breathe deep, stuff it down, and ignore it.

It's just that I've barely even heard him mention the Jack-Laurences before, let alone claim interest in their *things*. I mean, it's nothing to be ashamed of—they're basically the wealthiest family around, and ever since his dad married Charlotte and moved to Streetlight, Aaron's technically one of them. But he doesn't talk about it. He holds it close, acts like it's sacrilegious, practically. *Thou shalt not speak thy rich stepmom's name in vain.*

"You know," Aaron starts. "The IVs do this thing. Scope out the guys they want and then slip this fancy little letter in their mailboxes. An invitation to join, like one of those preapproved credit card notices. And when I got mine, I had no idea who the hell they were. I was just some kid from Philly, you know? But Charlotte thought it'd be good for me, get in with some of the local guys." He shrugs. "So I did it. I didn't want her worrying about me. And then they gave us matching blazers and called us brothers.

"But the thing is . . . all these other guys . . . this is all they know." He looks around, like everything about Streetlight that matters, that *exists*, is wrapped up in our little Halloween carnival. "And their families do it with them—it's like year after year they breed more IV Boys. And that's everything to them. Staying here and controlling every single second of everybody's lives . . . that's all that's ever gonna matter. And I don't wanna do this forever. I don't want you doing it forever, either . . ."

And now I really want to know if he decided all this years ago or days ago, when he called me to Iverson to tell me there were rumors. We've always joked about the IVs, and Aaron's made it plenty obvious that his life was more like mine before he came to Streetlight. But I never got the vibe that he didn't want to *be* them. Every IV wants to be IV.

God, I want to know what he was talking to those Boys about.

I don't ask, though. Because even if Aaron doesn't want to be IV forever, he's still IV for now. And I know what that means. It's the same thing it means with Nik. That he'll change the subject, or pretend he didn't hear me, or straight up tell me *no* if I'm asking for answers that belong more to them than they do to me. And it sucks when that happens—when they remind me, no matter how close I get, I'm still not close enough.

"Well, I hate to break it to you," I tell Aaron. "But I don't think I'll be following you to Vanderbilt."

He chuckles, and it airs out this moment like opening a window. "It doesn't have to be Vanderbilt. It can be thirty minutes away. An hour. Put as much or as little time between you and this place as you want. Just go."

When some Iverson girls come over and choose to notice Aaron but not me, I sneak off to the bathroom.

It's easier to breathe now that I've wandered some. All of Spooks is outside, but it's densest at the center, like a star getting ready to explode. And now that I'm toward the outskirts—the row of porta potties are in the back behind the Ride a Real Donkey attraction for little kids—there's so much more room to move around. I stretch my arms out to my sides just because I can.

My phone vibrates, and it's Em. Shawn got the jacket. And Luka's number. She adds a heart-eyed emoji and a fingers-crossed emoji and a shooting star. She tells me to meet them at the dunk tanks.

A part of me was expecting her to be Nik. He hasn't texted me since two o'clock, when he got to his friend's house to watch college football. A friend I don't know—one he's made since he's been at Barnes. Donovan, I think it is. And I love that he's making new friends—that it's not just him and Hendricks in their apartment all the time, and that I've heard about these new people before they start showing up in group pics.

"Do you think they've heard about you?" Shawn asked me once, while we sat in my moonlit bedroom, because we'd been too lazy to turn on the lights. "Obviously," I said at the time.

But, honestly, I'm not sure.

According to Find My, Nik is somewhere near Barnes. Probably screaming at a TV with Donovan still. I slide my phone back against my hip.

The bathrooms are straight ahead, and there's a line outside all of them. When Nik still lived in Streetlight and we would come to Spooks, I'd hold our spot in line while he killed time. Buying sodas or foot-long hot dogs. Getting our tickets for the raffle that gives the winner free access to every Spooks attraction next year. He always bought ten—fifty dollars total. And we never won, but he'd hold me at midnight while we stood at the main stage and they called out the numbers. *Next time,* he always whispered.

It's our first year not having a next time.

There's a booth, and it looks so weird out here by itself. I stop walking and study it for a second. Built out of wood, with no flashing lights or arrows pointing its way. No giant prize wall or huge sign calling it *The Cyclone* or *The Toss-A-Whirl* or *The Greatest Game You'll Ever Play.* Just a bunch of empty glass jars, lined up in row after row.

And there's this man, sitting among it all. Wearing one of those flat caps like Grandpa does, with the same brown skin and the kind of beard that's probably soft if you rub it one direction and scratches like Velcro if you rub it the opposite. And even though there's no one in line, he isn't scrolling his phone like everyone else who's bored at a booth. He's just waiting, patiently. And when he sees me watching, he smiles.

"Hi," I say awkwardly across the short distance between us.

"Hello," he calls back.

I walk closer, crossing the dusty gravel while everything Spooks is supposed to be—the screams and laughs and blinding lights—carries on behind me. The man stands as I get nearer. He's in overalls underneath his red Spooks apron. "You looking for the bathroom, ma'am?" he kindly asks, like that's usually why people come talk to him.

"No, I—" I reach into my pocket for cash. "I wanted to play your game."

"Oh!" His pleasant surprise is all over his face, this face with cheeks that sag a little and eyes that sparkle like a diamond I shouldn't touch. "First timer, I believe?"

"Is that okay?" I drop five dollars into his jar.

"Of course! Pleasure to have you. Just want to make sure I go over all the rules, that's all. Haven't had to in a while." He squats behind his booth, and when he stands again, he's holding a cardboard box full of red balls that are a little bit smaller than my palm. "Good news is, my game's as easy as they come. Like most things, really, once you know the parts that matter. So, for *my* game, these are the parts that matter." He starts setting one ball after another in front of me. "You'll have five balls—no more, no less. And for each ball you get in one of those jars you see back there, you'll get to pick a number from zero to nine. Each number corresponds to a prize, so the more balls you land, the bigger your prize will be." Now that my five balls are in front of me, he slides the cardboard box back where he got it from. "I say bigger and not better, because what's better to one person can be real different for someone else. That's the funny thing about the things we want—some people may not want them at all." He dusts his palms against each other before he lets out a satisfied sigh. "So. Did all that make sense? I don't want to go confusing you when you were nice enough to wander over here in the first place."

It's like a game that came out of a carnival decades ago. When girls wore those dog skirts and people went on dates to get soda. That's why no one's over here. Because it's like being zapped back in time.

The jars are ten or so feet away—all of them exactly the same. And the balls in front of me are hard and squeezable at the same time—like rocks wrapped in rubber.

"Does it matter if I get it in the same jar twice?" I ask.

His forehead crinkles, and, for a moment, he's watching me so closely that I almost pretend I have to cough, just so I have a reason to turn away. He seems to realize something. "You know, no one's ever asked me that."

And, for some reason, it feels like I need to apologize. "Since I've never played before, I just wasn't really sure . . ."

"Oh no, no," he assures me. "It's good to ask questions. And that was a *very* good question." He nods to reinforce it. "Yes, you can get each ball in a different jar, or more than one ball in the same jar. Whatever happens." And that glimmer in his eyes is back again, something that feels good and bad—warm and cold—at the same time. Like everything around here. "Any other questions?"

A breeze blows. A whiff of cotton candy and one of my long braids tickle my nose at the same time. "No more questions."

He nods. He smiles. He holds his arm out to his jars like he's presenting me with the whole world. And then he tells me, "Take your shot."

I pick up one of the balls, feel its weight, roll it over in my palms. There're a bunch of jars—maybe twelve rows deep? More than that many wide. Instinctively, I want to shoot underhand—because it's a softer toss. But after years of games at Spooks with Nik, and being his sober cornhole and beer pong partner at five million different IV parties, I've been trained:

Underhand for anything that won't bounce, overhand for anything that will, he's always said.

So I aim like I'm staring at a bunch of red plastic cups and flick the ball from my wrist. It bounces off the rim of one jar and into another.

"Well, would you look at that," the man encourages me. "What's your first number gonna be?"

"One?"

"One it is. Take your next shot."

Four more times, I aim and shoot like I did on my first try. Two balls end up in the same jar, and three end up in others, but they all land. He's so proud of me that it makes me proud of myself. And I'm glad that I came over, that I didn't keep walking.

"So few play, and even fewer win," he tells me, after my last ball goes in. "What's gonna be your final number tonight?"

So far, I've said one, nine, two, and three. "Four?"

"You said *four*?" He exhales like he couldn't be more impressed. "My, my. It certainly is a winning night for you. For both of us, as luck may have it." He taps the side of his nose two times. "I'll be back in a jiffy."

I hug myself as he disappears to the other side of the jars and begins digging in a box underneath the table they've been set up on. I glance over my shoulder at how empty it is on this side of the fairgrounds, but still not as empty as where I'm standing now. Behind me, there's energy and life again, a pair of zombies stumbling after two girls who are running away screaming and laughing. Kids eating funnel cakes from the famous pie shop that got a booth here for the first time when I was in middle school. It reminds me where I actually am. Spooks. Frightening Streetlight since 1968.

"You've gone and won yourself my biggest prize," the man says, and his voice whips my attention back to this lonely booth. There's a plastic sandwich bag in his hand now, the kind you fold closed instead of zip-locking. And inside are dozens of little, round candies. Like a bunch of blue Smarties. He holds them between us. "You mind if I ask your name?"

I stare at the baggie, the wrong kind of prize for Spooks. Spooks is giant teddy bears, hats that don't fit, a puffer jacket none of us ever knew existed. But this bag, that this man promises is the biggest prize he has to give, is the only thing I see right now. "I'm . . . Kady." I force myself to blink, to look at him instead. "Can I ask yours?"

"Why, of course you can. It's real nice of you to wonder." He tips his hat at me. "I'm the Timekeeper. TK for short. And my, how it's been a pleasure having you play my game tonight, Kady." He shakes the baggie a little, and my stare zips back to it like a dog who hears treats. "You see, these are my *magic* candies."

I try not to smile. "Magic candies," I repeat.

"Absolutely indeed." He gives me one firm nod. "And it's a real honor being able to share them with you." He sets the baggie on the surface of the booth and clasps his hands. "But before I let you run off and start using them, there's a few things you gotta know. You got your listening ears on, Kady?" He waits for me to answer, so I nod. "Good. Because the first thing you've gotta know is exactly what these things do.

"Well, they change things. Time, more specifically. And with them, as long as you follow the rules, it can always be whatever time you want it to be. Assuming that time has already passed. No going forward, only back."

"Time travel," I summarize, so he believes I'm listening.

"*Exactly*. Now, how will you do it? Just like this: Place a single candy on your tongue, say a date and time that's already passed, and when the candy dissolves—which it tends to do quickly—you'll be right back where you want to be. But there's a distinction to be made."

My phone vibrates against my hip; probably Em wondering where I've gone. And honestly, so am I. "Okay," I say.

"*Changing* time doesn't mean *erasing* time. There's a difference, and it's my job to make sure you understand it. Because your memories of what's happened—they'll stay. But the *evidence* of what's happened—that's what you're getting rid of. Let's see . . . how can I give you a good enough example?" And then he snaps his fingers. "Alright, imagine you buy an ice cream cone, and then you choose to go back five minutes earlier. You'll remember the ice cream cone, how it tasted and how it felt. You'll just no longer *have* the ice cream cone. Unless, of course, you choose to go back and have it again. It's real interesting, you know. The choices you're gonna have. To go back so you can try a different ice cream, or get more of the kind you already had, or maybe you change your mind and don't get ice cream at all." He watches me close. "Does that all make sense, Kady? If it doesn't, I need you to tell me. Alright?"

I nod. "Yeah. Yeah, that makes sense." My phone buzzes again.

"*Wonderful.* Now, we've talked about *your* memories. How they'll travel where you go. *But what about everyone else's memories?* Well, the moment you accept this prize"—he jiggles the bag of candies—"there's gonna be two types of people in your life. The ones who have traveled with you, and the ones who have not. Now, when someone *has* traveled with you, they'll keep all their memories, just like you. And all you have to do for them to travel with you is be touching them when the candy fully dissolves. So those are the first kinds of people you'll have in your life—the ones you bring with you.

"The second kind of people will be *everybody else.* And you may wonder what happens with them, if you're traveling and they're not. Well." TK takes a breath. "It's interesting, really—how their memories will work. On some occasions, they'll completely cease to exist—and that's usually how it goes for tinier moments, the sorts of things they weren't trying to remember in the first place. But with bigger moments . . . Have you taken a chemistry course yet, Kady?"

I hug myself against the chill and force myself to hold his gaze, to let him finish. I don't want to be rude. "Last year I did."

"Oh great," TK says. "So this next example won't be a waste. Because their bigger memories—they don't disappear so much as they . . . evaporate, if you will. They exist, just in a different form. In a way that's harder to grab, that's harder to reach. Like water that's become a cloud." He squints at me again, and with this edge of concern in his voice, he asks, "All that still making sense, Kady?"

He holds the bag of candies out to me like—as long as I say yes—all of them are mine. The biggest, craziest, most impossible prize he has to give.

Just maybe not the best.

I take the bag. It's warm. Like his hands, I bet. "Yes, it makes sense."

"Alright." He sighs, satisfied. "Then last but not least, let's talk about the rules. There are only a couple, but I want you to follow them. Now firstly, these candies are meant to be used only in Streetlight. Nowhere else. Ever. And secondly, I need you to make sure you never use a candy to go back to a date earlier than this Halloween, and that you've used them all before the next."

I look up from the bag in my hand. "They're only good for a year?"

"From Halloween to Halloween." He nods.

I don't know why that sounds like the most ridiculous part. Not this little rickety booth that has no bright lights or big signs, not this wizardy man Em would be obsessed with, not the fact that he's convinced he's giving me the power to time travel on Halloween night. But the fact that it has a stipulation like *that*. A sell-by date, like magic spoils just as easily as milk. "*Why?*"

"Because that's what they decided." TK smiles like things are just funny sometimes. "But don't you worry about that. You can always come back next year if you're jonesin' for some more."

My phone vibrates again, and I know I have to go, but I'd stand here all night, if I could. Figuring out who TK is and what he knows. Why he freaks me out but also makes me want to stay. I'd force him to put a candy on his tongue at the same time I do, just in case it's poison—and with my dying breath, ask why he chose to poison *me*? Right when Shawn just met a really cute boy, and Aaron said *Jack-Laurence* out loud for the first time ever, and when this was the year that I really, *finally* might get to go to the ball? And after he choked out an answer, or maybe he wouldn't have time to, I'd go off and haunt Em, just like I promised.

"Any other questions, Kady?" TK asks.

"No—" I answer, slipping the bag into the waistband of my leggings, the side where my phone isn't already. "Not really, I just . . ." I peek at him, one of my braids falling into my face. I push it back. "What other prizes do you *have* back there?"

Like, if he wasn't allegedly handing me time on a platter, would I have gotten a genie instead? The power to fly? A Tesla?

"Oh, lots of things," TK assures me. "Card decks. Yo-yos. A game of jacks." He slips his hands into his pockets. "Anything else I might be helping you with tonight?"

"Um . . . no. No, I don't think so. Thanks."

I turn to leave, to wander back into reality and finally go to the bathroom. There are gimmicks all over Spooks. The woman whose hair is a different neon color every year and says she can tell you, down to the second, when you're gonna die. And another woman who gives out beads that she says can grant any wish. And the family with the full magic act in the tent by the Ferris wheel.

But none of them feel like TK, so patient and calm and unassuming. Without an outfit or a schtick. And I know it's probably just in my head, but my hip—where those candies are—almost feels like it's tingling.

"Oh, Kady?" TK calls.

I freeze like I stole something. "Yeah?" I turn back around.

"Try to avoid using those with chewing gum in your mouth. Or right after brushing your teeth. They'll work alright, but something about minty flavors makes for a real nasty aftertaste."

"Hey," someone says, putting a hand on my elbow.

My heart lunges into my throat as I spin around.

Aaron and his trippy eyes.

I grip my chest. "*Shit!* You scared me."

"My bad." He smiles, holding his hands up in surrender. "What are you doing back here?"

"I was . . . I just . . ." I glance over my shoulder at TK, but not long enough for my eyes to focus on him before I turn back to Aaron. "I was playing that guy's game over there. He looked like he hadn't had anyone come by all night. So, yeah."

Aaron smirks, like I'm being weird. *Because I'm being weird.* "I thought you were going to the bathroom."

"I am. Now." And I shove him so he'll quit looking at me like that. "Stop. What are *you* doing back here?"

He shrugs, slides his hands into his pockets, and glances at that weird little booth before he tells me, "I have to go to the bathroom, too."

Kady
Saturday, October 31

On the other side of Streetlight, Spooks rages on, while Shawn, Em, and I stand shoulder to shoulder in an elevator so tiny that Owen and Milo had to carry their sofa up the stairwell when they moved in.

The Spot bag that Em's hugging to her chest crinkles as she takes a deep breath.

"Is that rat shit?" Shawn peers at the corner on my side of the elevator.

My gaze follows his. "Mouse shit," I correct, because they aren't that big.

"*No* . . ." Em insists, leaning into me to have a better look. The Spot bag I'm holding by my side crunches as it presses into the wall. "I think it's just like . . . chocolate sprinkles."

Shawn squints like there is literally *no way*. "Why would chocolate sprinkles just be chillin' on the floor right where rat shit would be?"

"Mouse shit," I correct again. "And because they're not sprinkles."

"You don't *know* that," Em argues.

"I mean . . . I don't *know* this shitty elevator won't crap out and kill us all before we can get to the guys' apartment," Shawn says, and I bite back my laugh. "But I'm taking my chances."

Em doesn't want to join the dark side. She does everything she can not to laugh. But Shawn bumps her lightly into me, and I bump her lightly back into him, and finally her giggle bounces off the walls of this gross elevator as she says, "My boyfriend lives here, okay?"

I shrug. "My brother lives here."

"I know," Shawn assures us. "They're my two favorite people."

"Hey!" Em snaps, and because she has no free hands, she digs her teeth into Shawn's shoulder instead.

"Asshole," I mutter, but it sounds like a good thing, because it is.

Shawn smiles and rubs his shoulder with the hand that isn't holding our third bag from The Spot. We stare at the numbers as they light up over the door.

Then Shawn says, "Still doesn't change the fact that that's rat shit."

"Mouse shit."

He yawns. "Whatever."

The elevator doors creak open on the seventh floor, to the long hallway that's never had enough overhead lights. We turn left and head toward the guys' apartment, which is the very last one on this side of the hall.

Shawn tries again to take my and Em's food bags, but we reject him for the third time since we left The Spot and hopped on the bus to get here. It was the same moment when we officially split off from Aaron—left him happily forking his to-go tray, the perfect companion for his long walk home.

We've been all over Streetlight tonight. Besides the temperature, it almost feels exactly like one of those humid summer nights when we had nowhere to be and anywhere to go. I'd FaceTime Nik, and he'd be wherever I was within ten minutes. And he'd kiss me, or trace me in the road with Em's little sister's chalk, or let me arm-wrestle him and pretend I won. Stupid, pointless stuff. Because time didn't matter, as long as we were together. Time didn't *exist*.

I brush my hip just to make sure the candies are still there.

Em knocks twice on 7K.

Milo opens the door, flashing us his perfect smile. He's in a white tank top and blue basketball shorts, and his shoulder-length dreads are tied back. "Hey, hey, what's up, what's up." He steps aside so we can walk in. A hug for me, a hand slap for Shawn. Em gets a kiss—my five-foot-two friend on tiptoes while her six-foot-two soulmate breaks his neck just to reach her. SZA is playing from the Bluetooth speaker in the kitchen, which means Owen's phone is around here somewhere, and Owen must be, too. My brother can't breathe without music.

Milo glances between us and the food bags in our hands. "I thought you went to Spooks?"

"We did." Em shimmies behind her giant paper bag of food. "Hungry?"

He smirks, taking her bag with one hand and using the other to close and lock the door behind us. Always all three. The knob, the dead bolt, the chain. "Real questions only." He sets the food on the counter, and Em laughs. "Y'all didn't win anything? Not even at the shot clock?" He claps his huge hand against Shawn's back. "You've got a shot like Curry."

"Oh, you know I crushed it," Shawn says as Milo takes his bag next. "Our stuff's just at Kady's."

"We needed both hands to feed you with," Em insists.

Milo kisses her again. "Love you," he says. Then he tells Shawn and me, "Love you guys, too," as he grabs my bag last.

"Speaking of love," I say, plopping into one of the three chairs at their "dining" table. "*Someone* left Spooks with a whole new boyfriend tonight."

Shawn's eyes shoot me daggers, and I blow him a kiss.

"Whoa, whoa, whoa." Milo freezes while Em starts digging into

bags, taking out food. He does a quick mental inventory, trying to figure out which of us I could be talking about. But his eyes go wide when
they land on Shawn. "You?"

"He's not my *boyfriend*," Shawn insists.

"Who's not your boyfriend?" Owen asks, his voice suddenly tow-
ering over me, his palm rubbing the top of my head like he's trying to
generate enough static electricity to make lightning. I slam my elbow
into his ribs, and he jumps back.

"STOP," I snap.

"Yo, chill," he says, and steals one more chance to pull my hair,
because he's faster than me. He slaps hands with Shawn and gives Em
a one-armed hug. "Wow, y'all brought everything," he says, eyeing the
feast Em's still unpacking.

"I think my man Shawn got himself a boyfriend tonight." Milo
catches Owen up.

Owen raises his eyebrows. I'm pretty sure he just got out of the
shower. He smelled clean while he was attacking me, and he still has
the pick in his hair. "For real?"

"And I repeat," Shawn says, "*he's not my boyfriend*. Because I'm
not a complete psychopath." He slaps my knees so I'll stand. He sits
and I sit on his lap, careful that my baggie doesn't slip free from my
waistband.

"What is he, then?" I laugh as Shawn pinches the back of my elbow.
"*Ow!* You're mean when you're in love."

He doesn't want to smile, but he does. "Shut up."

"Okay, maybe he's not your boyfriend . . . *yet*," Em says, folding
the empty paper bags. "But it *is* really, really fun luck."

The apartment is old and not in that lots-of-character way that they
talk about on HGTV. It has chipping paint and ancient appliances and
a window-unit AC. But it is big—a legit two bedroom with a living

room. Their furniture is a mix between Grandma and Grandpa's storage unit and the Salvation Army, and their only decorations are a few
posters and the sports trophies they won in high school. Shawn and
I talk a lot of shit about this place, about the way it shakes when the
train goes by or the way the cabinets are missing knobs, but the truth
is that I love it here. It's a place I can exist that isn't my parents' house
or Nik's gorgeous mansion. It's okay to spill things or break things or
stay as long as I want. Even if Owen asks me when the hell am I going
home, he doesn't mean it. Not for real.

And while Owen and Milo eat, Shawn tells them about this new boy
Luka. That he loves *The Walking Dead*. And he's the biggest Shakira
stan. That he's from LA.

"LA?" Owen repeats.

"I know," Shawn says, reaching past me for a rice ball, because I'm
still on his lap. "Weird."

Milo points out that their economics professor at Street U is from
Delaware. And Owen mentions this guy they graduated with who came
from Florida. Em says there's a manager at The Spot, and she isn't sure
where he came from, but she knows it's not from here.

"Aaron," I add. "He's from Philly."

And then we're quiet, thinking, trying to remember if there's anyone else.

But I guess not.

It's after midnight. I've been watching the clock.

Never use a candy to go back to a date earlier than this Halloween.

It's officially not Halloween anymore.

Owen and I are on the couch, in the same spots we claimed as little
kids when this sofa was at our grandparents' house and we had bowls
of cereal and footie pajamas. Our bodies are forever imprinted in a

way that makes me fit better in this spot—curled up next to the arm on the left side—than I fit anywhere else in the world.

Owen is pretending to be awake even though he's really not. He'll lie all the way down once I decide to go to bed, but, for now, it's just his legs that are stretched out on the cushions while an episode of *Everybody Hates Chris* that we've seen a million times plays on the TV.

Em and Milo said goodnight and went into Milo's room about thirty minutes ago. Shawn went to Owen's room a couple of minutes after that. That's how we sleep whenever we're here—Shawn and me in Owen's bed and Owen on the couch, because Owen insists that's how it should be no matter how many times Shawn and I have tried to argue with him.

My phone starts vibrating on the couch next to me. A FaceTime call from Nik. I glance at Owen before I answer. His eyes are closed.

I hold my phone in front of me and tap the green icon. I smile the moment Nik's face is on-screen.

"Hi," I softly say.

"Hi."

"Where are you going?" I can tell he's driving—he has the overhead light on so that I can see him, and there's air whooshing by like he has a window cracked.

"Home," he says, watching the road. But he knows his mistake—what him coming home does to my heart—so he quickly amends, "Back to the apartment, I mean."

"Oh." I settle deeper into my imprint. "How was Donovan's?"

"It was cool," he says, and he glances at me, lips twisted into an accusatory smile. "How was Spooks?"

I laugh into my pillow so I don't wake up Owen. "It was fine. Why are you looking like that?"

"I'm just looking. What'd you do?"

I shrug. "Ate a lot. Played games. Aaron came with us; you should feel good about that."

"Good guy." Nik nods his approval.

He's watching the road, so I look down for a minute instead, picking at my blanket. "Oh! And Shawn met a cute boy. His name is Luka. He's from out west."

"Like by the highway?"

"No, like LA."

"Yeah? How'd that happen?"

So I recount what I know, what Luka told us, and what Shawn told Owen and Milo. That Luka has family in Lake Ridge, like forty-five minutes from Streetlight, and his parents wanted to be closer to them. His dad's a teacher at the elementary school now.

"Wow, good for him," Nik says, and I'm not sure if he means good for Shawn meeting a cool new guy, or good for Luka finding himself in Streetlight of all places. "So that's it? Anything else?"

I look up from my blanket, and even though he's watching the road, his tongue is pushing through his cheek—a tic when he wants to say something but isn't. "Should there be anything else?"

He smiles again, glances at me. "Were you good?"

I hug myself. This was my first time since we started dating that I ever went to Spooks without him. It was my first time riding those rides, devouring that cotton candy, meeting a new boy from out of town without him there, doing it, too. And yeah, he's been gone two months now, and I'm slowly getting used to the little things I have to tell him because he wasn't there to see them. But Spooks is our biggest thing yet that I've done without him by my side. That he won't know about if I don't tell him.

"Perfect," I promise.

He tells me he loves me.

We talk for another minute, as he parks at his apartment and takes me with him in the elevator. He's looking back at me now, with those eyes that I'd float in forever, if I could.

"Have you thought any more about the ball?" I ask.

His keys are jingling as he stops in front of his door. He smiles. "Have you?"

I hold my hand up so he can see my thumb and pointer a millimeter apart.

Nik laughs. "Yeah? Well, if that's all you've been thinking about it, then that makes it easy. No need for you to go."

I frown. "Don't be mean."

So he turns on that voice that he uses when he doesn't want me to worry. *Yes, I'll be there at eight. Yes, I'll remember to call you tonight. Yes, there's enough room for Em and Shawn.*

"Yes, I've been thinking about it," he says.

I smile. "Good."

He tells me he's gonna go. That he'll text me when he wakes up. That he loves me. Again.

"I love you, too," I answer.

He hangs up first.

I bite back my smile as I thumb through my apps for a second. No reason, really. Just to feel like I'm holding Nik close for a little longer.

"I'ma start telling that kid you have a curfew," Owen murmurs.

I lock my phone. "You're supposed to be asleep."

"You too." His eyes are open now, barely. Watching the TV. "So how's all that stuff going?"

He means me dating an IV Boy. Nik being at college now. Seeing him once every couple of weeks, on weekends only. Stuff.

Owen has never loved any of that stuff.

"It's good." I hug my knees to my chest and hope I sound convincing.

"You know." He closes his eyes again. "There's a lot of girls at Street U. I thought I knew everyone around here until I got there. And it's wild sometimes, what it feels like. Because I've got this place now. All these girls I never knew before. Stuff I can keep to myself way easier, if I want to. It's different. You know what I mean?"

He sits there, on his side, eyes closed, just like when we were little and he never wanted to fall asleep first.

"Yeah," I tell him. "I know what you mean."

I roll off the couch and leave my blanket at his feet. In the next five minutes, he'll be fully tucked in, completely passed out.

"Night, O," I say.

"Night, K," he answers.

I walk down the hall to Owen's bedroom, where the door is closed and the light is out. I twist the knob and shove a little. The doors stick when the building turns the heat on.

Owen's room is just a full-size bed with a dresser and a desk, both random hand-me-downs like everything else in this apartment. Shawn's on the bed, on his phone—in the same sweats and sweatshirt he changed into before we came here. I shove the door closed again and join him, resting my head on his shoulder, staring at whatever he's staring at. It takes me a second to recognize it—*The Crown*. An obsession he developed back in middle school when they let us watch Harry and Meghan's wedding in class.

"Question?" Shawn asks, while we both stare at his screen.

"'Kay." I tilt his phone in his hand so I stop catching the glare.

"Do you ever feel like maybe Aaron is in love with you." But it's barely a question, the way he asks. Just a thought meandering through his mind.

"Nah." I frown. "He's just IV, that's all. More than he realizes."

"Hm," Shawn accepts, and we keep staring at his screen.

This is always how it's easiest to talk—not that it's ever *hard* to talk. But when it's in between nighttime and morning, and we're alone in the dark with just the idea of each other's faces in our minds, it's like our bodies disappear and only the thoughts are left, floating like clouds until they drift away with the next breath.

"There is this rumor, though." I keep my head on his shoulder.

"The one about Julie Edmonds peeing all over the football field?"

"No, about me. And Aaron. Kissing. They've been whispering about it at Iverson."

"*Why?*" he asks. I can't see his face, but I can imagine it. Scrunched.

"No idea. Aaron told me. That night I met him after *Final Destination.*"

"People will talk about the dumbest shit," Shawn mumbles.

"Yeah," I agree. Princess Margaret's crying on-screen. "Do you think Julie really peed on the football field?"

"Eh. Probably."

For a few seconds, we just breathe, watch *The Crown*, drift.

"Remember in *Tenet?* How they could go back in time and relive the same moment twice?"

Shawn yawns. "I swear to God if you try to explain *Tenet* to me again, I'm going headfirst out that window."

"I won't. But tonight, at Spooks, I played this game and met this man. He gave me these candies that he says can change time. Like *Tenet* stuff. Time travel."

"Was he the booth next to the woman who tells you when you're gonna die?"

"No, he was toward the back." I reach into the waistband of my leggings and pull my baggie free, the first time in hours. My hip misses its warm kiss already.

I drop it on Shawn's chest, in front of his screen. He lays his phone down and picks up the bag, studying it with the only light we have: the ambient glow of *The Crown* and the moon peeking through the blinds.

"This looks like the kind of shit guys put in girls' drinks." He hands them over to me and picks his phone back up.

I sit up and cross my legs, holding the candies in my palm. I should've thrown them away. I shouldn't have taken them in the first place. "I wanna try them."

Shawn turns to me, the light from the changing scenes flickering across his face. "But it's obviously cocaine."

"Cocaine doesn't come in tablets." I don't think. "And no one's giving away this much of it for free." I'm pretty sure.

Shawn squints like he couldn't care less. "Kady, throw that shit away."

I should. I should have hours ago.

But I scoot to the other side of the mattress and put one on my tongue instead.

"*Kady, what the hell—*" Shawn starts, but a second later it's like I'm listening to him underwater.

The bed, the floor, the walls—they fall away first. And then I'm weightless, little bright lights dotting my vision.

Stars? Death?

I close my eyes and open them again.

November first, 12:37 a.m. is the time I whispered.

And, all of a sudden, that's the time it *is*.

Again.

With Nik on FaceTime, telling me he loves me.

Aaron
Sunday, November 1

---

48 DAYS BEFORE THE BALL

The walkway. *Covered in leaves so dead that they shatter under my feet like glass.*

The path lights. *All lit except for the third one from the end.*

The air. *Pierced by sirens heading somewhere. Not cops. Fire trucks.*

I yawned as I jogged up the steps to the chapel. It was on west campus, all by itself except for some benches and trees. There wasn't even parking, so all the dudes were walking up from east campus, north campus, south campus.

But I didn't drive. I walked straight from the fairgrounds.

The air inside the chapel smelled like they'd just turned on the heat—thick and sort of like fire. All the lights were on, and most of the guys were here already. Doing rounds on the dartboard, the beer pong table, cornhole. Aim-and-shoot games, every meeting. So no matter who they played, or where they were, they'd never lose.

The coolers were full of ice and sitting open at the altar while guys sat around drinking beers. I didn't grab one, didn't want one. I took an empty pew toward the back. I pulled out my phone and scrolled TikTok while I waited. A few guys slapped my shoulder as they walked up the aisle.

The IV Boys weren't a brotherhood. Not the way they advertised it to be when Charlotte really wanted me to think about joining. A few of the guys' moms made it sound so good to her that she didn't even care that her family would give her a hard time. She just wanted me to like it here, have dudes I could trust, kick it with. And they told her that's what the IVs were. *Brothers.*

But my boys back in Philly—*those* were brothers. This? These guys wouldn't even be friends if they weren't so scared of each other. It was all just some big calculation for them—I could see them doing the math behind their eyes. *If we stay good with the Reynolds family, and we're also cool with the Spencers, is that enough goodwill to get Dad on that advisory board?*

Those moms never really wanted me. They wanted Charlotte Jack-Laurence.

"What's up, man?" I asked, after Bobby O'Grady slapped my shoulder and said it first. He grabbed a seat in the pew in front of me.

Someone pulled the chapel door closed. I heard it, but I felt it more. The fresh air went away.

Before Hendricks left for Barnes, he'd led these meetings. Gave me this whole speech when I was new about how creating the IVs pretty much made his family Streetlight's own Christopher Columbus.

Yeah? So who had the IVs before y'all stole it from them? I joked at the time. Hendricks didn't laugh, though.

That was when I started saving all my jokes for KD.

But, with Hendricks gone, Perry Washington was leading our annual post-Spooks meeting. He walked up to the altar and sat next to the cooler. Everyone playing games stopped. The guys got quiet in their pews—all closer to the front than I was.

Perry went first. Pressed record on his voice memos and started telling us about his night—what he'd seen, what we should know. He laughed, and most of the guys did, too. While he talked about a bunch of people who'd never be inside this chapel.

When he was done, he'd nominate the next person to go. They'd record theirs, too. Then the next person. And the next. When we finished, we'd all email him our memos, and he'd send them back around as meeting notes, stashed on a password-protected Dropbox. Nik said, back in the day, they used to have a note keeper who'd make copies and give them to each of the guys in the morning. But this was easier. And these guys weren't big readers.

So I listened, like I did every year, and waited for my turn. I'd probably be last tonight, since I was alone in the back. And then, after me, we'd vote this year's blood brothers. And then, after that, we'd start planning the ball. And then, one by one, before we got to go home, we'd walk up to the altar and drop off our annual dues.

Kady
Sunday, November 1

---

48 DAYS BEFORE THE BALL

Streetlight changes from Halloween to the holidays, overnight, every year. When we were little, Em believed it was elves and witches, coming together, friends for only one night. Turning jack-o'-lanterns into Christmas trees and cobwebs into twinkle lights. She believed it so much, told me to *just imagine* so convincingly that I did—pictured them flying around on broomsticks and sleighs, swapping Halloween candy for candy canes. It's fun dreaming with Em. She does it better than anyone I've ever known.

One year, we decided to stay awake and watch. We stacked pillows next to her window and wrapped ourselves in blankets for the wait. She fell asleep, though—probably around midnight. Respectable, really, for an eight-year-old. But I stayed up, watched as the witches didn't come, and the elves never appeared, but the trucks that get the garbage rumbled slowly down the street. Men—normal men, with no powers or pointy ears—hopped off the back and stripped the lampposts of their decorations, and the street corners of their pumpkins, and tossed them into the truck's giant mouth. Until they reached the end of our road and another one followed to hang the lights.

In the morning, I told Em I'd fallen asleep, too.

Kady

Friday, November 6

---

43 DAYS BEFORE THE BALL

I have sixty-seven candies. I'm so used to their weight that I think I'd know the difference if there were only sixty-six or sixty-five. They're warm—close to hot, sometimes. It almost makes me scared to try them again, scared it's gonna hurt or leave a burn. But the first time it was spicy cold like an Altoid and vanished on my tongue like it never even existed.

I haven't tried again yet. I'm saving them for when Nik comes home.

"Yeah?" Shawn asks, studying himself in the mirror hanging behind his bedroom door. Requesting our opinions. "I don't look like some solo act on *America's Got Talent* that's about to get thrown into a boy band?"

It is slightly boy-bandish, now that I'm paying attention again. A flannel with the collar popped. Black skinny jeans. An oversize jean jacket that's been razor-bladed all over. I sit up on Shawn's bed. "Kind of . . . but not like the lead-singing pouty virgin one. Like the bad one in the back who only gets solos on slow songs."

Em nods, hugging her knees while she sits on the floor against his dresser. "Yeah."

Shawn squints as he cocks his head, studying his reflection. His unsettled opinion on how he feels about his outfit slowly dissolves. "Cool," he finally decides.

Thank God. We were so screwed if we had to start at ground zero again.

I smile. Em squeals. "I'm so excited," she declares.

Shawn and Luka have been texting ever since Spooks—six days. About their mutual love for fast-food-hack videos or stuff that has to do with penguins or the *Lion King* soundtrack. They both think *Friends* is super overrated, and they both actually like Tootsie Rolls. Luka once broke his pinkie so bad that he needed surgery, and Shawn has a certifiable fear of anything ever happening to appendages. So the fact that Luka survived kind of makes him supernatural, as far as Shawn is concerned.

Tonight, they have their first date.

It's nothing fancy—just a meetup at Freeze Street, this ice cream pop-up we have in Streetlight every year from November to March. Luka has a job there, and he invited Shawn to come by tonight. Em and me, too.

"Alright," Shawn says, taking a deep breath, pushing it out. We're not supposed to be talking about how this is Shawn's first date. How he kissed Jake Reilly when we were in fifth grade, but Jake has amnesia about it now that he "only likes girls." And there are only so many boys—so many *people*—in Streetlight, that if you're not in love by sixteen, you won't be. That's what everyone says. Unless, of course, there's a new boy from out of state . . .

But we're not supposed to be talking about all that. Too much pressure. Too high a likelihood of jinxing everything.

Shawn pulls Em off the floor. "Ready to go?" he asks us both.

"Ready to go," we answer.

My candies warm my hip as Em, Shawn, and I walk toward the center of Streetlight. It wasn't witches or elves but men who set up the giant Christmas tree in the middle of Old Town, and the outdoor ice-skating rink that circles around its perimeter.

I wonder where The IV Boys are.

It's quieter than it would be if they were on the ice or wandering through town. If they were part of life tonight in Streetlight, there'd be a hum of something part electric and part real. Their big voices and revving engines mixed with a whiff of what it's like to be carefree. Maybe there's a party somewhere, just for them. Or a meeting. I miss knowing for sure.

Aaron would tell me, I think. I hope. But we haven't talked since Tuesday. I almost texted him today to ask him what was up, but I stopped myself because I realized how weird it was. How Aaron and me talking every day is a recent thing, not a *normal* thing. So I can't start showing up on his phone, asking where he is just because he isn't with us.

I'm honestly not even sure when I started *noticing* the times when Aaron wasn't with us.

"It's quiet tonight," Em says.

"Yeah," Shawn answers. "Finally."

He pulls open the door to Freeze Street, and the warm air smells like fresh waffle cones. There are a couple of round tables that can seat three or four, but there are only a few people in here; no one really hangs out inside. You take your ice cream to go, sit on the curb outside, or walk the frigid streets with it. That's the whole point. Ice cream so good that you want it even when it's freezing.

"Hey!" Luka calls at us from behind the glass displays of ice cream. There's only one other person working tonight, and she's behind the register. She smiles at us, too. She's a sophomore at our school.

Shawn smiles back at her before he says "Hey" to Luka. "Uniform looks good on you," he adds for fun.

It's the same outfit the Freeze Street staff wear every year. White shorts. White T-shirts that say WORTH THE FROSTBITE. A white visor that Luka's wearing upside down and backward. He looks at himself, frowns. "Uniform? Pulled this right out of my closet."

Shawn smirks.

"Luka, it smells *so good* in here . . ." Em runs her fingers along the display case of waffle cone options. Ones shaped as bowls and ones laced in sprinkles and ones dipped in chocolate or caramel.

"I've been making cones since I got here tonight," Luka tells her. "Spit in my batch so they're extra tasty."

"He didn't . . . mean that . . ." Shawn clarifies to the woman who looks up from paying for her order.

Luka sneaks a look at Em like he kind of did.

"Have you OD'd on ice cream yet?" I lean against the glass.

Luka smiles. "Kady. The button on these shorts is hanging on *by a thread*. Did you know we have a flavor that's basically just stuffed with—"

"*Scream Queen,*" Shawn, Em, and I say on top of one another.

"They say they make it out of all the uneaten candy people drop off after Halloween," I add.

"They don't train you on that?" Shawn asks.

Luka studies us, the same careful eyes he wore at Spooks when he didn't want to risk being the gullible new kid who fell for all our jokes. But, really, they were never jokes. Just the parts of Streetlight that taste funny to anyone who's trying us for the first time.

He smiles slowly, a giddiness behind his curled lips. "It's weird here," he says.

Em grins. Shawn sighs. I graze my hip with my fingers.

"I know," we answer.

Luka scoops us ice cream while he insists that we tell him more, while he asks about Streetlight like we're a myth or some old, haunted legend. I've never met anyone who cared before, anyone who believed that Streetlight was any more significant than our namesake. They say the whole reason our town was called Streetlight in the first place is because that's how quickly you'll pass it—that we're no more significant than a lamppost on a corner. And, yeah, there are times when that seems like nonsense—when the happiness is so explosive or the kisses so consuming that I'm positive there's nowhere on the planet bigger than here. But then there are nights like this one—when the Boys are somewhere without us, and it's dark and still and quiet—when Streetlight does seem small. Just a mistake on a map that people pass through before they realize they were ever here at all.

It's not that way to Luka, though. Or maybe it is, and he just *likes* that it is. Everybody knows LA, what it's like and what they do. They don't have secrets, rituals, things that only belong to them. At least, that's what Luka says.

"You have Disneyland," Em points out, spooning more of her ice cream into her mouth.

"Nope," Luka sighs. "That's Anaheim."

She frowns and then brightens again. "You have stars."

"Ooh." Luka leans against the counter, resting his forearms on the surface. "I do love stars." He lets his gaze drift to the ceiling like he can see the night sky through it. "Just not the Hollywood kind."

She smiles.

"You're right," Shawn decides. "LA is a wasteland."

Luka laughs.

The bell over the door dings, and a group of boys walks in, sweaty with cleats and soccer uniforms under their sweatshirts and coats.

They're younger than us—middle school or something—and one of their moms is digging into her purse for her wallet. Luka peels himself away from our conversation to greet them.

I pull out my phone while he takes orders. Since we're not supposed to talk about it, I'm not gonna say it, but this has already been such a good night. Easy. Fun. The sweet way that Luka listens to whichever one of us is talking, but his neck gets a little pink when it's Shawn. Em snuck a pinch to my wrist one time when it was happening, so I know she notices, too.

"Smile," I tell her, as I hold up my phone.

She does, posing easily with her waffle cone bowl. Then she asks, "Is this live?"

"Nah, just a video," I tell her, and pan over to Shawn next. "Smile."

He opens his mouth full of ice cream instead. I laugh and get a shot of my ice cream cone next—half-eaten but still pure food porn.

I stop recording, watch what I made, listen to Shawn and Em google how far Anaheim is from LA. I work on posting to Reels while they figure it out. Tagging Freeze Street. Tagging Streetlight. The boys in line tell Luka their orders step by step. *A scoop of cake batter. A scoop of reindeer tracks. Caramel sauce. Marshmallow fluff. More fluff. Please.*

I put my phone down, and a few seconds later, my first notification pops up. Then another, and another. "How far is it?" I ask Shawn and Em. Anaheim from LA, I mean.

"Like forty minutes," Em says.

"That's not *that* far," I insist.

"If you drove forty minutes outside of Streetlight, they wouldn't have even *heard* of Streetlight," Shawn points out.

I lick from my cone. "Fair."

Luka finishes with the orders, and the girl who goes to school with us starts ringing it all up. He asks if we want seconds, now that he's gotten some practice in. But he's kidding, because these portions are ridiculous.

I tap one of my notifications, glance at my phone so it has a chance to recognize my face. The screen unlocks, I read the comment, and then I go back to my ice cream.

Then I read the comment again.

hey cheater

I squint and scroll to the next one.

slut lol

"I'll be back," I announce, pretending to answer my phone. "Nik's calling."

"*Hi, Nik . . .*" Em calls sweetly.

And Luka asks, "Who's Nik?"

Nik Rios. Boyfriend. Have-Lot. IV Boy. The first guy who made my heart race and my breath stop. The one who showed me what love— what *magic*—feels like, how it makes my skin tingle and my throat dry, all because he took my hand.

The door closes before I can hear how Shawn and Em answer.

The air outside is colder than I remember, or maybe it really is colder now that it's later in the night. I step around to the side of the building so they can't see that I'm not talking on my phone, that I'm staring at it instead, scrolling these comments and trying to understand. It's Alex Vine. Nate Bullock. Cason Rowland. More. Nik's friends. Aaron's friends, too. Commenting one after another, bot-speed. All their messages basically the same. Kady Dixon is a monster and a liar and a cheater and a slut.

My throat gets tight, and my stomach does, too, like every one of their comments is grabbing a different part of me and squeezing from the inside. I've given these Boys a million truths to believe about me. That I'll smile through all their parties no matter how ready I am to leave. That I won't make a big deal about them calling a last-minute meeting, even when it's on my birthday. That it's okay that Nik keeps all their secrets. But they've never commented about any of that—in real life or on my page. They've never said, *Kady, you're great* or *We know Nik is happy* or even just *Cool pic*—so why say something now? When they're lies and they're awful?

My number of comments keeps growing. My phone vibrates by the second with new notifications. I have to talk to Aaron before they get to Nik.

I close Instagram and go to my contacts instead, a chill trickling down my spine that the cold didn't cause. I hover over Aaron's name but stop just before I press it.

My candies tingle against my hip like a gentle, friendly poke. And, for a moment, everything slows down.

I pull them from my waistband and squeeze them in my palm. They're . . . glowing? A faint blue haze like starlight. They're heating up by the second, and it feels so good, because my fingers are ice. I told myself I wasn't gonna use one until Nik got home. And once he did, I'd be able to give us so much more time together before he had to go back to school. We could relive a few days. Turn a weekend into a week. We could talk about the ball until he gave me an emphatic *yes*.

But right now, my candies tickle my left palm while my vibrating phone tickles my right. And the candies . . . they're better than any idea Aaron will have.

I check the time I posted the Reel and slide my phone into my back pocket. I pull a candy from the bag and glance up and down the lonely street, where there's no one but me and the parked cars.

I hold the candy I'm gonna take in one hand and the baggie with the rest of them in the other. Weighing the difference. Between sixty-seven and sixty-six. I really think I notice. One less. How I miss it before it's even gone.

But right now, I need it.

So I whisper the date and the time it was one minute before I posted, and I place the candy on my tongue.

It's gone—and I'm gone—before I can even taste it.

Kady
Saturday, November 7

I get it now, what TK meant about memories. How they shape-shift but never really go away. The evidence is gone, yeah—my Instagram is completely devoid of any onslaught of comments from those Boys last night. But I still know it happened. Even though it didn't. *Except it did.* Didn't it? For me, at least. Their words that never existed but are still so real floated into bed with me after I got home, suffocated me as I tried to fall asleep. They're still here now, making me hot, even under the guise of fresh daylight.

My phone vibrates, and my stomach drops through my mattress.

Aaron. A text. Probably wanting to talk about what happened last night, because he saw it, or they said something to him—

No, last night never happened.

I close my eyes and press my hand into my forehead. *It isn't real. It never happened.*

You getting into anything today?

That's all his text says. I stop holding my breath.

It's a little bit after nine. I've been up since eight, but there was no reason to get out of bed. So I'm here, still. Waiting and thinking way too freaking much.

Nope. What's up?

A few seconds later, he writes me back.

Wanna help me study? I'm at home

I frown. Aaron's never asked me to help him study before. Neither has Nik. I just figured they didn't need to. Not because they're geniuses or anything, but because I assumed tests weren't real things at Iverson.

But a reason to get out of bed is good for me right now, and seeing Aaron is a chance to ask him about this rumor, figure out if they're still talking about it or if what *didn't* happen last night was just some random sneak attack.

I text back and tell him sure, that I just need to get ready and then I can come.

Then I shed Nik's ratty old Iverson T-shirt, leave it in a ball on my bed, and dig in my dresser for something to wear.

Aaron lives on the Have-Lot side of Streetlight but in a different neighborhood than Nik's family does. The houses where Nik is are newer, all built in the past twenty years or so. But Aaron's in the part that's existed forever. Where the insides have been renovated, but the old bones are still standing.

You wouldn't expect Aaron to be in the old neighborhood, with neighbors like Hendricks and Saige. He doesn't come off like that at all. But it's the Jack-Laurence in him.

I jog up the front steps to his brick house. I knock and shove my hands back into my pockets, warming my left one against the glow of the candies. Tucked safely, yet again, in the waistband of my jeans.

Aaron opens the door in gray sweats and a hoodie, a beanie on his head. He smiles and gives me a one-armed hug as he lets me inside. I kick off my shoes by the door—not because they have a rule about it, but because they *don't* have a rule about it. Aaron's is the chillest Iverson house I've ever been inside of.

"Hungry?" he asks. "I have DiGiorno."

I'm pretty sure it's not even noon yet, but yes. Starved. "Yes, please."

"Dope," he says. "It's stuffed crust."

I follow him into the kitchen, this big open space that connects the dining room and living room without a single wall in sight. There's a giant island with waterfall edges, and on it are a bunch of Aaron's spiral notebooks. I slide onto a stool while Aaron starts the oven.

"So, what are you studying for?" I ask as he opens the freezer. "Doesn't Iverson just hand you the grades you want on a silver platter with a thank-you note for donating all these years?"

I know he's smiling, even though his back is to me. Busy digging into the DiGiorno box.

"AP tests," he says. "For Vandy." I twist my mouth, less interested in this study session now. But he can't see me, so he just keeps talking. "The dudes aren't gonna be all that down to help me, you know, renege on an entire IV tradition, so." He shrugs. *I've got you,* he says without saying it. "Plus, I haven't seen you in a minute."

So he noticed, too. That it's been a couple of days.

"Which AP test?" I ask as he shuts the oven door.

"US History." He faces me again and slides onto a barstool on the other side of the island. "Know anything about that?"

"Francis Scott Key. Three separate but equal powers. The Civil Rights Act of 1964?"

"Damn, KD. You wanna sit for this test instead of me? We can get you a nice fade so no one notices."

I scoop my braids into a ponytail and let them fall back on my shoulders. "You're learning way harder stuff than that."

"How do you mean?"

"I mean, this is AP." I pull one of his notebooks toward me, a yellow one, and run my thumb down the side of the pages. "My school barely even *has* AP."

"What's *barely* mean?" Aaron asks.

"Just AP Physics. That they groom, like, ten kids a year to be ready for. The rest of our brains aren't big enough."

"Nah." Aaron folds his arms on the countertop. "Physics is just rules. Not even about being all that smart, you just have to be willing to accept them all. How fast light goes. How to measure space. How time works. Always the same." He frowns. "But I don't know. I don't think I believe that. There's an exception out there. There's gotta be."

He watches me like he's ready to get deep about it. I smile. "You sound like Em."

"*Em.*" He snaps his fingers. "*That's* who I should have asked to help me study."

I'd kick him, but the island is in the way.

"You guys get into anything good last night?" he asks.

It takes me a second to remember that there were good parts about last night, too. Parts when we laughed so hard, and told stories we hadn't told in years, and witnessed Shawn and Luka try to say bye to each other, as much as they didn't want to. I smile and lower my voice even though I'm pretty sure we're the only ones home. "Remember that guy Shawn met at Spooks? Luka?" Aaron nods and I go on, "Well, he works at Freeze Street, and we went to hang out with him last night."

Aaron raises his eyebrows. "And?"

"*Anddddd . . .*" I bite back my smile. "I think they really like each other."

"*Let's go.*" Aaron grins. "What about the jury, though? You guys gotta give a verdict."

"Em and I like him a lot, too."

"Wow, really?"

So I nod and tell him about the only version of last night that exists anymore. How we stayed at Freeze Street until they closed at ten. Then we waited for Luka to change back into jeans before we took him on a walking tour of Streetlight. He's only been here for two months and hasn't seen much, so we walked him through Old Town and past The Drive-In. We brought him to the edge of this neighborhood, too, but it's weird to tell Aaron that his life is basically a tourist attraction, so I don't.

Em showed him The Spot from the outside, because they were closed already, and promised she'd bring him back soon. To hold him over, Shawn started telling him all the best things they make, and the list was so long that it almost got us all the way back to Luka's house. He's in the townhomes not far from the guys' apartment—just him and his parents, like Shawn. Luka hugged Em and me, and then he hugged Shawn last, and on our walk home we counted all the ways he's good for us. He hates mushrooms, like me. Knows all the zodiacs, like Em. Loves cooking reality shows, like Shawn. And a million other things.

Recounting the night as it officially happened, in all its Netflix-movie perfection, calms me down. Makes me realize that my shoulders were tight now that they're not anymore. Aaron smiles the whole time I'm talking, and when I finish, he says, "That's what's up. I'm happy for you guys."

"What about you?" I ask, swigging from the water bottle that he handed me halfway through my story. "Do anything last night?"

He twists his mouth. Shrugs. "The guys wanted to get together for a few hours. Get fucked up." He watches his hand as he slides it along the marble. "I didn't hang around long."

I nod. Maybe that's why they felt bold enough to attack me on social media. There have been too many nights to count now when Aaron and I have been the only sober ones in a mansion.

"Turned in early so you could nerd out for this AP test?" I smile.

"Yeah, buddy." He slides the rest of his notebooks over to me, so I have all of them now—including the yellow one I grabbed earlier.

"So how should we start?" I flip through his notebooks. "Do you have questions anywhere?"

"Yeah, so." He slides off his seat and rounds the island to get to me. He leans in. Close enough that the scent of his mouthwash warms the inside of my nose. "Each of these is a different unit." He grabs a blue notebook and flips it open. "And each page has one practice question on it. You don't have to go in order or anything. You can skip pages, even go back and forth between notebooks, if you want. It's probably better that way, honestly. To see if I really know it."

The first page in this blue notebook has a question written in black Sharpie, right in the middle. There are four answer choices below it, and the right one has been brushed with a yellow highlighter. But on the rest of the page are all these squiggly lines in purple pen. A few straight ones that were drawn so hard that they've left dents in the paper. A random blue circle sticker in the bottom corner of the page.

I flip to the next one. Another question in the middle, multiple choice answers underneath, but the rest of the page has been dotted with different-colored markers. Like confetti, or something. And the entire long edge has been carefully ripped away, so it's a torn edge instead of a straight one. I flip again. Another question. More answers. This one with a giant rainbow and all the corners folded. I can't stop staring. And flipping. Each page is so particularly designed and yet completely chaotic. And as I'm looking at it, I can almost hear Aaron scraping his foot or tapping his fingers or cracking his knuckles. I can practically see him looking off or looking through me. All his little tics, all his fidgeting, vomited in full color onto page after page. "What *is* all this stuff?" I ask.

"*Stuff?* You mean my art?" He squints at me, waiting for me to say I was joking, or that it's beautiful, or that I'm sorry. My throat goes dry the moment before his straight face breaks. I shove him and he laughs. "Nah, they're just tactics. To help me remember."

The oven timer goes off, and it makes me jump—the first sound that Aaron or I haven't caused since I got here. "What do you mean, *tactics?*"

He walks back around the island and grabs a pot holder from a drawer. "Like little things for my brain to hold on to. So it's easier to remember what was on the page." He says it like it's nothing, like it's normal, as he opens the oven. For half a second, his back is to me—before he turns around and sets the pizza on the island.

"You know"—he grabs a cutter from the same drawer the pot holder came from and starts slicing—"a lot of people think the best way to make stuff stick is to focus on it. Drill it into their brains over and over again." He shakes his head while he watches what he's doing, while he rolls the cutter two or three times in the same place, just to slide it through the hot dough. "But that's only half of it. One-fifth of it, I guess. Because really, the best thing you can do? Is give the rest of your senses something to hold on to, too. Like, right now. You're listening to me, right? But it also smells like this dope-ass pizza I slaved over." I smile as he goes on. "And this counter?" He sets down the pizza cutter and runs his fingertips over the polished stone. "Smooth. Cold. And the way it sounds? There are those wind chimes outside." He nods over his shoulder toward the sliding back doors, and I hear it now—the dainty dinging. "It's stuff like that. Making some tiny piece of information big enough to actually wrap your arms around. So on all those pages . . ." He nods at the notebook that's still in my hands. "I did that. Gave myself something to look at besides just words. Something to feel. Something bigger to remember. Bigger than just a bunch of dates, I mean." He nudges the sheet pan with our pizza on it a little bit closer to me. "Plate?" he offers.

I shake my head and grab a slice. "Where'd you learn all that?"

He takes a slice, too. "A tutor I had once." He bites into his piece, and I bite into mine.

The cheese glues itself to the roof of my mouth. "Ow," I say around a bite of steaming pizza.

Aaron closes his eyes and hops from one foot to the other, it hurts that bad. "Good, though," he declares when he can form words again.

"So good."

We both take second bites.

"Eat then study?" Aaron suggests.

"We'll eat this entire pizza, then study," I agree.

"There is *no way* you're about to help me finish this entire pizza."

"Get out of here. Owen and I used to crush a Domino's large and eat dinner three hours later."

"Stuffed crust, though?"

"Look, if you're trying to watch your figure for the girls at Vanderbilt"—Aaron snorts, but I don't stop—"I get it. First impressions are a big thing."

"Alright." He leans on his side of the island, holding my gaze, matching my smile. "We go slice for slice until this whole thing's gone. Or until someone's in the bathroom."

"What do I get when I win?"

"*If* you win . . ." Aaron looks around his kitchen, into the dining room, into the living room. Thinking of a good enough prize. "If Nik won't take you to the ball this year, I won't go, either. Bet?"

What? Aaron doesn't talk about the ball any more than he talks about his family. But I guess it's just gotten that pathetic—how badly I've wanted to go and how I've still never been.

I study him. Why does it feel like he already knows I'm about to be let down again?

"What happens if you win?" I ask instead.

He thinks for a second, rubbing at a spot on the island. "I wanna pick a movie at The Drive-In."

"No one gets to pick a movie at The Drive-In."

His mouth is half-full. "So y'all just happen to play *Erin Brockovich* on Shawn's birthday every year since I got here?"

I watch my pizza instead of him and try not to laugh. But I feel him across the island, smirking.

"Fine. Bet."

He holds out his fist, and I bump his with mine. "Bet," he agrees.

And for a little while, we just eat.

"Can I ask you something?" I finally say.

He groans like he'd rather take medicine.

It's enough to make me smile into my slice, even though I'm nervous. "That rumor . . . are they still talking about it?"

It takes a second, but he admits, "Yeah. They're still talking."

In my periphery, he's looking at me, but it's easier if I don't look back. "What if it gets worse? What if they . . . I don't know. Go to Nik? Or start saying stuff all around Streetlight? Or make a bunch of comments on my posts, or something?"

I want him to say that they won't. So it's not completely delusional for me to hope that maybe—somehow—what I did last night was enough to erase their words permanently.

"Would you tell me if they did?" he asks instead.

I finally look up from my pizza, while he leans against the island,

and his forearms rest on the surface. His eyes are the color of storm clouds.

I don't know if I'd tell him. I'd *want* to. Last night, I almost did. But as long as I have candies . . . as long as I can rewind and avoid the land mines on my own . . .

"Would you want to know?" I ask.

"*Of course* I'd want to know. We're in this together, right?" He watches me steadily as he chews.

I reach for my water again, but I'm not really thirsty. I just need to squeeze something, swish it around. "It's such a stupid rumor."

"I know."

"I never kissed you."

"I know."

But something twists in me after I say it, the part that aches whenever I lie.

Aaron
Saturday, November 7

The page. *Ripped long edge. X's in a circle. Diagonal lines drawn corner to corner.*

The colors. *Cool ones. Blue. Green. Purple.*

The question. *What was the Cold War?*

After KD left, I kept studying at my desk with the TV turned to the game. That helped, too, sometimes. Adding sound to the words. Completely unrelated sound, but still. It gave all this stuff dimension, other details to tug at when it was time to remember what I knew.

I closed my eyes and pictured the page in my head. I mumbled the answer out loud as it came to me. The buzzwords. The ones that flashed through my brain like cheap motel signs.

"Named by Orwell. After World War Two. When the alliance fell apart. Communism. NATO. Enough bombs to destroy the world. Not a real war, but it could've been—"

My phone went off. I answered on speaker.

"Hey, Pops."

"Hey, kid. You alright? You at the house?"

He was using his car audio—his voice had that thing about it.

"Yeah, studying for this AP History test. You with Charlotte? How was the fundraiser?"

They'd been in White Cove all day for a book drive, one of the charities Charlotte supported. She let them use her name and likeness for promos, but she also showed up for as many events as she could. Talked to families. Read to kids. She was made for that stuff.

"Aw, man, it was great," Pops said, still in awe. "Turnout was huge. They had to have gotten a thousand books in just a couple hours. And yeah, I'm with her now. She can hear you."

"Hey, honey," Charlotte said, her voice far away like Pops's.

"Hey, Char," I answered. "Glad it went well today."

"Me too," she said. "We missed you, though. How's studying?"

I'd been rubbing the torn edge of this page since I answered the phone. "It's good. I've been at it all day, though. I'll probably quit soon."

"Well, are you hungry?" Charlotte asked. "We were gonna stop by the Whole Foods over here so I could cook us some dinner once we got home. Are you craving anything?"

My real mom never stuck around—she was young, and about that party life, and gave Pops full custody when I was a few months old. But I didn't think about it too much. It was easier not to, plus we were good—we had each other, our apartment in South Philly, Hulu Live with the sports package. The only thing I thought a mom would bring us that we didn't have on our own was food. Pops and I had frozen meals and takeout, period. That Little Caesars carryout deal was religion.

I never thought I'd miss how we used to eat until I got to Streetlight, and all they had was local shit. Not a major chain in sight. Man, I could go for a Cheesy Gordita Crunch. But I couldn't ask for that. Charlotte loved cooking for us.

"Whatever you guys want," I promised. "Maybe not pizza."

I could hear her smile. "Okay, I won't make a pizza."

"Alright, kid," Pops cut back in. "We'll see you soon. Give us an hour."

"Bet. Love you guys."

Their words got muffled on top of each other, but I knew they said it back.

The call went dead. The time shined back at me. Six o'clock. I looked down at my page. *What was the Cold War?*

My phone went off again. They'd probably decided what they wanted to make and needed me to check the kitchen for what we already had. Garlic? Onions? Potatoes?

Hendricks.

I frowned. We didn't talk like that. Not in the kind of way where he'd call me and I wouldn't know why. Maybe I forgot about something. A party tonight and blood brothers were driving. Or an alumni meeting I was late for.

I racked my brain. Nope.

I pushed back from my desk and stared at the TV instead. " 'Sup, man?" I answered on speaker.

"There he is," Hendricks said on the other end. "The man everyone's been talking about."

Andddd *here we go*. No telling what stories had made it back to Barnes, but I knew he'd be glad to tell me all about it. That was the thing about talking to Hendricks—he barely needed you to be there for most of the conversation. Just wanted to remind you what he knew and who he was and why he was so damn convinced the rest of us should care.

But at the end of the day, all he was was a fourth-generation IV Boy, and the only place that mattered was here. He wasn't all-powerful anywhere else. Just lucky for him he'd never been *around* anyone from anywhere else.

Except for me.

"Yeah?" I said, sitting back in my chair, splitting my attention between this phone call and the basketball game. Collecting details. "Appreciate y'all thinking about me."

"Pleasure's ours, brother."

Brother. I tensed up whenever he said it. Especially when he said it to me. It sounded different than it did with everyone else, *because it was.* Because there was everyone else, and then there was Nik, and then there was me.

I ignored it tonight like I always did. *Mavericks up seven.*

"A birdie told me you're trying to go to Vanderbilt," he finished.

I relaxed a little bit when it was nothing more than that, even though I had no idea how word got out. I hadn't said anything to anyone besides KD, and I knew she didn't go snitch. It could've been Charlotte; it wouldn't have been her fault. Just her being proud, talking about me to one of the other moms, loving me like I was hers all along. Or maybe not. It didn't take much in Streetlight. It could've just been the wind.

"It's never a guarantee anyone's getting into Vanderbilt," I said, because I wasn't ready to talk about it yet.

Celtics score. Mavs up by five.

"You know our Boys go to Barnes," Hendricks said like he shouldn't have to remind me. "And then we come back. You trying to not come back?" He was smirking. I could hear it. "What'd we do, scare you away?"

"That's years from now, man." *Mavericks up eight.* "I don't even know what I'm having for dinner."

"Well, this is something you should know. It should be easy. Because it's not really a question about whether you're coming back to Streetlight or not. The question is whether you want to stay IV or not."

Time-out. "And you decided you needed to have that answer to-night?" I asked.

"Look, we're supposed to be on the same team, right?" Even though he wasn't, I felt him getting closer. Like, if he'd been here, he would have been leaning in. Watching me dead in the eye. "Looking out for each other? And last I checked, your last name was still Johnson. It wasn't Jack-Laurence."

"Damn, you over there doing research for my memoir?"

I forced a laugh, pretending like it didn't bother me. Annoyed at myself that even when I knew Hendricks was nonsense, he still got to me sometimes.

"Your name matters," he went on, like he loved being the one to have to tell me. "And the Jack-Laurences—you know I've known them my whole life, right?—they're gonna look out for each other *way* before they worry about some kid named Johnson. They're gonna make sure Sophie and Chad get those legacy spots at Vandy before you do." Charlotte's cousin Phil's kids, who were my age. "That's the point of a name—that's what it's for. And that's what the IVs are supposed to be for you. At Barnes. In Streetlight. That's the whole reason we created all this to begin with."

It was funny, because there were all these times when I was *too Jack-Laurence*, as far as Hendricks was concerned. Because I didn't want to get fucked up with the guys that night, or I missed a meeting because the family had something going on. Any time I didn't feel like being blindly IV, Hendricks got all in his feelings and said I was *too Jack-Laurence.*

And now here he was, telling me all the reasons why I'd never be Jack-Laurence enough.

Maybe he was right.

I mean, I didn't stand up at that altar as Pops's best man and automatically assume that made me one of them. *Of course* I worried about not being Jack-Laurence enough. But not because of some admissions decision. I was worried I wasn't Jack-Laurence enough to be a family.

But Hendricks didn't care about any of that.

"Look, Charlotte just finished cooking, so I gotta go," I said. *Mavs up eleven.*

"I'm sure she did." Hendricks chuckled into the phone. "Well, you have a good dinner, brother. I'm sure we'll talk more about this real soon."

Celtics at the line.

I hung up and slid my thumb over my phone, wiping away a smudge and the truth that I'd never told anyone. That, yeah—I wanted to leave the IVs. I'd wanted to since the moment I survived that first ball. And I didn't know if it was gonna be Vanderbilt, or some other school, or just going back to Philly. But I was done with them as soon as I could be. That part I knew for sure.

Mavericks up nine.

I rolled back over to my desk and rubbed my neck first, then my eyes.

The page. *Ripped long edge. X's in a circle. Diagonal lines drawn corner to corner.*

The colors. *Cool ones. Blue. Green. Purple.*

The question. *What was the Cold War?*

I closed my eyes and mumbled, "After World War Two. When the alliance fell apart. Enough bombs to destroy the world. Not a real war, but it could've been . . ."

Kady

Friday, November 13

I would have walked here tonight, but Nik isn't a walker.

Not even to Old Town, with its cobblestone sidewalks and all the nice stores. Not even now that it's all dressed up for the holidays, with evergreen garlands that wrap all the way up to the tops of the lampposts and string lights in all the storefronts.

We walked all summer, he insisted again tonight. But that's an irrelevant argument. Because it's not summer anymore.

We only drive around the block once before he finds a spot across the street from Bianchi's, the restaurant where Saige is hosting her birthday dinner. A bunch of her friends are home this weekend for the party she's having tonight in a giant tent on her family's patio, equipped with heat lamps and lanterns, according to the post on Instagram that she only shared with Close Friends. But people like Nik—and, by association, me—were invited to the dinner she's hosting beforehand. It started at seven.

It's 7:17.

I unfasten my seat belt, but Nik says, "Hold on."

He hops out of the driver's seat and closes his door behind him. I smile as he rounds the front of his Range Rover to come get me. His headlights are still on because they have this fancy feature where they stay lit for sixty seconds, even after the car is off. So, as he passes, it's like his perfection is glowing beneath the spotlight it deserves. Khaki chinos. His blue button-down under his black Iverson pullover. Lightly gelled hair. Suede shoes.

He opens my car door, smiling at me as he does. I'm not even sure which one of us starts it—if he chuckles, or if I giggle, or if it happens at the exact same second because we're exactly the same—but suddenly, we can't stop laughing, and I'm hopping into his arms instead of taking the hand he offered to help me out of the car.

I wrap my legs around his waist and my arms around his neck, and he holds me up with one arm while he pushes my door closed with the other.

"This what I get for trying to be a gentleman?" he asks as I tug his ears out to the side so he looks like Dumbo.

"It's what you get for assuming I'm gonna be a lady."

He shakes my hands off and kisses my mouth instead. Under the lampposts. Under the starlight. My legs still around his waist. I wonder if he feels it, too. The way my heart is pirouetting in my chest, and that *thing* in the air. Like the stars are shedding billions of particles too small to see, but they glitter on my skin when they land.

I can't wait to do this again. To put a candy on my tongue and vanish for just a second until I'm back in this exact, perfect moment.

"You look really good tonight," he says. I pulled my braids into a top bun, and Nik always likes it when I do that.

"You told me that already," I remind him.

"Did I?" He sets me down. "I must really mean it, then."

I'm in black skinny jeans and a white blouse with sheer sleeves. I borrowed a pair of shoes from Em that have a tiny heel on them—all in an effort to look nice, but not *too* nice, for this dinner tonight.

Bianchi's isn't fun. It's a four-dollar-sign restaurant where the

Iverson kids are constantly having lunch or dinner or unsupervised drinks. There are harp-playing babies painted on the ceiling like you're eating in the Sistine Chapel. The giant windows at the front make it easy for anyone passing by to see all the men in blazers and women in cocktail dresses sitting happily at the tables they reserved weeks in advance. It's always a little too warm inside. At least, it has been the handful of times when Nik dragged me along.

I wish we could stay out here, where the wind blows, and the stars with their secret dust make me feel like I'm sparkling. But maybe we can do it that way later. When we do it again.

Nik pulls open the door and lets me walk in first. A girl with short brown hair greets us at the host stand. She looks a little bit older than us. In her white shirt and little black skirt, she says, "Welcome-to-Bianchi's-how-can-I-help-you," like it's one long word.

"Hey," Nik says, leaning closer so she can hear him over the soft classical music playing in the background. "We're with Saige Alexander."

"Saige-yep." The hostess grabs two menus. "You-can-follow-me-this-way."

She walks as fast as she talks, weaving us past all the happy tables. We're low-key jogging just to keep up with her, and I tug on Nik's arm as I whisper, "Is this the complimentary workout before dinner?"

His hands are in his pockets, and he's refusing to look at me, like he knows it'll get him laughing and it could be too hard to stop. "Shh," he gently tells me. And after a second, he adds, "You know nothing's complimentary at Bianchi's."

I smile into his bicep just as she stops walking and spins to face us. "Here-you-are." She hands us our menus. "Have-a-great-dinner." And then she Usain Bolts–it back to the host stand.

"Hey," Saige says, her smooth voice carrying through the hum of conversations.

I pull my face away from Nik's arm and pay attention to the table in front of us for the first time. Saige at the head and four chairs on each side. Hendricks on her right, then two girls next to him, and a Boy on the end. Then two more Boys, and the two seats closest to Saige on her left are open. Ours, I guess.

Their gaze snaps in our direction. Every single one of them. The conversations pause. The texting does, too. The stillness makes my neck hot. I want to drop a glass or knock silverware onto the floor. Something clangy and shattering and loud.

Saige is smiling, though, like nothing's weird at all. "I thought you went ghost," she says, with her chin in her hand.

She didn't really think that; that's why it's so easy for her to say it without sounding embarrassed. She knows Nik would have to be lying in a ditch somewhere before he'd miss her birthday.

Nik rests a hand on her back and kisses her cheek. "Sorry we're late."

Their exchange breaks the trance, as the table says hi to Nik and Saige stands to give me a hug. "Hey, Kady," she says.

"Happy birthday." My muscles relax, and I dig into my clutch for the card that I made Nik stop at the drugstore for on our way here tonight. He said we didn't need it, but I insisted that we did, even if Saige and I aren't close. Or maybe because of it.

"Aw, you're so sweet!" She takes it from me and turns it over in her hands like she's never seen a real-live card before. She looks me in the eyes. "Thank you."

"Of course. I know Nik already said it, but I'm sorry, too, that we're late."

She's in a short, fitted, maroon dress. Long-sleeved. Mock turtleneck. Lacy. Her hair's in a bun, and diamonds the size of marbles glitter from her ears. I can't see her shoes—they're mostly hidden by the table—but they're something with a heel, because she's taller.

"That's okay." She slides the card onto the corner of the table and assures me, "I blame Nik, anyway."

"Typical," Nik says as he takes my hand and tugs a little so that I'll sit down. I'm not sure he's even heard us except for the part at the end, and Saige laughs but doesn't disagree. He takes the seat next to her, and I take the seat next to him.

There's wine in green bottles and dark liquid in short glasses, little splash marks on the white tablecloth like confetti. It reminds me of Aaron's study pages, covered in dots and spots and details that make all the sense in the world to him. Before I even realize it, I'm trying to make the imprints on my mind that he can make on his.

"Do you know everyone, Kady?" Saige asks, now that she's sitting, too. I don't, but she does a round of quick introductions without me having to say so. She starts on my left. "Chris, Jacob, Brian, Hannah, Elle."

"What about me?" Hendricks smirks at her.

"You?" Saige brings her wineglass to her lips. "The man who needs no introduction?"

He doesn't look at me again, doesn't offer a smile—and, in a way, it makes me feel better. Normal, at least. Hendricks has never cared to acknowledge all the ways that our lives bump up against each other's. And I always thought that that annoyed the hell out of me, the way he could ignore me like the stop signs he blows past on Main Street. But, right now, I'll take it—if it means he and his friends aren't glaring at me like they were when we first walked in.

He leans in close and mumbles something to Saige that makes her laugh into her glass.

I'm vaguely familiar with the other Boys, the same way I am with most of the IVs. I don't know the girls at all and have already forgotten which one is Hannah and which one is Elle, but they smile at me and I smile back. The Boys don't. They talk to each other, muttering things I can't hear.

Suddenly, I catch a whiff of something. Not the garlic that's a little bit of everywhere. It's the memory of the night I erased—how those comments, when they existed, made me nauseous.

Who were the Boys who posted? I can't remember. Did I even really look? At the time, it didn't matter. It just had to go away.

But maybe it was them. The ones who know the rumor. The ones who actually believe it.

And now here we are, tucked into the same lavish dinner, and they're sitting all around me. Hungry.

They order a bunch of appetizers—breads with dips, calamari, olives for eight dollars that come five to an order. Hendricks and Nik are paying, apparently, which was either previously understood or just very easily accepted by Nik when Hendricks announced it for the table to hear. They request more drinks, pour more wine. Nik settles on a light beer, because I hate it when he drinks and drives, and he considers that to be a compromise. I get the vibe that he's trying not to make this dinner any harder for me than it already is, because he feels it, too. How different the guys are being. How they've taken turns looking at me all night, smirking over their glasses. Like I'm in a house of mirrors, and any time I dare to look up, I'm faced with another one of their stares.

It makes my palms sweat and my throat burn, this deep and embarrassing instinct to let the tears come, but I refuse. Shawn hates when people stare. He says there are only two kinds of people who would ever dare look at another human being like that, like they're just some caged thing at a zoo.

The crazy ones, he says. *Or the ones who've decided they're better than you.*

With one arm hanging over the back of his seat, and his navy blue sweater tied around his shoulders, Hendricks says, "Let's play Drop Cup."

I don't have to say anything—just like they did with the appetizers and the last round of drinks, they decide it's a good idea on their own.

It's not, though. Drop Cup is the most disgusting game ever, and Saige seems to be the only one who kind of remembers that, but in a coy and smiley way, so everyone knows she's not gonna fight it. It's truth or dare, basically, except when you don't want to tell the truth, you have to drink from the Drop Cup. And the Drop Cup is full of whatever random liquid-ish things people drop into it after their turn is over.

They use Nik's basically empty pint glass to get started.

They go around the table, asking each other questions about a bunch of people I don't know. I'm not expected to participate, and I don't want to, anyway. Instead, I wonder what Aaron is doing, and if he's gonna be at Saige's house later. I almost text and ask, but it feels like I'd be tempting fate too much. Giving the guy next to me a chance to see Aaron's name pop up on my screen and notice how long our text thread is. Bringing Aaron into a dinner—even if it's just on my phone—that he absolutely needs to stay out of.

"Hey, Kady." Hendricks juts his chin at me, getting my attention. Then he says it again, smiling like a prick, his tone changing so it sounds like he's actually saying hi this time. "Hey, Kady." His green eyes glisten with rich-boy snark and alcohol.

"Yeah?" I ask.

"It's your turn," he tells me.

This cup has passed over me a dozen times, while they asked each other questions and filled it with wine and calamari and all the other scraps on this table. But he watches me now—*stares at me now*—like I'm the one who's mistaken. Like I've been a part of the worst game ever all along.

"She's not playing tonight, man." Nik squeezes my knee.

But Hendricks keeps his eyes on me and says, "Everyone's playing." He nods in Saige's direction. "It's her birthday."

Saige smiles and promises me, "You don't have to—"

"Why *wouldn't* you play?" Hendricks asks before she can fully get the words out. He doesn't have to speak up for everyone to be listening to him more than they're listening to her. It's the way he smirks and glares, like he wishes you were more of a challenge. The way he doesn't bother to raise his voice, like you aren't worth the energy. It's the same way he is with a ton of people, the same way I've seen him at a million parties, but there's an extra edge tonight. Or maybe it's this moment stacked on top of the others. The way he treated me in front of Nik's house before they drove back to Barnes. The way that Boy at Spooks looked at me when he felt me watching their conversation with Aaron. And the way they all watched when I got here tonight—eyes whipping in my direction like they were magnetized.

The glances that have kept happening all dinner. And now, it's like I'm all he sees, all he cares about, for the first time I can ever remember.

Everything, stacked on top of each other, littlest to biggest, top-heavy now and ready to crash to the ground.

"I don't like this game," I answer.

He shrugs, frowns. "Don't we all put up with things we don't like?"

The Boys at the table snicker. Elle-and-Hannah smile with them. Saige rolls her eyes. "Hendricks . . ."

He laughs a little. "What?"

"Come on, I'll go." Nik takes the glass from in front of me and sets it in front of himself. "My turn." But when the table stays quiet, Nik insists, "Come on, someone ask me something. Everybody's shy all of a sudden?"

One of the Boys starts to come up with a question, leans forward so it's easier to hear him. But Hendricks, in that same, easy voice that made everyone stop and listen the first time, tells me, "You don't want to play because you know what I'm gonna ask."

My heart slides, slow, down my body.

"It's true," he goes on, like it's just us, like I can be real with him. "Isn't it? The stuff that's going around? I mean, why would you care, if it wasn't? Why not just play, if it wasn't?" He laughs again. At me.

Saige's gaze darts around the table, searching for someone who understands. Then she squints at Hendricks. "*What's* true?"

But he shrugs, like it's boring. Like lying about me is boring. Like destroying my life is boring. "She's been hooking up with Aaron."

"*What?*" Saige cries.

"*No I'm not!*" I insist, but Elle-and-Hannah are already covering their mouths, trying to catch up while the Boys whisper to them about what they've missed. My throat tightens just thinking about the words they could be saying, the ones that were left on my Reel. *Cheater. Liar. Slut.* "I would never, ever do that . . ."

Hendricks glares at me across the table. "No?"

From the corner of my eye, I see Nik's gaze fall into his lap. I want to squeeze my hands over his ears and force him to look away. But if this rumor is here—in the middle of Saige's birthday dinner—it's already everywhere.

I grip the edge of the table so my hands stop shaking, while Hendricks sits there, completely still. "*No!* Anyone with a pulse knows this is completely ridiculous, so *why* are you listening to it? Why don't you just tell the guy who started it to shut the hell up already?"

Hendricks raises his eyebrows. "You think he'd listen?"

"*Make* him listen."

"Okay." He stares. "Make me."

I wait for him to laugh some more and tell me to lighten up—that of course he isn't the one who started this, that he'd have to give a shit about me before he'd invest any kind of effort in ruining me. But he doesn't. He just stares, because he can—because he's so sure he's better than I'll ever be.

Our two waiters come over and start clearing off our table, asking if we're ready for entrees or refills. They shuffle around like blurred extras in a movie, but all I see is Hendricks.

Nik's chair scrapes the floor, reacting before either of us has a chance to fully process what I'm about to do. "Kades—"

But he can't stop me. I grab the Drop Cup and throw everything that's inside it in Hendricks's unfazed face.

Elle-and-Hannah gasp like someone's been shot, and Saige's big brown eyes go even bigger. Within seconds, waiters are everywhere. They start wiping him dry, apologizing, offering him for free all the things he can easily afford. *Do accept our apologies, Mr. Hendricks. Might we offer you a panna cotta?*

They tell me I need to go. And I *want* to go—I'm just trying to slow down enough to get my coat back on and not break down under the stares of this entire restaurant.

And when I push open the heavy wooden door, the cold nighttime swallows me whole.

My eyes are wet, and I try to catch my breath, but my lungs are sieves. My trembling fingers pull my phone from my pocket, and I check my Instagram, TikTok. But there are no new comments.

They've never gotten me to break before. I've refused the bait for years. Been the model-fucking-girlfriend so no one could point to any real reason why Nik and I weren't good together, or why he shouldn't be proud of me, or why I didn't belong at the ball. And in the time it took to douse Hendricks, all of it came undone.

I shove my phone away and scramble for my candies, hotter even than what I've gotten used to. I have to get out of here. I have to make sure that whatever the hell just happened never really happens, and I close my eyes and try to breathe and try to think. Going back to earlier in the dinner isn't gonna stop Hendricks from saying what he said, probably not even going back to earlier in the day. I need to skip dinner altogether somehow, give Nik an excuse and bail. So maybe I go back to yesterday? When did he ask me to come? It was Monday. No . . . Tuesday . . .

"Hey." Nik's flat voice cracks in the darkness.

He's behind me somewhere, and I push my candies back into my waistband as discreetly as I can. Like I'm just cold. Fumbling around. I rub my arms next. And pray he didn't see anything.

I turn around.

His hands are in his coat pockets. His breath comes out white, little ghosts escaping his lips. He isn't smiling, and he isn't frowning. He's just there—right outside the restaurant while I've walked up the side-walk a bit—out of arm's reach.

I swallow and force myself to say, "There's this rumor that's been going around."

He nods. "I know about the rumor."

I squint, his face unchanging. "Why didn't you say anything?"

He shrugs, glances around, down toward the stoplight that's almost always red. "I never believed it."

He walks to the curb and has a seat. I hug myself and sit down next to him.

It's quiet out here, and I'm just now realizing it. The stores all closed. A car hasn't driven by. It's the opposite of what we've left inside Bianchi's. I finally catch my breath.

"I'm glad you don't believe it," I tell him. "But it also isn't true."

He holds that thought for a second, trying to decide—I think—how different the two are. But he nods and laces his fingers through mine. "They're just talking shit."

"*Why*, though?" I study the side of his face, desperate for something that makes sense. "They're supposed to be your friends. They're supposed to be *Aaron's* friends. You and I have been together for *three years now*, and Hendricks thinks this is okay? *You* think this is okay?"

"It's just what it is, Kades." He sounds like he's tired. "You can't freak out about it. You can't let it get to you. We're brothers. We mess with each other. Always have."

I wish I could tell him about the social media stuff, or the way Aaron looks whenever we talk about the rumor. Because that doesn't feel like just messing around. Like brothers being brothers. "It's only gonna get worse," I whisper, because it's so quiet that I feel like I have to. "Now that I just threw a cup full of sewage in Hendricks's face."

Nik nods to himself, like I've made better decisions. But he tells me, "He's had worse things in his face."

And the way Nik somehow always manages to do, he actually makes me smile. "I only did it because I didn't want him to hurt you."

We sit there a little while longer in the quiet cold, and my mind drifts to all the things I really would do for him. All the things I already have. The parties I hate to go to, the friends I've never liked to be around, tracking his location like a video game so I always know that he's okay. The time we've spent together, the endless days and infinite nights.

I'm not gonna use one of my candies, not to try to undo this dinner. Not if this is how it ends. Because if he's okay, I am.

"Come on." He stands up. "Let's go home."

He starts walking across the street. The lights on his Range Rover flash twice.

"What about Saige's party?" I ask from the curb.

He laughs, and the sound bounces down the street. Like he's sure I've lost my mind. "You're not going to that." He doesn't even turn around to say it.

Kady

Saturday, November 14

"Hello, miss. Welcome. May I take your coat?" something invisible asks.

And then my arms are bare, my shawl drifting weightlessly into the darkness.

I'm floating in a world with no walls. Tinted with galactic purples and midnight blues and sparkly whites. The air snakes through my fingers when I try to touch them. The kinds of colors that live among the stars.

Do we?

There are hundreds of them—people?—maybe thousands. In tuxedos that are so black they hardly exist, so pressed that their edges are sharper than knives. In gowns that shimmer and flow like they're half-liquid. Honey, maybe. Smooth and slowly dripping. But they don't have faces, only eyes. Sparkling jewels and fluorescent feathers where their noses and cheeks and mouths should be.

Maybe they don't eat. Maybe they don't breathe. Bewitching and alien. Beautiful and perfect.

And they blink. Blink, blink, blink. At me. At who I am.

Who am I?

My fingertips brush my face, my neck. My soft skin. My heavenly dress. The skirt stretches farther than I can see, to the next world, to the next galaxy. I spin and it twirls, and magic shimmers off me, mixing with the colors in the air. I hope it lands on earth and makes another girl shine.

They clap. They cheer. Whatever they are, they love me. I keep turning. I spread my arms. Can I fly?

"NO!" *one shouts.*

I collapse on a hard, dark ground.

I grab my stomach. My hands are wet. Blood. My blood. Every-where.

It hurts.

God, it hurts.

The faceless things float above me. Growing. Stretching as tall as trees as they hover over my aching body. Their applause becomes laughter. Deafening laughter—booming like thunder, and I'm the center of the storm.

Was it always laughter? I hear it, but I don't see it. Because they have no mouths, only eyes. Twinkling eyes.

Even while I bleed, they're beautiful.

No. They're evil.

Blink, blink, blink.

One pushes its way to the front, wearing those sharp tuxedo edges. It shrinks until it's small, like me.

It drifts to the ground—a phantom. A ghost.

No. Those eyes.

Aaron?

It takes my bloody hands. It puts its palms on my cheeks. When our skin connects, its face forms, like some sort of chemical reaction.

Aaron.

"I'm sorry," *he whispers. Somehow, it's louder than everything else. He kisses me with lips that burn like fire.*

I jump awake like I've been falling.

Nik's room is filled with bluey starlight and silence. Cars don't drive past late where he lives. There's no honking. No sirens. Just big, sleepy houses keeping their people warm and safe.

My heart is beating so hard it hurts. It was just a nightmare—but it felt so, *so* real . . .

I slide my hands under Nik's duvet and pat my stomach through his Iverson T-shirt. Dry.

Nik is on his back, head cocked to the side, passed out. How long have we been asleep? When we got home from the disaster at Bianchi's, we came straight to his room. Closed the door. Messed around a little and then slipped into pajamas. A T-shirt for me and boxers for him. Then he turned on *Family Guy*, but the TV is off now.

I pull my phone from beneath my pillow and check the time: 2:57. I wonder if people are still at Saige's.

I lock my phone and slide it back under my pillow, roll onto my side, and try to clear my head. There's something across the room, though . . . what is that? This dull glow coming from my sleepover bag . . .

Shit.

I freeze for a second before I get out of bed, to listen to Nik's breath, to make sure it's low and slow. He's asleep, for sure, and I slide from under the covers and tiptoe across his rug.

My bag is on his desk chair, and I dig inside. My candies glow like a flashlight. They're beautiful, and, for a second, all I can do is stare. But I can't let him wake up and see this, so I grab a pair of socks from his drawer and shove my candies inside them. I ball them up and stuff them into the bottom of my bag. Zip it up. Take a step back.

No glow.

I tiptoe across his room and crawl into bed. I scoot up against him and rest my head on his bare chest. He shifts a little, slides his arm down and rests it over my shoulders.

Outside his giant arched window, stars peek through wispy clouds. The color reminds me of my nightmare. And that reminds me of the blood. And of the kiss.

I hug my stomach. I close my eyes. I swear it's only been a minute. But when I open my eyes again, it's daylight.

Kady

Saturday, November 21

I'd rather peel off my fingernails than be at Tipsy Crew tonight. Not just because all the IVs will be there. I've always hated this place, with its beer-sticky wood floors and dank air that's heavy with sweat and vomit. But Nik and his friends are in love with this bar—even though it's nothing more than a hole-in-the-wall across from Street U. I think— for them—it feels far away when it's not, so separate from their legacies and last names, so disconnected from anything they'd ever actually become, that it's like spending a night on Mars.

I wish I were with Em at the guys' apartment, where she's probably helping them study or playing *Halo*. I wish I were the third wheel with Shawn and Luka. They're at The Drive-In for our doubleheader of *The Preacher's Wife* and *Soul Food*, Luka's first time ever going. I wish Nik and I had just stayed home, curled behind his locked bedroom door, playing cards and kissing every time one of us had Uno.

I wish, I wish, I wish.

Em would say just find the brightest star. But it's cloudy tonight.

I peer out the window of Aaron's back seat, trying anyway. We've been inching forward, creeping backward, and inching forward again for the past thirty seconds, trying to squeeze into this street spot between a U-Haul and a yellow cab. He wasn't gonna worry about it—told Nik and me to hop out and he'd find a spot and meet us inside. But Nik said he wasn't in a rush (that made two of us) and pointed out this spot on the corner. That yeah, we could fit in. Technically. If we were being lowered by a crane.

"Alright, man, you're good over here," Nik says, sticking his head out the passenger window and eyeing the curb.

"Nice." Aaron waits for Nik to finish rolling up his window and cuts the engine. He opens his door, and the cold outside takes over. It's in the twenties tonight.

The three of us hop out. Aaron's our DD, even though Nik and I don't need one. I could always drive us home, but that's not the point. It's about rituals. *Tradition.* And tonight, all the blood brothers are driving. A gift for the Boys who are officially back home for Thanksgiving break.

Nik takes my hand as we step off the curb.

"You think it's gonna snow?" I ask. Doug Hillman on Channel Four has been saying there's a chance.

Aaron holds his head back for a second. "Doesn't smell like it."

I take a deep breath. He's right.

Aaron saunters into the street, leading as we jaywalk our way to Tipsy Crew's main doors. Headlights turn the corner, and Aaron holds up a hand to stop them, animatedly positioning himself like a crossing guard and waving Nik and me ahead of him as the car slows to let us pass. "Your safety, then mine," Aaron says.

Nik claps a hand against Aaron's shoulder and promises him, "I'd jump in front of a car going five miles an hour for you, too, man."

Aaron chuckles and walks with us the rest of the way across the street.

When I told Aaron what happened at Bianchi's, I wanted him to laugh. To make it seem small and stupid so it was easier for me to sleep at night. But he ripped a page from his notebook and crumpled it in his hands until it was tight as a ball. He said I can't freak out like that, not with Hendricks, not again. And it left a taste in my mouth like metal.

"Why?" I asked. I meant it a dozen ways, though—why was he being such an IV, why did I have to be such an idiot, why was he tearing out another page just to crumple up and leave on his kitchen island?

"Because Hendricks never forgets anything," he answered.

We walk inside of Tipsy Crew, just as sticky and musty as it's always been. There's a song playing so loud I can practically taste it—some kind of old rock and roll. The lights—shining from these low-hanging chandeliers covered in green glass—are too dim to see anything real, like faces or freckles, or if someone's eyes are actively hating you.

There's a bar with stools on the right, old arcade games on the left, a pool table that I've never seen anyone use. This place is packed with Iverson kids and people home from Barnes, drinking and laughing and being generally obsessed with one another. A couple of girls call Aaron's name as soon as we walk in and drag him over to talk. Seeing him go to them feels like someone pulled the wrong piece in Jenga.

As he leaves, the Boys turn and watch him. One after another, like dominoes. I'm too scared to look over my own shoulder. I don't want to know what's happening behind me.

"Why does it always smell like wet throw-up in here?" I groan into Nik's ear.

"Because there's no such thing as dry throw-up?" he offers. He rests a hand on my lower back, and it sends a tingle down my legs. "Come on, I'm gonna grab something to drink."

He stays close as we walk through the dense crowd, stopping to hug every girl he notices and shake hands with the guys. But his hand always finds its way back to me, one magnet to another, whether they smile at me or not.

It never used to be this way. We all weren't friends, but we weren't this weird. The girls would make small talk with me about lip gloss and the IVs—two of the only things we had in common, but we always made it count. And the Boys would smirk like creepy uncles and make harmless jokes about me being with Nik, like letting him know when it was ten o'clock, because he had to have me home by midnight. Pretending like it took that long to get to my side of Streetlight.

As much as I see it, as I feel what's happening, calling attention to it is worse, bringing it up to Nik like I can't deal on my own.

We reach the bar, finally. TVs hanging from the ceiling, tuned to some basketball. Nik slides in next to two men with beers and their eyes on the game. Regulars, probably.

"Hey," he says easily to the bartender, used to ordering drinks in public. "Can I get a whiskey sour and a seltzer?"

I hug his arm. I didn't ask for it, but the seltzer water is for me.

A hand grips my shoulder, and the voice comes a moment after. "Hey, EV, that you?"

EV. Shorthand for External Venture. Bobby O'Grady is the one who says it, a junior at Iverson this year. His brother Brady is a year ahead of Nik at Barnes and was the first Boy who ever called me that.

"Hey." I force a smile while Nik waits on the bartender and glance at Bobby's milky-white drink in the dim lighting. "Is that a piña colada?"

He swirls his cocktail in his hand. "A White Russian." He has a sip and holds it out to me. "Cheers?" he offers, eyebrows raised, but I can't tell if he actually means it.

"Oh." I shake my head. "I don't drink."

He laughs. At me. I think. "What are you doing at a bar, then?"

"She's here with me," Nik says, sliding his wallet into his back pocket and handing me my bubbly water. "That cool?" But he says it like it better be, even though his tone is easy.

"You tell me," Bobby says, while he and Nik slap hands.

"Alright," Nik says. "Well, I'm telling you."

Bobby smirks; he nods; they tap glasses. And whatever Bobby came over to do, it's over before it started.

It goes like that all night. The Boys slapping Nik's hand while they remind me I shouldn't be here. Staring at me like they know what I did.

Where's Aaron? I'd do anything to laugh with him about IV bullshit right now. But it probably is better that we're not hanging out together in front of all these people.

Luckily for me, the drunker they get, the less they care that I'm here. They get busy taking shots, and pretty soon I don't matter.

"I'm going to the bathroom," I say, leaning into Nik's ear. "I'll be back."

The girls' bathroom only has one stall, but it's open when I walk in. There's a weird fluorescent light overhead, and the walls are drenched in notes from the past. Girls signing their names or leaving their numbers or making hearts. There's a Sharpie in a plastic cup on the sink with a Post-it that says *Use Me!!*

Maybe I shouldn't.

But whatever.

I uncap the marker and scrawl over the mosaic of faded notes. On an angle, right above the sink.

Fuck IV Boys, I write.

Then I put the Sharpie back and go into the stall.

It's almost eleven o'clock. I haven't gotten a vibe yet for when Nik's gonna want to leave. I hope we're not here until they close at two.

My candies are resting in a nook in my pants while I pee, and I pick them up and hold them in my hands. Warm. And mine. Magic that no one would ever believe could exist, even if I told them exactly how it happened. Even Em would barely believe it, unless I let her travel with me. Maybe I should. Maybe it would be okay.

I've thought about it.

But I stop myself, every time. And right now, I squeeze my candies tighter. It doesn't seem possible, or *fair*, that I'm holding the greatest thing that anyone ever decided deserved to be mine—maybe the greatest thing that's ever existed at all—and I'm still trapped in a world I don't want to be in.

I stand up, flush, tuck my candies safely back against my hip. I unlock the stall and open it.

"Oh my God." My heart stops.

It's Saige, holding her wineglass with both hands. In a plaid skirt and tights and a white sweater. Standing *right there*—her brown eyes staring into mine the second I open the door, the buzzing fluorescent light turning her white skin a sickly yellow. A pretty, staring, dead girl. That's what she looks like.

She snaps out of it. Blinks, finally. "Sorry! Did I scare you?"

My blood starts flowing again. She's not a haunting. Just drunk.

"Yeah, but"—a chill passes from my neck to my ankles—"it's fine."

"I saw you walk in here, and I wanted to talk. I have to pee, though." She raises her eyebrows. "Will you wait for me?"

"Yeah, of course." I step aside so she can use the bathroom.

The door squeals as she closes it behind her, and the rusty lock slides into place. I stand at the sink while I let her finish.

The mirror is faded and spotted with water stains. But through it, my skin looks bad, too. Waxy.

"Hey, Saige?" I start, hesitant to bug her before she's done, but the words are ready now. "I'm really sorry, by the way. About your birthday."

I thought about texting her a few times this week. Or DMing her, in case the number I have is wrong. I don't know, because I've never actually used it.

The toilet flushes, and I wait for her to say something. After a second, the stall door opens, and our eyes meet in the reflection of the mirror. "That was awful," she insists.

I squeeze myself as I turn around to face her. "I'm so sorry—I like, saw red, and I shouldn't have—"

"Not what *you* did," she tells me. "What Hendricks was doing *to you*. I had no idea about the rumors, or what he was getting at until he finally said it. I swear." Her eyes are glassy the way drunk eyes always are. But I believe her, believe that this isn't the kind of talk that's happening because she's been drinking, but in spite of it.

"*You* shouldn't feel bad about that . . . I literally ruined your birthday dinner."

She flicks her wrist as she sips more wine. *A mutilated eight-hundred-dollar dinner. So what?* "I honestly didn't expect to see you here." She says it like I'm braver than she is.

That's when it hits me that she's the first person who's really talked to *me* all night. My voice threatens to break, and I really don't want it to. "I came for Nik."

"Good for you. Those Boys are always whispering about something. Like a bunch of gossipy little bitches." She smiles as she says it, like she gets it, like it's okay. "And it's a shame. Because Nik really is obsessed with you."

One of the pointy toes of her brown booties twists into the moldy floor tile, killing a bug that isn't there.

"I'm obsessed with him, too," I tell her, my voice soft.

Her red-polished pointer traces the rim of her glass, her pupils pricking mine. "Hendricks kind of kept going after you two left. It was *weird*. I've never seen him like that. He's just *so convinced* you're messing around. No matter what you say about it." She squints at me, the end of one word just barely bleeding into the beginning of the next. "But he's wrong, isn't he? I told him he was. I see how you look at Nik. I know how much you care about him—you wouldn't lie."

This faucet leaks. Has it been doing it this whole time? *Drip, drip, drip* like a ticking clock. "I'm not lying." But my fidgeting fingers tear my cuticle to the quick.

"I told him so."

She takes the last swallow of her wine and disappears into the stall. Then she comes back and hands me a small wad of toilet paper. I press it to my bleeding thumb.

"Thanks," I softly tell her, but all she does is seal this moment with a wink.

She steps up to the mirror and teases her back-length hair with her fingertips. She looks at me in the reflection. "Should we keep talking?"

She offers like she means it, like we could absolutely huddle in this disgusting bathroom as long as I want to.

Is it weird that there's a part of me that might actually want to?

But that's not what Saige and I do.

"We can go back out," I tell her. "So you can get another glass."

She smiles. Then she glances around the sink—probably for the soap that isn't there and the paper towels that don't exist.

But before she turns back toward the door, her fingers graze the words I scrawled. Bright black and brand new. *Fuck IV Boys.* My stomach drops, and I squeeze my thumb tighter.

"Hm," she says. "This one's fresh."

She doesn't ask me if it's mine.

Nik isn't where I left him. I check my phone and I scan the room, but I still don't see him anywhere. So I wander.

It's even hotter in here now than it was when we first showed up, this suffocating combination of more bodies and some manager who probably thought the best thing to do on a chilly November night would be bump up the heat.

I step outside.

The cold air shocks me down to my bones, but it feels so good. Like I can breathe again. It's quiet out here, the restaurants next door are closed, and the Street U building on the corner is sleepy except for a few lights shining through certain windows, the kind that stay on all night.

In a minute, I'll text Nik. Ask him where he went and tell him to meet me at the door. But for now, I just want to be cold and remind myself where I am. I'm not lost, and this isn't Mars. It's just Streetlight.

There are voices coming from the alley. I start to ignore them, but I recognize them.

I peek around the corner of the bar.

It's Nik, with one of those whiskey sours in his hand, and Hendricks, with a cigarette in his. I haven't seen him all night—or at all, since I doused him—and my stomach knots. Aaron's with them, too, holding nothing.

"That's bullshit," Hendricks definitively says, drawing on his cigarette and flicking off the ash.

"Come on, man, perk up," Aaron dryly comments. "I told you I'd write from Vandy."

Hendricks takes another drag. "You think I give a shit where you end up?"

Nik chuckles and tells Hendricks, "He's kidding, dude."

Hendricks shrugs. "You guys are sitting here talking about 'rumors this,' 'rumors that'—like I don't know what a rumor feels like. Like I'm brand new and don't know the difference." He isn't looking at either one of them because he's busy buffing his nails on his sleeve. "And you sound like a couple of dumbasses."

Nik's smile fades. "Man, what's with you lately?"

Hendricks looks up from his sleeve, but not to see Nik. He's peering at Aaron. And as if he should know the answer, Hendricks echoes, "What's with me lately?"

"Lately?" Aaron says.

"Relax," Nik mutters to him.

"No, for real," Aaron goes on. "Because we know what this is about. This is a takedown." He faces Hendricks. "You guys just don't like her. Don't like that she doesn't come from all this and she still got close to us. Because you're scared. Of what it means if the IVs aren't exclusive anymore. Of what that means for your secrets. And for your power. And you figured, once he was gone"—Aaron holds an arm out to Nik—"that she'd disappear, too. That they'd end things, or whatever, and you'd be done with her. But it didn't end anything. So now you want to end it yourself." He raises his eyebrows. "Right?"

None of them grabbed their jackets. Neither did I. Their breath is white like mine, but we don't feel it. We don't care.

Hendricks has another drag of his cigarette, smirking as he does. Like he likes being analyzed. Accused. "And why would that have anything to do with you?"

"Eh." Aaron makes the same impartial sound he did when I asked if he liked Froot Loops. *What's the point of the colors if they all taste the same?* he asked then. "Because you don't like me all that much, either."

He knows it and he doesn't care—that's what it sounds like to me, at least. I never knew he felt that way, but Hendricks doesn't seem surprised.

Nik glances at the ground, and I imagine this is one of those things they've talked about, one of the reasons why Aaron always tells me that Nik's not like the rest of the Boys.

"Not to break your heart, but I'm not really here to talk about *our relationship*." Hendricks says the last part like a bully on a playground. Then he takes a cool step forward, like he is one. "What I meant when I asked what any of this has to do with you"—he's close enough to Aaron to spit on him if he wanted—"is what does *all of this*"—he spins his pointer in the air like he's twirling the whole universe around his finger—"have to do *with you*."

But Aaron doesn't answer, because he's so busy doing that thing he does, where he isn't really looking at you but through you. He's doing it to Hendricks.

"Get it now?" Hendricks presses two fingers into Aaron's chest. Not like a push. Like he's waking him back up. "Because if nothing ever happened—if you never kissed her, never crossed a line—why am I so sure you did?"

My fingers get twitchy, like they did in the bathroom and when I reached for that Drop Cup. But I force myself to stay where I am. He and Nik are *friends*. They *live together*. This happens all the time without me. It kills me, but it's true.

Nik slides an arm between them. "Dude, you're losing it," he declares. "You're talking about Kady and Aaron. *Kady and Aaron*."

Thank God Nik gets it.

"Yeah?" Hendricks goes back to leaning against the bricks. "And what if it happened when they were fucked up?"

My eyes and Aaron's eyes squint at the same time.

"They don't *get* fucked up," Nik insists.

"*All that time she spends with you?*" Hendricks snaps. He looks back at Aaron and sucks his teeth. "And I've seen you get fucked up before. Don't stand there like you're some kind of prude."

"It's been a long time since I've gotten fucked up," Aaron tells him.

But Hendricks shrugs, takes a drag, watches him. "What's time?"

"Look," Nik cuts in like he's tired, and faces Aaron. "Brother to brother, you to me. Did anything ever go down between you and Kades?"

Aaron looks him in the eyes and shakes his head, and when Nik waits to hear the actual words, Aaron tells him, "Never."

"Never," Nik repeats. He turns back to Hendricks, who's standing there unimpressed. "Never. Okay? Alright?" He holds out his hand to shake on it, to end it.

But Hendricks doesn't take his hand. He finishes his cigarette and flicks it on the ground.

"No," he says.

And *that's* what ends it.

Aaron
Saturday, November 21

---

28 DAYS BEFORE THE BALL

Tipsy Crew was always busted as hell, don't get me wrong. But I liked it there. The guys were different at that place. Whenever they were partying at one of their houses instead, it felt like some low-key IV meeting. Lights on and everyone a little bit on guard. Calculating. Thinking. About what they needed from each other. What someone else might need from them. Who had the power in that moment, and what that meant for the rest of us. But Tipsy Crew was the universal equalizer. You couldn't talk about your dad's lunch with the mayor and breathe air laced with throw-up at the same time. So they got there, and they forgot for a little bit. About who they were and what that meant. And, for a few hours, they were the people they didn't want to be when the lights were on. A lot of them could be pretty cool, when they got like that.

But we were on our way home now. Nik and KD in the back while I drove. Normal, once Nik had a few in him. He wanted to sit next to her, tell her how pretty she was, be her seat belt. Sometimes, KD and I would catch eyes in the rearview when he got like that. Sober person to sober person. She'd roll her eyes. Or mouth *Who brought this guy?* and smile. I'd wipe my mouth so Nik wouldn't notice me laughing, and she'd let him kiss her so he wouldn't notice it from her, either.

Tonight, though, KD and I weren't stealing looks at each other. She was quiet, and so was I. So was the road.

The moon. *Blurry behind the clouds. Almost a perfect half sphere.*

The ground. *Freshly paved. Practically too smooth to feel.*

The stop sign. *Slanted. Like someone hit the metal pole but not hard enough to knock it down.*

"The guys were weird tonight," she said.

I almost forgot they were back there. Got busy thinking about how chummy Hendricks had been with me all night, how he could almost be kind of decent when he wanted to be—telling me how great Barnes was and all the reasons to choose the guys over Vanderbilt. But KD's words landed in the silence like she'd dropped a dumbbell. I never heard her like that before. This voice that was lacking . . . *anything.* Just that statement—flat and heavy: *The guys were weird tonight.*

She wasn't talking to me, and I had no idea what she was talking about, but I believed her.

"No they weren't," Nik said. His mouth was so buried in her neck it was like he was talking into a pillow.

"They were looking at me funny," she went on. "Like they didn't want me there."

I rested my head against the seat and ran my hand up and down the steering wheel. Stitched leather that'd be softer if it wasn't so cold out tonight.

Lamppost. *Flickering at the end of the block. So fast that it's almost like something's wrong with me instead of with it.*

Bird. *Big, black, alone. Perched on top of the broken light.*

"I was with you all night," Nik said. "No one was looking at you funny." I could hear him kissing her. "What?" he said after a few seconds, laughing. "They weren't." And then, after a few more: "So you're just gonna be pissed now?"

I tried to meet her eyes in the rearview, so she'd know that I'd heard her. That whatever she saw tonight, or felt, she wasn't wrong. Nik was just drunk. We both knew what that meant. He couldn't talk about anything real when he was buzzed.

But she was too busy gazing out the window to see me.

"Nik," she said. "I want to go to the ball."

I closed my eyes for a second at the stoplight. Everyone was thinking about the ball right now. The Iverson girls were clawing for an invite, too. Guys like me—who weren't boo'd up and spoken for—were kings in their eyes. They baked me stuff. Left test answers in my locker with lip prints on them. Sent pics all day—late night, first thing in the morning, in class.

But I didn't take dates to the ball. I didn't want to add to the problem. The mess I was so ready to leave behind. A whole bunch of people just fighting for status.

Nik groaned, and I glanced at him in the mirror. He'd pulled away from her. Leaned back in the middle seat and watched the ceiling instead. "Kades, I don't want to talk about this right now."

"Why?" she insisted.

"Because we just had a good night—"

"*I* didn't have a good night," she argued. "Because all your friends were looking at me like they don't get why I hang out with them. And if you'd just take me to the freaking ball already, and show them how serious we are, and how much you love me, then maybe they'd finally accept the fact that I'm not going anywhere . . ."

I ran my hand down my face and watched the road. Man, I just wanted her to be happy. And if this was what it took, I wanted her to have it. Even if the guys would never get over it, even if she'd wish she'd never gone at all, I wanted her to have the ball if it meant she wasn't sitting in my back seat feeling like she did right now.

"I'm not taking you to the ball," Nik said. Nothing to talk about. That was it.

For a second, they were quiet. And then she whispered, "You said maybe."

I scratched the steering wheel and watched the road. Coaching Nik from my mind. *Come on, man. Say something decent.*

But he was annoyed. Drunk. "Well, now I'm saying no."

"*You can't do that—*"

"Yeah, I can," he answered. "Because the thing is, I can't have fun if you're there."

I chuckled—it was too ridiculous not to. But neither of them heard me. They were too busy being mad.

"*You can't have fun if I'm there?*" she whispered.

"No. And I'm sorry, but you'll ruin it. Okay? If you're there, you'll ruin it for me."

A second later, I felt her fingertips on my shoulders and her breath on my ear. "Can you take me home?" she asked.

"I got you," I muttered, too soft for Nik to hear.

I'd never dropped them off separately at the end of the night. And it made me want to pull over and take her outside, and make her notice the shape of the moon and the smell in the air and the car we just passed with the flat. And once she was grounded in this moment and nothing else, I wanted to tell her the truth.

I didn't know for sure when Nik realized I'd started heading to her house instead of his. He didn't say anything about it, even after I pulled up to her driveway. She climbed out without saying bye to him, and he didn't say bye to her.

"Thanks, Aaron," she told me before the door shut behind her, and her voice broke when she did.

I broke a little, too. "Hang in there, KD," I said, but the words felt like they met the door more than her ears.

I started to pull off, but Nik said, "Hold on. Let me get up there with you."

I left my foot on the brake while he got out the back seat and climbed in the front instead. He shut the door and brought a gust of cold air with him. Then he sprawled out in the seat like he'd run a marathon and there was nothing left in him.

I started to drive again.

"No cap, man, that was pretty bad," I said.

"I mean, what the hell am I supposed do with her?" he insisted, and stared out the window like maybe the answer was somewhere out there instead.

Nik was my boy, and I had his back. No matter what, I was showing up for that guy. He'd been good to me since day one, and I knew it wasn't transactional—in part, because he knew me well enough to know I didn't come with perks. I didn't know anything about this life when I first showed up. But he taught me the things I needed, told me who to watch out for, how to keep the peace. He hooked me up with a pass I could flash any time I was late and showed me how to game the system so I got first pick of classes.

And when he had the chance to hurt me—shove a knife straight into my back—he didn't.

The blood-brother thing was always the little doing stuff for the big. Driving them around, picking up food late-night, carrying a bunch of stuff they didn't feel like carrying themselves. Nik was the only guy who ever made it mutual. Who said I was family and then acted like it. Asked about Philly. Asked about Pops. Remembered the names of my boys back home.

And I took that seriously, for real. Even when he was drunk.

"What if you just brought her?" I asked, watching the road. I really meant it. Not like I was talking about the simple decision, but the scope of it. All the interlocking parts of it and things that came undone.

Nik shook his head, and I knew he was thinking about all that stuff, too. "You know I can't bring her."

The sound. *A dog barking. Outside. Somewhere on the left.*

The air. *Minty with that hair gel he uses, now that he's sitting up front.*

"Maybe you should tell her why," I said.

But he sighed. "You know I can't do that, either."

Kady
Sunday, November 22

---

27 DAYS BEFORE THE BALL

Aaron's taillights blur, bright red watercolors. I blink, but the tears fall anyway.

"Keep your stupid ball!" I yell after them, but my voice is too hoarse from my fight with Nik to carry. It disappears into the air, insignificant and broken.

I go to my front door, hands shaking as I pat my pockets for my house key. *Please let me have it.* It's the worst night ever to get locked out. I finally find it in my jacket pocket, tucked under my glove. I slide it in the lock and let myself inside.

It's just after midnight and Mom and Dad are still at The Drive-In. The *Soul Food* showing only ended a couple of minutes ago, and they'll be there until the field is empty and every car pulls out of the lot. Which is a relief. They hate it when I cry.

I walk up the steps and go to my room, crawl on my bed, and curl into a ball. Before Owen moved out, we shared the wall behind my headboard. When Nik and I would fight back then—when I would lie in the dark, crying about it—I'd always wonder if he heard me, the same way I heard his TV or the music he was playing. He never acted like he did, never mentioned it in the morning, but Owen has better ears than anyone I know. He hears alternate melodies in songs that I never would have even noticed. He always sits up a little straighter and says, *What's that?* when I swear nothing even happened. So I like to believe he did hear me in here and chose to just keep carrying on. Like nothing was happening. Like everything was okay. To remind me that, in the morning, everything would be.

It's quiet in here tonight, though.

I pull my candies from my waistband and set them on my comforter. Their blue glow makes me feel like a moth in the summertime that's too dumb—too weak—to resist the light that could kill it. But going back to earlier tonight sounds like shit, too. I guess I could go back and not go to the bathroom, so I could try to keep Nik from going into that alley, and then try asking him about the ball again, when he's in a better mood. Or maybe I could just go back to the car ride and ask differently, or not ask at all. That's the thing—there're too many ways to do it again, too many ways to mess up again. And none of it fixes what I already know, what I'll *always* know. That even if I change what's happened, it doesn't change what I'll remember. The way Hendricks talked about me in the alley. The way Nik's words were a knife in that car. The way mine sliced right back.

I pick up my phone and call Em.

It rings once, twice. If she doesn't answer, I'll use a candy. It's a sign. That I'm not supposed to spend the rest of the night talking to her about what did happen, but I'm supposed to *do* something about it. Make the story the one that I want it to be.

"Hi, baby," she says.

My throat instantly clenches.

"Kady?" Em tries again. "*Helloooo?*"

"He doesn't want me at the ball." The tears slide down my cheeks.

"*No . . .*" I can tell by the rustling in the speaker that she's moving now. Off the guys' couch. Or maybe out of Milo's bed. "What do you mean, he doesn't want you there?"

"He told me no. I asked him again tonight, and—" My voice catches. "He said no."

She doesn't say anything, and neither do I. But I imagine her behind the closed door of the guys' bathroom, on the toilet with the lid down, hunched over her phone and wishing she could crawl through it. She doesn't ask me why he said no—he's said it so many times now that deep down she's probably as used to it as I am. I just wish it'd been like the other times, when he blamed things like head counts or forgetting to give them my RSVP. But no, this time he told the truth, and this time was for sure the worst time of all.

She finally whispers, "What a dumb boy."

It breaks me; I don't know why. It's a mallet to my cracked chest, and, just like that, it shatters. I haven't cried in so long, not like this. Not even when Nik was leaving for Barnes, after the best summer of our lives, and I was so scared we'd never be that perfect ever again.

Em's words on the other end are the same hug she'd give me if she were here—comforting and patient and soft: "Why do you think you want to go so much?" And then I feel even worse, because I don't even know.

"I bet that ball sucks so bad," she promises me. "That's probably why he doesn't want you to come, because he's embarrassed. It's probably hot, and full of Bingo, and shoes that hurt your feet. Stuffy Have-Lot nonsense. You hate that stuff—you don't want to be there."

I bet it's the absolute opposite. Glamorous. Mysterious.

Blood.

My nightmare slams into me so hard that it steals my breath.

"Oh, I have an idea!" Em goes on. "Let's throw our own party—a total rebellion. Like the third-class passengers on the *Titanic*—you remember. How Rose's party sucked while Jack was getting lit with all his friends. Well, we're just about as third-class as anybody else. Let's throw our own ball."

I smile a little. "An anti-ball?"

"An anti-ball." I can hear her smiling, too. "Same day, same time. I guarantee it'll be *way* more fun. I bet we can do it here." The guys' apartment, she means. "I'll decorate and everything. We'll invite who-ever we want."

"Aaron made a bet with me the other day." I forgot about it until now. "Over who could eat the most pizza."

Em slides into my subject change like it's nothing. "Oh no, did he hurt himself?"

"I mean, I wasn't gonna let him have to get his stomach pumped or anything."

Em giggles. "Hero."

I laugh, too, through my stuffed-up nose. "But since I won, he said he'd skip the ball this year if Nik didn't invite me." I hold my bag of candies in my hand, shift it from one palm to the other and then back again. Double-checking. It's still sixty-six. I can tell. "Obviously, I'm not gonna let him. But he offered. Almost like he knew this was coming."

"He's nice to you."

"Yeah." I set my candies back down. "He is."

"Come over," she insists. "I don't want you to be alone when you're sad. We have leftover pizza bagels, and we can start planning our anti-ball."

I glance out my window, at the stars trying to peek through the clouds. I don't want to be alone, either. But I'm tired after tonight, and these tears just completely wore me out. "I think I'm gonna stay here. But thank you for talking to me. I love you. Text me when you wake up."

"Are you sure?"

I know she's disappointed, but I promise her, "I'm sure."

When we hang up, I leave my candies where they are, on the left side of my mattress, and scoot over to the right side to give them space. They'd be even prettier in the dark, but I'm too lazy to get up to turn off the light. So I gaze at them from where I am, at their quiet radiance, until my puffy eyes finally close.

I try not to think about Nik, which is kind of like trying not to breathe.

My phone starts vibrating. Has it been minutes or hours? I check the time—12:57. It's Em calling.

I fumble to answer it. "Are you okay?"

"Will you let me in? I'm outside."

I frown and roll out of bed, go to my window. She's bundled up like a snowboarder and looks up like she knew I'd peek. She blows me a kiss.

I hang up and throw on a sweatshirt as I hurry to get her, but stop in my bedroom doorway and turn back to face my bed. My candies are still there, sparkling. And I could leave them, let Em stumble upon them and ask me what they are. Tell her the truth and figure this out together— what day to go back to, what moment to redo to keep this night from ever happening. Em's so good at that stuff. At puzzles. At fixing.

I grab my candies and hide them in my nightstand drawer.

I jog down the steps and tug my front door open, pull her inside, and squeeze her around the neck. "What are you doing?" I insist. "It's freezing out."

"Milo dropped me off. The heat in the car just takes a while to start working," she says, hugging me back. "I never want you to be sad by yourself."

The words threaten to choke me up all over again. I swallow hard and let her go. She lets me go, too.

"We didn't tell Owen he was bringing me here," she adds. *So he won't get suspicious. So I don't have to worry about explaining myself. So he won't worry about me*—are the parts she leaves out. "Oh!" She digs into the canvas bag hanging on her shoulder, the one she uses to stow underwear, deodorant, and floss when she's staying at the guys' place. She pulls out a paper plate wrapped in foil. "I brought pizza bagels."

I take the plate in one hand and squeeze her around the neck one more time, her hair still cold against my cheek. "Do you want a sweat-shirt?" I offer, ready to take off this one so she can have it.

"I'm okay," she promises, shedding her layers. Unzipping her coat, peeling off her scarf, tugging off her hat, yanking off her boots. "It feels funny out there tonight, you know?"

She's in her socks and sweatpants and a T-shirt now, strands of staticky hair floating on their own.

"Funny how?" I ask.

She takes a second, deciding on the words she wants, as I hand her the plate back and gather her shedded clothes. I start to drape them over the banister, leave her boots on the step.

Her voice is behind me when it comes, wistful and thoughtful and sure that it's right. "Like something wants to tickle you, but it won't."

I turn around to see her face—to understand if that's good or bad, or just one of those things—but she's already wandered to the kitchen instead.

When Mom and Dad get home, Em and I are still in the kitchen. Mom kisses Em's head, and Dad steals a bagel for himself before they leave us at the table and go up to bed. All we have is the kitchen light and the leftovers. My phone isn't even downstairs. I haven't seen Em touch hers since she got here.

I was so tired, and now I don't even want to sleep. It has to be close to one thirty if Mom and Dad are home. But I just want to sit here, laughing with Em, planning with her, pretending like time isn't real and the sun isn't gonna rise. Believing that we can do this as long as we want, and it doesn't matter.

I'm in my usual seat, the one that faces the front door, with my legs tucked under me and my fifth pizza bagel on my fingertips. There was no dinner tonight. Just IV Boys and booze. "I know why I wanted to go so bad," I realize, picking at the baby pepperonis that Em shaped like hearts.

"To the ball," she fills in, from the seat across from me. The one that's always Mom's. I nod, and she asks me, "Why?"

"Because, I think . . ." I take a breath. "I think the day that Nik believes I'm good enough to be there, then maybe I'll finally believe it, too."

I look at her, ready to be reprimanded for being like this. For needing him like that. For not knowing who I am unless he tells me. But she doesn't give me some big speech or insist that I'm already perfect. She doesn't say that he shouldn't matter or try to talk me out of how I feel. She just moves to the seat that used to be Owen's and scoots it close enough that the wooden legs tap together, and eats pizza bagels with me until there aren't any left.

Kady
Sunday, November 22

"Okay, well, just let me know," Em says as she zips her coat. The sun beams through the three little windows above my front door, and I hold up my hand to block it. "I need to shower and stuff—"

"Same," I agree.

"But we can do it after that?" Shopping for the anti-ball, she means. She reaches for the doorknob and pulls. "Like this afternoon?"

The sun has been up for hours, but there's still frost on the grass. White smoke pours from the exhaust of the Range Rover parked in front of my house.

Em smiles. "*Orrrr* we could go tomorrow."

"What's he doing here?" I wonder out loud, staring at the car as the driver's-side window goes down.

"Apologizing?" Em shrugs. "You deserve it." She squeezes my hand as she starts to leave. "Good luck, okay?"

"I'll call you."

She nods, and by the time she turns around again, Nik's window is all the way down. He smiles at her, the same charming way he smiles at parents or in pictures. "Hey, Em."

"Hey, Nik . . ."

"You need a ride?"

"No, I'm just going home." She crosses my lawn toward the street but smiles at him as she passes. "Be good to my girl."

"Forever," Nik promises, and turns to me instead. Pouting on purpose, because it's cute when he does. "I got here a minute ago. Was just about to text you. Can we talk?"

I check on Em, officially to the road now, walking up the middle. She'll be home in two minutes. I hug myself and stay in my doorway, squinting against the morning sun. "We didn't talk last night?"

"I don't know if I'd call that talking. So I thought we could try again?" He reaches into the seat next to him and reveals a greasy paper bag. "I've got a French toast stick for every minute you're willing to give me."

I don't want to smile, but I start to. Not to mention it's getting cold, just standing here in what I slept in. A long-sleeved T-shirt. A pair of sweatpants.

I step into the boots that I keep by the front door and jog outside, around the front of his car, and hop into the passenger's side. The whole thing takes less than ten seconds, but my teeth are chattering by the time I close the door behind me.

Nik rolls up his window, and I pull my feet onto the seat as I rest my back against my door. I hold out my hand. "Stick."

He digs into the bag and gives me one, sets a plastic syrup cup in my lap. "Careful with the seats," he pleads.

I frown like he's lost his mind as I tear off the top of the syrup. I've never once cared about these seats.

I take a bite and realize, "You went to Mom's." The restaurant next to the library. I can tell, because these are custardy and the ones from Dad's are doughnutty. They're across the street from each other. Exact same menus with completely different recipes. The Nicholsons—an IV family—own the buildings, and the Jacksons rent the spaces. Em's parents rent from them, too.

"Well, it's your favorite," he says, even though his loyalty is to Dad's. I can feel him looking at me as I dip my next bite. "It's nice to know you're still sleeping with me, by the way."

I glance at him, but his eyes have wandered to what I'm wearing, and it makes me look, too. An Iverson shirt. Iverson sweats.

"I didn't sleep in this," I lie.

He glances at the clock on his touch-screen radio: 9:17 a.m. But he just smirks out the windshield. "Okay."

I roll my eyes and hold my hand out for my next stick. "Way to waste a whole minute."

It'll take a while before my neighborhood really wakes up. It's slow here on Sundays while people sleep in and take it easy in the morning. Almost everyone who goes to church is there by now—the nine o'clock service has already started, and barely anyone goes to the one at noon. Even The Drive-In is closed on Sundays. And it's too cold for the kids who would be playing outside or the people who'd be washing their cars. So it's really just Nik and me, on my empty road.

He hands me another stick. I'm not hungry, but I eat it anyway.

"I love you," Nik says finally, while he studies the steering wheel. "But that doesn't mean that everyone's gonna love us."

I frown straight ahead. "Is that supposed to be an apology?"

"I can't apologize for that, Kades. That's just how it is—that's life. I can't apologize for life."

I fold my arms and sit back in this heated seat, facing all these vents that work, in this car that lives in a temp-controlled garage whenever it's back in town. I don't need Nik blaming last night on "life." On this ambiguous, untouchable *thing* that we can't yell at or control.

"*You're* the one who doesn't love us right now, though. You're the one who doesn't want me there. It's not life. It's *you*." I'm due for another French toast stick, but I don't want it. "There's nothing . . .

nothing I've ever done that I thought would have been worse if you were there. I don't even think that's what love *is*. What's the point, if it works that way?"

"Kades." From the corner of my eye, I see him turn to me, this sweet smile on his face like I'm being too silly not to laugh at. "Come on. You know how crazy I am about you. We've been at this for *years*." He takes a breath like he's deciding whether or not to say what comes next. "A couple weeks ago, I had people over, and we were playing this game. I got asked who my first kiss was, and I said you. Saige gave me so much shit for that. Not for real, but you know what I mean. Because for me it *was* you. It still is. And of course I'm sorry. I don't want you to be sad. Come on." He reaches for my chin and nudges me to face him. "Look at me. I'm sorry. I am."

For a second, it feels like summer again, when we'd park in his car with my steak-house-style burger from Mom's and his super-smashed burger from Dad's and sneak into the back seat under the protection of his tinted windows. When we'd stay in here forever and forget everyone else, addicted to the moment and each other. The most magical summer of my life.

I wish we could go back. Before Barnes. Before the rumor. Before last night.

We could . . .

But no. TK's rules sock me in the ribs. I can't go back any earlier than this Halloween. *After* everything already started.

His stunning brown eyes squeeze my heart, and they're full of all our goodness, our happiness, our magic.

"Do you know how thrilled I'd be if you and the IVs loved each other the way I love you both?" he sadly whispers.

I tear my gaze away from his. "Stick."

He digs into the bag and hands me another one. "Last night . . ." he starts, as he rolls the bag back up. "Kades, that had nothing to do with you. That had nothing to do with *me*. There are just rules . . . traditions that have lasted way longer than I've been a part of them. And if I could change them, I would, but I don't have that power—no one does.

"The guys extend the invites." He shrugs like it's out of his control. "Our guest list is limited to Iverson kids and alumni. And even when it comes to them, only a handful get in. It's the way they want it, and it's the way they're gonna keep it. And I'm sorry, Kades, I really am. But just because you don't belong there doesn't mean you don't belong with me.

"And maybe I should have explained all that to you years ago, and never let you believe that this time could be different. But I didn't, because I never wanted to see you like *this*. Maybe it's a cop-out, but it's true. I hate telling you no. I'd tell you yes to everything, if I could."

"We've never exploded at each other like that before." I whisper it because maybe that was the worst part of all. We got so loud that Aaron pulled over and told us to stop. Made Nik sit up front with him for the rest of the ride.

"I never want to again," Nik says, and I'm sure he means it more than anything.

I study my French toast stick, holding it in one hand and using the other to tear off bits to eat. It leaves grease on my fingertips that smells like maple and cinnamon.

"These really are better than Dad's."

"Jokes."

"You wanna make up?" I threaten, holding out my thumb, slicked in buttery oil. "Taste."

He smiles and cringes at the same time. Then he opens his mouth and sucks my thumb. *"Mmmm,"* he lies.

I take my thumb back. I rip my stick in half and watch myself do it. "I get what you're saying."

It changes something in the car, releases the tension like a deflating air mattress. "Come on," Nik says. "I wanna hug you."

He crawls over the console into the back seat, and I follow him, leaving breakfast behind. He rests his back against the door on the driver's side and stretches his legs out so I can fit between them. I wrap my arms around him and rest my head on his chest. My Iverson pajamas pressed against his Iverson sweatshirt, mixed with a whiff of his Ivory soap.

"I want you to come for Thanksgiving this year," Nik says, his heart beating softly in my ear. "With me and my family and our friends. We don't eat until late—like seven. And you guys eat early, right? So you would be able to do both."

I know it's a trade—*I'm not bringing you to the ball but how about Thanksgiving instead?* It's a good one, though. A huge one. I've never been to his house for a holiday before, and he's never had me around for one of his famous dinner parties. Until he left, I was at Nik's house as often as I'm at my own, but only behind some closed and locked door. Keeping the twins out. His parents out. Like I was a toy too precious to share. Or a secret too dirty to show.

I don't know what I'll wear around those people, what I'll say around them, how to act. Do I need to go shopping? Or learn how to pronounce *hors d'oeuvres*? Nik wouldn't ask me if I had to change. Would he?

I perch up on his chest, and he slides my braids behind my ear. "You really want me there?"

"Bad," he promises, stroking my hair.

"You know what I'm thinking."

Nik nods. "Yeah, he'll be there. Don't worry about it, though. He's fine."

Nik still doesn't know what I saw in that alley last night. That I know, firsthand, that Hendricks is still very much *not fine*. But around their families, it'll be different. I think. I hope.

I smile. Nik grabs the backs of my thighs and shakes me. "Is that a yes?"

I laugh. "Stop—"

"Looks like a yes," he says. I cuddle back into his chest, and he wraps his arms around me like that's where they were always meant to be. "Feels like a yes, too."

We lie there for a few seconds, quiet and better. I think I hear a car drive by. Maybe church is over.

"Remember how much time we spent in here this summer?" Nik says. "Felt like years, sometimes."

"We had so much fun." I draw circles on his shoulder with my pointer. "Would you do it again?"

"Yeah. For sure." He sighs. "But things change, you know? We had to move on. It was time."

It almost makes me want to tell him that it doesn't have to be. That we can regress, be exactly who we once were, because I have the candies now. And we can stay in his car for as long as we want, or at least for as long as sixty-six candies buys us, if we just hold hands and do it together. He doesn't have to go to Barnes. Or to Thanksgiving. Or even to the ball. We can just be here, tucked on my quiet little street forever.

But no, he might hate it. Hate *me*. Freak out and call me crazy or worse. And it's not worth breaking this moment—the first one in weeks that feels good enough to be worth doing again.

So I lie here with him for now, in his back seat where we belong. And, eventually, Hendricks will call him, or Saige will, or his mom will need him to do something. And once he kisses me goodbye, and as I watch him go, I'll sneak my next candy. I'll take us back to 9:17 this morning so we can do it all again. And maybe again after that. And maybe again after that.

And Nik can just be happy. That's all he needs to know.

I have sixty candies left.

I used six before I finally let Nik go home, before I finally went inside and stayed there. I could have easily used six more—*I could have used all of them*—but I didn't. What if there's an even better moment that we deserve to keep forever? What if we need magic, and I've spent it all?

So I stopped.

But now I'm so disoriented—so tripped out about what day it is, what time it is—that I call and ask Em if we can go shopping for the anti-ball tomorrow instead of today. She's been thinking, and she wants to make it Gatsby themed. She's always loved the book and the movie with Leonardo DiCaprio. She bets we can make really good costumes out of the things we find at the thrift store.

"Of course we can shop tomorrow," she says. "We can shop whenever you want."

I tell her I can't wait, that her theme sounds amazing, that I love her.

And then I lie down, close my eyes, and try to stop the spinning.

Kady
Wednesday, November 25

The line at Honey Ham is already to the edge of the shopping center, and it's only eight in the morning. Owen and I have a spot right outside the drugstore, with about twenty people behind us and a million people in front of us. Any other time of year, this store is running half-off ham sandwich deals just to get people in the door. But when it's Thanksgiving, the line is so unreal that you'd think they're giving out cash.

Mom and Dad made this my and Owen's job years ago. Get up early. Get in line. Get ham. It requires layers of clothes and a fully charged phone battery to be out here for the sometimes-longer-than-an-hour wait.

Owen yawns. "Cold," he mutters, his face the only skin peeking out between his beanie and winter coat.

"Freezing," I agree, except for my hip.

He glances over his shoulder, as more people get in line. By the afternoon, it'll loop around this parking lot twice. "So what's the deal with you tomorrow again?"

I've told him twice already. Once on Monday, when he texted asking if we should drive to the Target in White Cove Thursday night for their doorbuster sale to get Dad AirPods for Christmas. And again last night, when I slept over at the apartment so we could be in line early today.

"I'm gonna get to Nik's at like seven," I tell him, burying my chin as far as I can into my scarf. "And I feel like that'll last a few hours. You're sleeping at our house, right?"

Owen nods. "Do you have to bring something?"

"What, to Nik's?"

"Yeah."

"I don't know . . ." I hadn't even thought about it. "Should I bring ham?"

Owen laughs and assures me, "You're not taking those rich people my ham."

I frown and hug myself. Maybe you do bring things to stuff like this. Maybe everyone knows it, and it's so obvious that Nik wouldn't even think he had to tell me. Not even after I gave him six extra chances to say something.

I have to remember to ask him.

"You can spare some ham," I insist.

"I'm not about to stand in this damn line, first thing in the morning, when it's too cold out here for the birds, and hand over my hard-earned ham." We creep forward in line. "You shouldn't, either." And he yawns again.

I yawn, too, catching it from him. I can't give Nik's mom a bunch of slices of ham on a plastic-wrapped paper plate, anyway.

"Have you seen the pajamas yet this year?" he asks. The ones Mom is gonna make us put on tomorrow night, so we all match when Dad pulls out our twenty-year-old Christmas tree and we start decorating it with twenty-year-old balls.

I squint at him, my cheeks numb. "Why are you smiling?"

"I'm just asking."

"Have you seen them?"

He frowns a little. Shrugs.

"O . . ." I take a threatening step closer, but he doesn't back away like Nik or Aaron would. He just smirks and dares me without saying a word.

"Show me." I smack his arm.

"I haven't seen anything," he lies. He and Mom are like this—conspirators. Whenever she has a secret she's too excited to keep, Owen gets the text, the picture, the whisper with a pinkie promise.

"Just tell me it's not onesies again," I beg. "Those things were so freaking hot."

Owen laughs. "Yo, remember how fast Dad sweat through his?"

I laugh, too. "The picture . . ."

"That picture." Owen shakes his head. The picture we took of Mom and Dad two years ago, in their furry reindeer onesies, with Dad's two shades darker because of how sweat-soaked it was. It's been stuck to our refrigerator ever since.

Owen laughs harder. Hard enough that he doesn't see the two IV Boys jog up to the Honey Ham door and pull it open. Skipping the line. Ignoring the rest of us. Or maybe you can't ignore what you can't see.

They'll be in and out fast. They always are. Another IV family—the Robertsons—owns this space, and Streetlight Pizza, and the dry cleaners, and the sandwich shop in Old Town that has the best pastrami, and the retirement home.

It'll happen again. More Boys. In and out, too fast to even get cold. And odds are, Owen will see it next time. Suck his teeth. Get pissed, like he has for the past four years.

That's why he doesn't want to share his ham.

Usually, the night before Thanksgiving, The IV Boys throw a rager, and the rest of us go to The Drive-In. Mom and Dad do this thing every year where they play all the Indiana Jones movies in chronological order. Dad says it's perfect, because nobody *needs* to see them, but everybody still loves it when they're on.

"Why is it orange?" I ask Luka, wrapped in an extra blanket and huddled on the lawn. He, Shawn, and I gaze at the sky while Em holds her breath for the truck chase on screen.

"Because it's cheese," Luka marvels, and I elbow him as Shawn laughs.

I tear my eyes from the moon—huge tonight with a hue that matches a sunset—and turn to Luka instead. "Tell me," I insist, laughing, too. He's obsessed with this stuff—like Em is, but differently. It's magic to him just like it is to her, but it's also science. He knows *the reasons*. The rules.

He smiles. "It's because it's been spinning, and we've been spinning, and it's closer to our horizon tonight." He leans in and points, so that I'll look, and from where I sit, he's holding the whole moon on the tip of his finger. "See how it's kind of low? It's shining through more of our atmosphere than usual—all our earthly gases and stuff. That's what makes it look orange."

"And they try to tell us pollution is bad." Shawn tosses a handful of popcorn in his mouth.

Luka grins. "You're the worst."

I lie back on our blanket so I can stare straight at the moon. Secretly, I squint, trying to see all the stuff between me and it that's strong enough to light it on fire.

My phone vibrates. So does Em's. So does Shawn's. I hear it as much as I feel it.

I pull mine from my pocket and hold it in front of my face. A massive group text.

"Dexter's parents rushed to the hospital?" I'm still on my back, still facing the sky. I say it out loud to make sure they got the same text I did.

"Wait, someone's in the hospital?" Luka asks.

Shawn's chewing; I can hear it. "His sister's just having her tenth baby—it's fine."

"*TENTH BABY?*" Luka cries.

I kick Shawn. "It's not her tenth baby."

He's probably shrugging. "All I know is she's been pregnant for half my life."

"His house will be empty indefinitely, so he's having a party," I explain, so Luka gets it. And then I add, "Should we go?"

"Let's do it," Shawn agrees.

"Luka?" I ask.

"Yes, please." He's never once told us no.

I peel myself off the blanket and sit up again, tucking my phone on the same side as my candies. Shawn stacks our empty cups of apple cider, and all around us, Fairmont kids fold up their blankets and head to the exit—the ones who got the same text that we did.

"Em, we're heading to Dexter's," I say, reaching past her to gather our trash.

"Okay," she says, but she isn't actually getting up. The bright lights flicker across her face while she keeps her eyes on the screen. I smile. She's seen these movies every year, just like Shawn and I have. But she always watches.

Shawn leans in to her ear, squeezing her shoulders and helping her stand at the same time. "Spoiler alert," he tells her. "He survives. And makes four more movies."

The IV Boys throw parties every other night, but we don't. They always have an empty house, parents who are off vacationing on some island—or are home and they just don't care. Nik used to take me to these mansions full of Iverson kids, and I'd pretend to have fun so that he could, too, but I always watched the clock. They'd drink for hours and file in and out of bathrooms, secretly ingesting things I'm never meant to know about. And it really didn't matter that there was so much space to move around, because it always felt like there was nowhere to go. Just a bunch of them and one of me, no matter what room I wandered into.

But it's so different at Dexter's, crammed into his two-bedroom house. We don't all fit, but no one wants to leave. We're sweaty and pressed against one another, but all we do is laugh about it. There's alcohol, but it didn't come in fancy bottles from cellars—people smuggled it from their parents' liquor cabinets and poured it into water bottles to get it here. They pass it through the crowd for everyone to share, and those of us who don't want any just pass it to the next person. People take turns propping their phones in Dexter's speaker and blasting a new song while we dance and scream the words.

And when Shawn and Luka kiss—even though it's the first time—it happens like it's the millionth.

Outside of this house, Dexter's sister is having not-her-tenth baby. The Drive-In is playing our Indiana Jones special, and the Iverson kids are partying the way they always have. The way they always get to. But this, for us, is special. And maybe that's why it feels like there's something contagious in here, like we're Elsewhere, and Streetlight is so far away. Maybe that's why it happens so easily, why Shawn's and Luka's mouths find each other like they've been together forever. Because wherever we are right now—wherever Dexter's house has transported us to—maybe they have been.

It's only a couple of seconds, but my head spins watching them, the way they smile before it happens and keep smiling once it's over, the way it doesn't matter that Em's been dancing between them, because they do it right over her head. It's the most perfect thing that's ever existed. The kind of moment I want them to have for longer.

So I reach into the waistband of my jeans, and I sneak free one of my candies as I keep dancing and twirling and sweating on our side of town. And when I rewind everything by one minute, it's like tripping without actually hitting the floor.

I open my eyes, and seconds later, they're kissing again, and my head is spinning again, and it's just as perfect as it was the moment before. They're just as happy as they were the moment before. And so is Em. And so am I.

So I do it again.

And again.

And again.

At one point, Luka looks at me. Like he feels something, but it feels *good*. And we're all so close together, maybe he was touching me one of the times I took a candy. Maybe he was touching me a few of the times. Maybe he knows his life is on repeat, but it's too impossible to believe, to actually say. It must be how hot it is. How loud it is. How lucky we are.

Yes, that explains it.

He pulls me in and keeps dancing.

Aaron
Wednesday, November 25

Every year, the day before Thanksgiving, the Jack-Laurences host their Warm Plates event. And, for the past four Thanksgivings—ever since the wedding—Pops and I have gone out to support.

It was a really dope thing they were doing. They rented out this banquet hall at the Waldorf Astoria in DC and dressed it up like some kind of fairy tale. They catered a ton of turkey, stuffing, macaroni, mashed potatoes, green beans . . . everything Thanksgiving is times ten. And then they opened the doors to anyone who needed it. No dress code, no questions. You made your way down the line buffet style, you grabbed a seat at a tableclothed table, and—if you wanted it—you got a to-go tray to take more food with you when you left.

I didn't really have a job when I was at Warm Plates. I guess none of us did. But Pops was hella in demand at these things ever since he and Charlotte got hitched, because press was everywhere, trying to get statements and pictures. Only from the recognizable Jack-Laurences, though. Pretty much all of them except for me.

I peeped Phil at one point, talking to a reporter. "Wouldn't families in need be just as happy with a warm dinner that wasn't accompanied by all the pomp and circumstance?" she asked.

Phil smiled like the answer was easy in his mind. "Just because the food is free doesn't mean the night shouldn't feel like a million bucks, right?"

I'd never seen money like Jack-Laurence money. Charlotte was modest about it, but still. This was the kind of money that could charter jets when one of them had to make a charity appearance in LA, or have a business meeting in New York, or get to the family vacation a day later than everyone else because they had work to do here. They had the kind of money that was so big it was invisible—because yeah, the homes were huge and the cars were nice, but the clothes were normal. The laptops a few years old. The iPhones, three or four generations behind. Like none of that stuff really mattered.

It was bigger than Streetlight money. The Jack-Laurences had more of it, and they did more with it, and sometimes I wondered if that was the real reason why all those guys were determined to stay back in Streetlight. Because they knew, in the real world, there were families like this one—families that weren't gonna make pacts and had never heard of the little shops and restaurants they owned. Families who didn't need their land or the IV brand—families who didn't even want it. That was the thing: All they'd built depreciated the second they reached the next town. And there were times I thought that was wild, and times I knew it was genius. Because it forced everything and everyone to stay right where they could always see them.

Staying in Streetlight—it was never about controlling everyone else. That was just a perk. The real reason why they did it was to keep tabs on themselves—to make sure they always needed each other, just enough to remember the truth: that they'd never survive in the real world on their own.

I spent most of my night talking to folks. I recognized a few of the kids serving food from around Streetlight—they went to Fairmont and

were easy to talk to once I told them I knew KD, Shawn, and Em. There
was a man there with his wife and kids—he'd gotten laid off a month
ago but got his first interview request on their drive over here tonight.
And there was a single mom there with her eight-year-old son—their
home had caught fire, and they'd lost just about everything. I remembered that story from the news; it was on while I was memorizing the
Cuban Missile Crisis. Page with bent corners, green stars all over it.

"The fire at Sycamore Apartments, right?" I asked.

She nodded. "There are a few of us here tonight." She pointed out
her neighbors at other tables. "None of us had come to this event before, but we are so very grateful for it this year."

"I'm so sorry about your home . . ." I didn't have the words, but I
hoped she saw it on my face. Looking at her and that little boy twisted
something inside me, something that was maybe never meant to be
untwisted in the first place.

She patted my leg. "Now, now, don't you be. Things can be re-
placed." Then she had another bite of her potatoes and insisted, "Tell
me about you."

I talked to her longest of anyone. Told her I was from Philly, and
she said she'd grown up spending her summers there with her favorite
aunt. I hadn't realized how much I missed it until we started talking
about it. She told me she'd have to take Cody—her son—there one
day. That I'd made her miss it, too, but he wasn't great at car rides. It
was why she'd gotten him the Nintendo Switch he'd been dying for, but
she lost it in the fire. It was supposed to be for Christmas. She laughed
and said that's what she gets for not procrastinating this year.

It was probably dumb and hella needy, but talking to this woman
with skin that looked like mine made me wonder if this was what it
felt like—being a normal kid with a normal mom. I didn't even know I
missed it, or that it was even possible to miss something I'd never had.

To miss something I *couldn't* have if I was gonna keep the life I'd loved with Pops and eventually the one I loved with Charlotte.

Maybe it didn't have to make sense, though.

I reached into my pocket and pulled out my wallet. Charlotte always wanted me to have cash. She was raised that way. Never knew who she'd have to tip.

I took out two hundred and forty bucks and handed it to her. "I want you to have this. It's all I've got, but I want you to have it."

"Boy, put that money away . . ." she threatened.

"No, ma'am, I want you to have it. It's better with you than it is with me, anyway. Trust me. My stepmom would want you to have it."

"This family has already given me *too much* . . ." she said, a sheen of wetness in her eyes. "I have to tell you, and your stepmom, *thank you*. But I can't take anything else."

"What if it's for Cody, then? This should get him a new Switch. He can't be raising all that hell while you're trying to drive him to Philly. Being on 95 will make you crazy as it is."

I held my hand closer, hidden by the table, so no one else would see, so it wouldn't turn into some photo op and she'd know I really meant it.

She closed her fist around my whole hand, money included. She sniffed and watched me dead in my eyes, and I wondered if my mom's eyes were amber brown like hers.

"Thank you for being our angel this year," she whispered.

But I didn't do anything. I just moved with Pops when he fell in love. Inherited that cash for existing, like every other guy I hung out with.

She took the money and sniffed again as she tucked it in her purse.

"Sycamore Apartments aren't in Streetlight, right?"

"No, baby." She zipped her purse shut once the money was inside. "Where's Streetlight?"

I shook my head and told her "Nowhere."

Seats. *Smooth leather. Heated. Headrest a little too high.*

Air. *Cinnamon-scented and warm. A red evergreen tree–shaped air freshener dangles from the rearview.*

The dash. *Soft, white light. Giant interactive map. Alexa capability. Netflix, too. 11:09 p.m.*

Phil asked me to ride back with him.

I came out here with Pops and Charlotte, but Phil said he'd take me home. He didn't make a big deal about it. Just wanted to catch up. So I said, "Bet. Thanks."

He drove an all-black Bentley sedan. I'd seen it enough times, but I'd never been inside. He started backing out of his spot, and it rode like we weren't even touching the ground.

My phone went off in my pocket.

"You're real popular tonight," Phil said, shifting to drive.

It was the third time my phone had gone off since we started heading to his car. "There's a party tonight. I'm on call to help drive people home when it's over."

Phil nodded and pulled out of the Waldorf's parking lot. "That's what being an IV gets you these days? A chance to be a personal valet?"

Bougie store after bougie store passed outside my window. Tiffany's. Coach. Hermès.

"Happy holidays to me," I said.

"Yeah, well, at my house tomorrow, you stuff your face with all the food you want and don't worry about driving everyone home afterward. Unless you want to make a buck. Because if you drive *my* friends around, they're at least gonna pay you." He reached over and rubbed my head.

Phil was a big guy. Built like Mark Cuban and some physique left over from when he used to ball in college. When his hand rubbed my head, his fingers could have touched my ears.

"Deal." I smiled to myself now that he was done. "The event to-night was lit, by the way. It's amazing how many people come out. And how many people need it, you know?"

But Phil just watched the road. He never liked taking credit, no matter what I praised him for. "I'm glad you could make it."

My phone went off again, but I ignored it. Blood brothers were always on call for Fucked-Up Wednesday.

"You know," Phil said, faking like he didn't notice me silence an-other call, "Charlotte was talking to me a couple weeks ago about how you're gonna apply to Vanderbilt."

I started gnawing on my cheek while we drove beneath the lamp-posts and the car went light, then dark, then light again. A part of me was glad she'd gone ahead and brought it up. She'd ripped off a Band-Aid that I probably would have left there to rot. But it also sucked— because now here we were, talking about Vandy, and he hadn't even heard it from me first.

"Yeah," I admitted. "I've been researching it for a while. I know you only have good things to say. I thought it might be a good option."

"It's a great school," he agreed. He glanced at me. "How're your grades?"

"Good," I told him. "I have a 3.8 unweighted. I got a 1470 the first time I took the SAT and a 1490 the second time. I have three AP tests coming up in the spring—history, bio, and English. I took stats last year and got a four."

He nodded. I'd seen Phil with his own kids, and I knew he wasn't easily impressed. I kind of liked that about him, to be honest. The tough-love thing.

"Not bad," he said. "I'll make a few calls."

He tapped the dash. Turned the heat down two degrees. And I

realized that was it. That was all it took when you had a name like Jack-Laurence. Just an unverified transcript and a few phone calls.

"The IVs . . ." Phil squinted at the road. "They've got a legacy somewhere, don't they?"

At first, I wasn't sure if he was really asking. He'd been around long enough to know the IVs ran Barnes. But then I thought about his house in White Cove, and how he didn't send his kids to Iverson, and how he had businesses and charities and a soccer team in Spain. And that's when I thought, *Nah, this man is way too busy to be keeping track of where the IVs go to school.*

"Yeah, at Barnes," I answered. "It's a long one, too."

He nodded like that sounded familiar as we zoomed past a minivan on the right.

The seconds ticked by. He turned on NPR.

"You don't want to know why I don't want to go to Barnes?"

"Son." He frowned and flicked on his blinker as we glided into the next lane. *"Vanderbilt versus Barnes?"*

I chuckled and watched out the window. *Fair.*

"What's the beef with the IVs, anyway? I mean, I know our family doesn't do it—" But I caught myself, swallowed the rest of what I was gonna say. Not *our* family. *His* family. The Jack-Laurences. Not the Johnsons.

Phil watched me as we slowed at a stoplight. He'd definitely heard what I said. He seemed like the kind of guy who remembered every word you ever spoke without having to rip edges or draw pictures and who could spit them back at you verbatim the second he felt like he needed to.

"But why?" he asked, finishing what I'd started.

"Yeah." I swallowed again, relieved he didn't harp on the "family" thing. "Why?"

The light turned green, and he tapped the gas pedal. We sped forward. "Charlotte never told you?"

I shook my head.

"Well, I'll have a good time giving her hell about that tomorrow," he said. But he was laughing about it, running his hand down his short beard. "So you don't know that my father—Charlotte's uncle—was in the IVs."

"What?"

Phil nodded, glanced at my pocket when my phone went off again, but ignored it. "He went to Iverson, was part of the IVs. In fact, my grandfather was, too. But my dad walked out in '68 and never looked back. Graduated from Vanderbilt and bought a house out in White Cove and didn't want us to have anything to do with what was going on over there." He rested his wrist on top of the steering wheel. "You know, Aaron, the IVs are strong. They've got families tied up in that organization who people would really listen to. But they don't want to talk about anything. They don't want to do anything. Except call you fifty goddamn times to drive their drunk asses home."

"Is that why your dad walked away from them?"

Phil nodded. "It bothered him his whole life. Sometimes I even think the reason he did as much good work as he did was to try and counteract all the work they *weren't* doing. He'd tell me the story about the day he walked away—they were having this debate about power. And you see, my dad knew what they were capable of, and he wanted them to rise to that occasion. Use all that privilege to change something. But they acted like he was out of his mind for thinking like that. Like it was damn near treason." Phil scoffed and shook his head. "One thing my father always told us growing up was that having power just to keep it all for yourself is the greatest sin a man can commit. And I'll tell you what—I believe him."

"Did he say anything else?" I asked, my heart thudding. I never knew Phil's dad, but it did feel like I knew what he meant. Like I'd seen what he'd seen. And if Phil was trying to protect me from it, he didn't need to. More than that. *I couldn't let him.* "About the power they had and the way they chose to use it? Because I've seen it—I mean, I really, *really* get that."

I watched his face, close. But it didn't twitch. Didn't change. "Just told me I was out of the will if I ever tried to join. And that went for my kids, too."

It was a rich-people threat, and I didn't know whether to believe it or not.

"I'm glad you're getting out of there, kid," he sincerely added. "Those boys need you, not the other way around."

He was probably the only one who could say that and make me believe it. "Thanks, Phil."

"And, you know," he said, glancing at me like he wanted to make sure I was listening, "you can always call me. Not a million times in a row like those kids do, give me a chance to call you back"—I smiled—"but really. You don't need permission or an invitation. Just pick up the phone. And that goes for Kat, too." Phil's wife. "She loves you, man. And Soph, Chad, and Sam." Their little brother. "Sam may be a little young for you, but Soph and Chad are always at your disposal. I know they can kind of be pains in the ass, but they're halfway decent once you smack 'em around enough."

We glided down the parkway, the river on the right and the trees on the left. Headed back to White Cove, and, about thirty minutes after that, I'd be back home. And while we drove, I started wondering how different even *that* would be. White Cove was just twenty miles away from Streetlight but a long twenty miles. Twenty miles that might as well be two thousand. Because they separated two completely different worlds. One where Phil was—where things changed and people left. Where there was no such thing as Spooks or the IVs. Where you could find a Nike Store or a KFC.

And on the other side of the highway was Streetlight.

"You think we could swing by McDonald's?" I asked once Phil took our exit.

He glanced at me like I should be slapped. "All that food we just left and you're thinking about McDonald's?"

But he'd never get it. Because he'd gotten out.

My mouth was watering already. "I really miss Big Macs."

He checked his blind spot and coasted into the other lane so we could turn into the drive-thru coming up on the left. He smirked and told me I ought to be checked for worms.

And then, mostly to himself, he added, "That's a real strange town you live in."

Kady
Thursday, November 26

Forty-eight candies left.

My fists squeeze my thumbs in the pockets of my jacket as I walk through Nik's neighborhood. His house is the one at the end of this long street, all brick with columns and black trim. Even from here, all the perfectly placed lights glitter in flawless synchronicity.

I walk slowly up Nik's long driveway, past the line of cars that are already parked. Ten, at least. Maybe more. Nik offered to pick me up, and Dad wanted to drop me off, but I lied and told each of them that I'd accepted the other's offer. Just so I could be on my own and feel the cold in my bones.

I hesitate when I reach the front door. Any other time, Nik would be outside waiting for me, or I'd text him and he'd jog down in a pair of Iverson shorts and a tank. But that's when it's just us, and I'm only here for him.

I press the doorbell. It gongs on the other side of the door, and it takes less than five seconds for it to swing open. A short, gray-haired man in a tuxedo is in front of me, smiling.

"Hello, miss. Welcome. May I take your coat?"

God, that sounds familiar. But it's a feeling too small to hold on to, a grain of sand falling through an hourglass before it disappears into all the rest.

He's behind me before I even say yes, helping me shrug off my jacket. It's warm in here, but I still shiver—shaking from my almost memory and the cold outside—now that I'm only wearing this thin gray turtleneck and the black jeans that Nik's always liked on me.

"May I have your name?" he asks.

I turn away from the giant chandelier that's sparkling from the peak of Nik's soaring ceilings. I've never seen it on before.

"Sorry?" I ask.

He smiles, and with my jacket draped over his arm, he repeats, "Your name?"

"Oh, I'm Kady." And when he reaches for an index card and a pen from the end table they keep next to the door, I spell it to be helpful. "K-A-D-Y. I like your bow tie, by the way." It's black with gold polka dots.

"Why, thank you," he says, jotting my name down the right way and sticking it to the sleeve of my coat with a safety pin.

"Of course," I answer, dusting off the front of my jeans. "What's yours?"

"Beg your pardon?"

He sounds so surprised that I look up just to make sure I didn't do something wrong. "Your name?"

"Oh." He clears his throat. "I'm Michael."

"M-I-C-H-A-E-L?" I ask. "I have a cousin who spells it with a K."

"Yes, miss."

"Well, it's nice to meet you, Michael. Thanks for taking my coat."

Before Michael can say anything back, Nik pokes his head into the foyer. He smiles and heads over when he sees that it's me. He's in skinny navy slacks and a light blue button-down, and his hair is slicked back the way it is in all his school pictures.

He kisses my mouth and starts to slip his hands onto my hips. But I lace his fingers through mine so that we're holding hands instead. A little bit because Michael is right here, and mostly because he just drifted dangerously close to my candies.

"Have you met Michael?"

Nik doesn't say yes and he doesn't say no, but he does smile at Michael and ask, "Everything okay so far?"

Michael smiles back, my jacket still draped over his arm. "Great, sir."

"Nice," Nik says, and then he turns to me instead, dark eyes glistening like he has a secret. "Come here. I wanna show you something."

He walks me through the living room, my fingers still tangled in his. It's full of people in cocktail dresses and suits with no ties being catered to by tuxedoed staff carrying trays of bite-size food. Christmas trees are in every corner, perfectly trimmed with white lights and red bows, and I want to stop and look at everything. But Nik doesn't slow down as he slides open his back door.

They have a heated porch, so it's warm even though we're outside now, and when Nik slides the door shut, the hum of all the people disappears, and it's only us.

His yard sits dark and quiet beyond the screens, and my mind slips back to this past summer, when everything was still so right that it shimmered. We dragged millions of pillows onto this porch and lay in the corner with his iPad where we were sure no one inside could see us. We streamed a thousand movies while he kissed me, and our fingers secretly drifted over each other's bodies until the sun set.

"It's dark out here . . ."

His white teeth glow in the moonlight as he smiles back. "It is?" He looks around like he hadn't noticed.

I shove my palm at him, but he catches it and laughs. "Shut up," I insist as he pulls me in for a hug. "You know what I mean. Why are we out here?" My voice echoes back into my ear while my head rests against his chest.

"I wanted to show you something real quick." He lets me go.

"Is it cool?" I ask, his shoes clunking on the wood as he walks across the deck.

"Nah, it sucks," he answers, and I bite back a smile. He reaches the far corner of the deck and calls across the distance between us, "You know how you've wanted to go to Sparks the past couple years but we never make it?"

Sparks is the next big event that'll be at our fairgrounds, a light display for the holidays that starts two weeks before Christmas and lasts until New Year's Day. When I was little, I used to go with Owen and my parents, because it's more of a family thing. But Nik always promised me that we'd go one day, too. So we can sing along off-key with the carolers and go to the hot chocolate stand that gives whole brownies as toppings.

"Are you finally gonna take me?"

"If you want me to," he says. "Or we can pretend like we're there right now."

He does something. Flips a switch or messes with a plug—he's too far away and the porch is too dark for me to know for sure. But suddenly, the entire yard lights up. Twinkling trees, blinking candy canes, a sleigh with flickering reindeer. Flawless enough to be in one of the storefront windows in Old Town.

Nik starts walking back to me. "I told Mom I wanted to wait to light up the backyard till you got here. I know it's not Sparks, but I thought maybe you'd like it anyway."

"Being rich is so cool," I say.

"Whatever." He wraps his arms around my shoulders and rests his chin on my head. His yard is prettier that way, somehow. Gazing at it while I'm buried in his hug. "Look, I know the ball stuff sucks, but I really do appreciate you cutting me a break. And I really am happy you're here, Kades—I just wanted to make sure you knew that."

And maybe he means that I'm here for Thanksgiving, or maybe he means that I'm here in his life. But however he means it, I mean it just as much. "I'm glad I'm here, too."

He kisses the top of my head, and, for a little while, we just stand where we are, the blinking lights dancing across our faces. It's so incredible that I'm not even sure what would be better:

Staying just like this with him, until they call us in for dinner.

Or undoing the whole thing just so we can do it again.

Dinner was quail.

And a salad with dried fruit and walnuts, some kind of roasted potatoes that flavor-bombed your mouth when you bit into them, squash casserole. There was a crab bisque and a New England clam chowder. Roast beef that they cut right in front of us. Lamb chops. Corn on the cob.

The food came out in rounds—*courses*, Mrs. Rios corrected me—plate after plate placed in front of us and swept away. Nik sat next to me, charming our side of the table, having easy conversations with all of his guests. He told me everybody's name and introduced me each time, but I still couldn't keep track of everything. Of their faces and their relationships, and all this different silverware. I hesitated before every new round—ugh, *course*—to see what fork or knife or spoon Nik would pick up next. And if he was too busy talking to act soon enough, I looked to Saige instead.

She was on the other end of the table, on the side across from us. She covered her mouth every time she laughed and never talked while she was chewing. She made her eyes big when a story was really good and only touched her hair to push it behind her ears. And every time they put a new plate in front of me, I picked the silverware that she did, because I knew that she'd be right.

I tried not to look too much, though, not get caught up in how graceful and distracting she was, because Hendricks was on her side of the table, too. And every time my eyes met his, his stare was so hot that it burned.

"Kady, dear." I turn around, and Mrs. Rios's hand is on my chair. "Will you help me cut the pie?"

She doesn't wait for me to say yes, just floats along the hardwood floor in her four-inch heels while she smiles and squeezes the shoulders of the people next to me as she passes. I turn to Nik, but he's watching her go, and I know that means he heard what she said.

"I'll be back," I tell him before he can offer to come with me. But he doesn't seem happy enough with that, so I add, "It's fine."

I stand up and follow her into the kitchen.

I've never seen it so . . . *used* before. It's usually polished and shiny with plates stacked perfectly in their see-through cabinets. But the island is full of the meats we didn't finish. The sink full of dishes from all our *courses*. People in tuxedos and chef coats are milling around, cleaning and preparing and scurrying. Mrs. Rios walks up to a woman who's slicing a pie and setting the pieces on tiny white plates.

"That looks lovely," Mrs. Rios tells her. And then she goes to have a seat at the table.

I wonder if that's what she considers "cutting the pie."

"Come, come." Mrs. Rios beckons me. "Sit."

I do.

"So," she says, settling in. "How did you like your dinner?"

She's in a white sweater and high-waisted black slacks, with her thick, dark hair coiled into a bun. Simple, sleek, modern. A diamond brooch glitters from her shoulder. A duck, I think. Maybe a swan.

My mouth is dry already. I've never really talked to Mrs. Rios before, nothing more than a smile-hello, or a smile-goodbye—and at first I thought it was *so weird*. I have full conversations with Em's parents when I'm there; Shawn's always have questions for us about the latest thing they saw on TikTok. But Mrs. Rios—and Mr. Rios, too—didn't exist to me for weeks, and then months. And now years.

Nik and I will run into her sometimes, in transit from the bedroom to the car. And when we do, she watches with this eerie stillness. Like she wants me to feel every second of it.

"Dinner was really good," I tell her, sliding my hands under my thighs so they don't sweat too much. "Those potatoes . . ."

She presses her hands against her flat stomach like she'll never eat again. "Every year I try to take them off the menu, but my husband would leave me for those potatoes if he could."

I laugh a little. She watches me do it. Then she smiles, just with her lips.

"Thank you for having me," I add, anxious to prove I have manners.

She fans me off. "It's long overdue. Your parents . . ." She squints like she's trying to place it. "They run that drive-in movie theater on the Wilshires' land, no?"

I can't tell if she thinks that's good or bad or just an impartial fact—like a birthday or the color of their eyes. "Yeah, they started it right after my brother was born. Have you ever been? I bet you'd like it."

"Oh, no," she says, like she's shamefully too old for something fun like movies. Even though I honestly have no idea how old she is. Maybe she's forty or maybe she's sixty. Nik told me one time that after thirty-five, she stopped counting. "But I'm sure it's lovely."

"You should come one day," I insist. "Let me host you."

"I'd love to find the time." She crosses one leg over the other before she goes on. "You know, Kady, when *I* was growing up, my parents owned a car wash." She nods a little when my eyebrows come together. "It was the kind you drive your car into and it scrubs the outside, and then people would park and my brothers and I would vacuum the inside. Every day of the week. Even when we had school, we'd work at the car wash afterward."

She smiles, like it isn't the worst memory. And I try to imagine Mrs. Rios working like that, working at all. Her perfectly trimmed nails are glossed with a pink so pale that any physical labor would stain them. She has staff floating around doing everything for her while we sit here, not cutting the pie. The dishes clang in the sink while someone cleans.

"Was it in Streetlight?" I ask.

"No, no. Albuquerque, actually." She folds her arms and rests them on the table. "I worked very hard. I was very smart. I got a scholarship to Barnes College, where I met Nik's father. And now I'm here today."

She pauses like a guest speaker, ready to take any questions. But the only one I have, I can't actually ask. Because what I *want* to know is which part was the hard work and which part was really smart? Was it the scholarship or going to college or ending up with Mr. Rios? Because she says it like it all exists together. One complete, entire truth.

"Whenever you're in my house," she goes on, gentle and strong at the same time, "you tiptoe around like a little mouse. Like you're barely here. My daughters call you Invisible Girl." She laughs, but my cheeks get warm with embarrassment. "And it's sweet—how respectful you try to be whenever you're here. I know that you're a sweet girl, Kady. But I'm also sure you're more than that. You remind me of myself." She sits up a little taller, proud of that part. "And seeing you with my son? It's like watching me with my husband all over again. That's why I'm glad you're here tonight. Sitting with us. Talking to us. Because with people like this"—and she's talking about everyone who's sitting in her dining room, as she glances around her dirty kitchen, at all the quiet, hardworking people who aren't—"you have to *make* them see you."

Her eyes shimmer as bright as the diamonds glittering from her brooch, the same unrelenting gaze that follows me when Nik leads me to his bedroom. And even though she's just across the table, close enough to touch, it feels like she's on a mountaintop, reaching over the edge with a single hand, offering to save my life.

This is how you get to be like me. She doesn't say it, but still. It pricks me all over.

How? I want to plead. *Tell me.*

"Peekaboo," someone says.

The voice is soft and coy as it tickles my ear, and I sense the hands on the back of my chair.

Peekaboo. I see you.

Mrs. Rios smiles over my head at whoever it is, and I turn around to see Saige, as bubbly as the champagne in her glass.

"Hello, my darling," Mrs. Rios says.

Saige dips her chin into her shoulder as she smiles. Her hair falls into her eyes. And then, as sincerely as if she were asking permission, she says, "I wanted to talk to Kady a little bit."

I turn back to Mrs. Rios to see if I'm allowed.

"Of course," she says. "You girls have fun." She glances disappointedly back at the kitchen. "I think dessert is going to take a minute longer than I thought. Everyone could probably use a moment to freshen up." She stands and gives my shoulder a squeeze, places her cheek against Saige's cheek, and floats back into the dining room.

I stay in my chair while Saige keeps standing in her black suede booties. She's in tights and a peplum leather skirt with a fitted red sweater.

"I saw Diana take you and I know how she can be, so I just wanted to make sure she hadn't unhinged her jaw or anything." She looks hesitant to say it, but she smiles when I laugh.

"No, she didn't bite."

"She can be sneaky, the way she does it," Saige admits, tucking one leg under her as she sinks into the seat that Nik's mom just left. "You think you're fine, and then you wake up with scars." She smiles into her glass before she takes another sip, remembering a moment that's hers and not mine. "I love Diana," she whispers, almost too softly to hear.

She pushes her hair behind her ear, swallows her glittering bubbles, sets the fragile glass down so gently that it pings.

"Thanks for checking on me," I tell her.

"Of course," she says like it's nothing. She tips her glass toward me. "Champagne?"

"I'm okay," I answer.

"That's right, you don't drink." She shakes her head to herself. "I always forget that."

"It's not a big deal," I promise.

"Can I ask how come?"

No one's asked me like that before—like they really care to know—and I hug myself under Saige's gaze as she waits patiently for my answer. She was actually there the one night that I did drink—at an IV party that Nik had taken me to my freshman year. It was at a Boy's house whose family had a full bar. There was a pool, and a few of the older guys were playing poker for money. Nik made me tequila Sprites, and we drank them together until he took me home. But it wasn't *better*. It wasn't even as good as what we already had, and the memories we already made, and the things we'd already done. I thought it'd be like magic, the way the Iverson kids loved to drink, the way their parents did, too. But it wasn't magic at all. Just a little bit of spinning.

Saige doesn't remember that night, I'm sure. Nik and I were so new back then that no one was expecting us to last; no one wasted their time remembering who I was or what I did or didn't drink. But I remember her. The first time I officially met the only girl he'd kissed besides me. The first time I witnessed how perfectly she fit into his world, how perfectly she fit with him.

"I just never really thought it was fun," I admit to Saige tonight.

"It's not," she agrees, and when I laugh, she does, too. "It's actually super stupid." She finishes off her glass, anyway, though; a final sip and then it's back on the table. *Ping.* "But you know what it *does* do?" She sits back in her seat and peers at me with a smirk on her pink lips. "Makes it easier to talk about the truth." She nods back at the dining room. "You know every person at that table has a story."

I squint. "What kind of story?"

"A bad one. Or a juicy one. Or one that's completely unhinged."

The kind of stories my friends and I always heard from someone, who heard from someone, who heard from someone. Always fragmented and distorted by the time they reached us. "As in . . ." I smile. "Gossip?"

"You can't spend an entire night in a house full of strangers," she passionately insists. "That's not very safe."

And then she leans over the table, her voice soft enough that the people she's talking about won't hear. Words that were allowed to be hers but never meant to be mine, until she tiptoed after me with a glass in her hand. But here we are now, becoming something to each other we've never been before, hovering so close that her hair tickles my cheek and mine almost drips into her empty glass, while she whispers to me with wet breath that smells like sweet champagne.

After dessert, I say goodbye.

I start to give Mrs. Rios a hug, but she squeezes my elbow instead and tells me she'll see me again soon. I let Saige know I'm leaving, and she pouts and insists no one else here appreciates her stories. I sneak out back with Nik again, and he kisses me for one perfect second after another.

"I'll drive you," he says.

"Owen is coming," I tell him.

But he's not.

At the door, I talk to Michael while he works his way through the coat closet to find mine. I sneak him the chocolate truffles I smuggled from one of the silver trays, because I'm pretty sure he hasn't eaten anything yet. He chuckles and says, "Miss, you're going to get me in trouble."

But I zip up my jacket and insist, "It's just chocolate."

And then I let myself out.

Tonight wasn't bad, but my shoulders are still tight. They'll loosen up on the walk, though. I take a breath so deep that it tugs at my insides.

"Reeks, doesn't it?" a voice says from the shadows.

I jump. It takes my eyes a second to adjust to the darkness. That movement in the driveway isn't just my imagination.

Hendricks pulls himself off the hood of a Lexus and starts over to me, nose in the air as he takes a breath that mimics mine. "You notice it, too?"

I frown, my skin tingling the closer he gets. "It doesn't smell like anything."

"Not so much a scent." He steps into the light of Nik's front door.

"More like a feeling." He leans his shoulder against the house, coatless and smug. "Can't believe you were about to leave without saying bye."

"Yeah, what a shocker."

His gaze shifts to his shoes and then out into the night. "You know, it's been a while since I've had a drink thrown in my face. Guess that means I hit a nerve, huh?"

He glares at me again, and I can't stand him watching me like that. Unbothered and mildly amused, a predator playing with his prey. He's losing his mind. Whatever he thinks he saw, he didn't. Whatever he thinks he knows, he doesn't. I want to tell him to shut the fuck up and seek help. But Aaron ripping those pages from his notebook when I told him about Bianchi's—the way the sound tore through his quiet kitchen like a whip—stops me.

"Look—" I insist. "We don't have to be friends, or get along, or even agree on what's real. But we care a lot about the same guy. He's the collateral damage. So can't we just . . . coexist?"

He doesn't answer, though. I'm not even sure he was listening. He just stares like an animal, taking one slow step after another. Getting closer and closer—

Blood.

I blink hard.

Laughter.

I blink harder.

But in the moment it takes me to remember that this isn't my nightmare, it's just Nik's front step, he's as close to me as he was to Aaron in that alley. He breathes and I do, too. It's the only sound in the entire world.

"There's something about you I can't shake lately." He stares into my eyes, as deep as Aaron does sometimes, but it's not the same at all. "Why can't I shake you, Kady?"

I refuse to step back, to just grant him the space he stole from me, no matter how much I hate how his breath is brushing my cheeks. "Maybe you're not trying hard enough."

"Is that it? I need to try harder?"

"Hendricks—"

"You look hot, by the way." He says it the same way he says everything, like he knows he can get away with it. Like he knows he's an asshole.

My eyes narrow. "You're disgusting."

He nods. "Pretty much."

I push past him. I'm going home.

He grabs my waist so fast that it stops my heart. I spin around, ready to knee him in the balls regardless of what Aaron says. But goose bumps are springing up all over my arms. His head is on a tilt as he watches me. Like I'm an exhibit behind glass. And that's when it hits me—he's not gripping my waist. He's gripping my hips.

Where I *am* hot. Where I'm always hot these days.

I shove his arms away.

He says, "You know they only burn because I don't want you to have them."

My stomach is suddenly nothing but bile.

"Oh, and for the record—" He backs away, satisfied. "My answer is no."

"No what?"

He winks. "We can't coexist."

I stare at him as he goes, the world cracking down the middle with every cool step he takes. My lungs can't hold on to the air long enough to speak. Maybe there *is* something wrong with it tonight.

And when his hand slides out of his pocket, it happens in slow motion. His thumb pressed to his pointer, pinching something that he brings straight to his mouth.

I run and grab his other wrist, but he yanks it away. And I only have seconds—*less than* seconds—

I slam my foot into the back of his legs, and then I grab his shoulders.

He peers up at me from his knees, his breath heavy, his eyes full of so much hate that I'm trembling.

But then he smiles. At the very moment that we slip away.

I open my eyes.

I pat my body, my pillows. I'm in bed. It's dark. Where's my phone?

I grab it from the other side of my mattress. It's three a.m. Thanksgiving morning.

"*Shit.*" I cover my eyes with my hands. "*Shit. Shit. Shit.*"

I yank open my nightstand drawer, desperate to breathe. And there, I find my candies. Right where they should be. Glowing peacefully in the dark.

Kady

Thursday, November 26— Sunday, November 29

I do Thanksgiving at Nik's all over again, too sick to eat, so I just push my food around my plate. I'm a doll—that's what it feels like. With legs and arms and a head that I once thought were mine, but tonight they aren't, and maybe they never were. It was always Hendricks, playing with me. Putting me right where he wanted me to be. All of us, really.

He smirks at me all night, like he's sure I get it now—that I know nothing about his world and that's the entire reason he doesn't want me in it. He's forced the medicine down my throat, and I hear his sneering voice every time his bold stare catches mine:

We can't coexist.

Saige steals me from Mrs. Rios again and whispers all the same stories. I don't listen, but I pretend to. Until she says, "Do you ever get déjà vu?"

My eyes drift from the grand piano and focus on her again. She's paused like she's heard a sound where one isn't supposed to be.

"Sometimes," I answer, my throat going dry.

She takes a deep breath and lets it out just as slowly, peering around the room. Swirling her champagne. I wait for it to hit her so hard that the blood drains from her face.

But she shrugs. She smiles.

"Me too," she says.

The rest of Thanksgiving break passes like a fever dream, me tucked under Nik, because it's the only place I feel safe. Is the time really passing, or did Hendricks just pop another candy somewhere? How does it even work when two people are using? Time can't be both of ours— Hendricks *has* to know that.

Hendricks has to *hate* that.

Did his candies come from Spooks, too? Has he been playing TK's game and calling those same numbers for years? Maybe the candies really *are* his. There's nothing around here that belongs to him and the rest of us, too.

Maybe Nik feels what Saige feels—this déjà vu that he can't explain. He wouldn't believe me if I tried to tell him why. *I* barely believe me. So I escape with him instead, locked away in his bedroom while we keep the rest of the world out. Like it's summer all over again—and, God, I wish it was. I want to be on Nik's screened-in porch while the sun shines and turns our skin even prettier shades of brown. I want to be on top of all those pillows, while he kisses me all over and I get tipsy off his fingertips. While our breaths grow heavy in one another's ears and our sweat melts together, sticky and salted. And we lie there with our hearts thudding, staring out at his acres of lawn. While I wait as long as I can before I finally insist, *Again*. And his lips part and take me back to the beginning.

Maybe if TK just understood how great things were. How perfect they could be. Maybe then I could actually ask him. Beg him—

Is it really so bad to go back to when everything was better?

Kady
Monday, November 30

On Monday night, Shawn, Em, and I are on the lawn at The Drive-In, with a blanket to sit on and extra ones to wrap ourselves in, while our Styrofoam cups of hot apple cider warm our hands. Luka isn't with us tonight. He has work.

The movie is *Inception*, which Em loves and Shawn swears is so smart that he loves it, too. Dreams within dreams within dreams. Just to plant the tiniest idea in someone's mind, so it can grow big enough to change the entire course of their life.

"Who should we incept?" Em wonders.

"Luka, so he stops eating mint chip?" Shawn suggests.

Em smiles, and then she takes a second to really decide. "I think I'd incept Milo to remember to restock the toilet paper at the apartment."

"That's a good inception," Shawn declares. "You should plant a seed to wash the toothpaste down the drain, too, while you're in there."

Em giggles and sips her cider. "Done." Then she adds, in the same floaty voice that asks us about superpowers or happily-ever-afters, "Do you think inception is real?"

"A hundred percent," Shawn says. "I mean, not like *this*. You can't dance around in people's dreams. But you can definitely make them think an idea was theirs when it was really yours."

Em's eyes glisten in the light of the big screen. "And then control their minds forever," she whispers.

Shawn swigs from his cup. "Or at least stop getting stranded in the bathroom with no toilet paper."

A chorus of car horns goes off—a kiss on-screen and a slew of IV Boys in the parking lot to witness it. They honk and flash their headlights for at least fifteen seconds.

When they finish, Em keeps talking like nothing even happened. "I'd let you guys incept me, if you wanted," she decides. "You have good ideas."

For a little bit, we just watch the movie with everyone else, the night sky clear enough that I can count the stars. This is the first time in days it feels like all of me exists in one place again, and I'm not so distracted that I can barely follow basic conversation. It's The Drive-In, I think, and being on this blanket with Shawn and Em. How we've done this forever and we're doing it still, like not a single thing has changed.

"*Slut!*" someone calls from the parking lot. It's short and sharp, like a bark.

Shawn glances over his shoulder. "That's new."

"*Whoooorrre!*" someone calls next.

On the screen, it's a chase scene—so that's not why they're reacting. Em turns around, too.

"*Stupid slut!*"

"*Lying slut!*"

"*Biiiiitchhhh!*"

More people in the field are turning around to look at the lot, at the rows of cars lurking in the darkness, as voices call out from faceless bodies. But I don't turn around, because I know what this is. Nik, Hendricks, and Saige drove back to Barnes yesterday afternoon, and Hendricks hasn't said a word to me since the first Thanksgiving. But these voices are for me, just like those Instagram comments were for me. The things Hendricks has all of his dolls do and say so I never forget who I belong to.

By the concessions, a flashlight pops on. Dad, I'm sure, ready to shine a light in the lot to get people to quiet down and, if they won't, make them leave. I start to sweat inside my coat.

"You guys," I whisper.

But Shawn and Em are busy looking at the lot with everyone else. "What the hell are they doing," Shawn says more than asks, like he'll never stop being amazed by how much IV Boys suck.

I pinch his cheek, because his face is the only bit of skin that's not covered.

"*Ow*," he says. "What?" He turns to me, annoyed. But then his eyes go soft, and he asks me, "What's wrong?"

"I think they're talking to me."

"What do you mean, you think they're talking to you? Em." He nudges her so she'll turn around. He asks me again, "What do you mean, you think they're talking to you?"

Shawn and Em study me, while the movie dances on their faces, and all the things they don't know dance through my mind. "The rumor." It's all I can think to say.

"What rumor?" Em asks.

"You're kidding me," Shawn declares. "From *weeks* ago?"

"What rumor?" Em asks again.

The voices behind us don't stop. They come from the left and the right, and far away and then so much closer. No one's watching the movie anymore. Parents in the lawn are covering little kids' ears.

"There's been this rumor going around the IVs," I tell her. "That Aaron and I kissed—I thought it would die on its own."

But it didn't, because it was never about that.

Em blinks. "Since when?"

"Halloween," I admit.

She squints. She probably thinks it's the longest amount of time that she's ever not known something about me. She shakes it off after a moment. A chill that just needed to run its course.

"So they never stopped," Shawn summarizes, jaw tight as he watches me. As the screen and the moon and the stars that are icy and bright turn his pale skin blue. "They've just kept at it for weeks."

Years, maybe. Since the moment I existed. I'm not even sure anymore—how much I've imagined and how much has been real. It slices through me when it's loud, when they're yelling or leaving comments. But what about all the times when it's been quiet—a whisper so soft that a breeze could blow it away? The glances, the External Venture jokes, the ball. Me, reading too far into things. Or just me with my eyes open.

I don't know anymore.

"Can we go?" I ask.

"Yeah." Em stands up, grabs the blanket she was wrapped in and then the one that I was. "Yeah, let's go."

But Shawn's anger is hot, his eyes narrowed on the parking lot like a snarling dog. He stands up, too, as he calls into the shadows: "*Why are you hiding in the dark like a bunch of bitch-ass little boys?*"

"We're not doing that," Em says, tugging his arm, taking his blanket. "Not in front of Mr. and Mrs. Dixon. Come on."

"What?" Shawn insists, still glaring at the lot. "They can act out, but I can't?" He cups his mouth and yells into the darkness, "*Fuck* you guys."

Two flashlights are bobbing around the lot now, hunting. Dad and maybe Julius, maybe Ryan—I'm pretty sure they're both working tonight. Mom is probably back at the concession stand, there for anyone who needs anything. Hoping Dad finds whoever these Boys are and gets them out of here. Disgusted that they'd come to The Drive-In just to ruin everyone else's night.

My heart aches at the thought of her ever finding out that I'm the reason why.

Em lassos her arm around Shawn's waist and drags him with us. She drops our blankets in the big wooden baskets that frame the exit, and finally the field is behind us, the voices a distant echo in the night.

"Do you wanna go to The Spot?" Em asks me, just offering ideas. "Or home?"

"Let's go home," I tell her, and she nods. I don't want to risk being anywhere that one of those Boys could see me.

"Okay," she agrees. "Home," she tells Shawn.

He nods, his hands shoved so deep in his coat pockets that their imprints are pushing through the bottoms. His cheeks are red, but it's not from the cold. "It's not okay, you know."

"You think I don't know that?" My voice breaks.

"For them to act like that," Shawn goes on, like he can't even hear me. "For them to think they can. Nik shouldn't get to have you *in spite* of all their bullshit. He should be the reason why there *is* no bullshit. He should be the one telling those guys to shut the hell up, and telling them that he's fucking *lucky* you pick him. Over and over. Every time. He should be telling them every second that it's never gonna get better for him than you. And when they do shit like that—" Shawn straightens his arm and points back at The Drive-In, his hand trembling. "He should be back here as fast as he can drive on the 403, and *he* should be the one picking those assholes off, one by one. Not your mom and dad."

We stand there, our white breaths meeting in the middle before they swirl and disappear. The hot tears pool in my eyes while my hot candies press on my hip, a reminder of Hendricks's threat.

They only burn because I don't want you to have them.
Shawn blurs as I blink.

He pulls me in and hugs me, and he pulls Em in, too. For a second, I let myself sob—just enough to release the tension, to give the rubber band a little slack before it snaps. I let my face contort into all the pain that I've felt, and the secrets that I've kept, and the lies I've told myself all this time. It's soundless, though, because I still don't want Em and Shawn to know how bad it's gotten. How it's even worse than this.

Shawn kisses me through my hair while he keeps hugging Em and me. "I just love you," he tells me. "I just actually know how to love you."

I lie in my bed that night, curled on my side, as small as I can make myself. My lights are out and my parents still aren't home, but I knew I wanted to pretend to be asleep by the time they got here. In case they want to talk about what happened tonight. How gross it was. How unfortunate.

The darkness in my room is a shade of sapphire—a combination of the moon, the stars, and the candies on my nightstand. I reach for my phone and open my Find My app. Nik's at his apartment, the one he shares with Hendricks, the one I've never seen. So I can't even picture what he might be doing—if there's a TV in the living room that maybe he's watching or a desk in his room where maybe he's studying. All I can imagine for sure is him with Hendricks. His best friend. His brother.

If I could crawl into a dream and plant a tiny seed, it wouldn't be in Luka's or Milo's. It'd be in Nik's, from the moment I met him. It'd be the size of a grain of salt, buried so deep in his mind—a dream within a dream within a dream within a dream—that I would've risked my entire life just to place it there. But it'd be the most worthwhile risk I'd ever taken, so that he knows the difference between games and what's real. So that his blood boils when his friends act like enemies. So that I don't have to tell him why it hurts, why I bleed.

I dig into my bag of candies and squeeze one in my palm. There's no use in erasing tonight, not while the Boys are after me. If they don't find me tonight, they'll find me next time, somewhere else. It's small here, but it's never felt like this. Like the invisible force field that surrounds this town is closing in—more and more—every second. Crushing. Suffocating. Until it leaves me flat.

But really, it's no different. Who we are. Where we are. In the same tiny town where those Boys are still watching even when they aren't looking, and just because I cover my eyes doesn't mean that they're not there. They're *always* there. Staring right at me the second I move my hands.

I place the candy on my tongue and whisper, "Eleven oh eight," one minute earlier. The walls go, then the bed; then the bright lights prick my eyes. When I blink, it's like I rolled out of one bed and landed gently in the next. Just a blip.

I do it again.

And again.

Until it rocks me to sleep.

Kady

Tuesday, December 1

Thirty-one candies left.

Aaron texted me while I was in class to see if I could meet him at Iverson's library and look at his Vanderbilt essay. Which sounded freaking miserable for multiple reasons. In part, because the last place I wanted to be after last night was that campus. But also because it did weird things to my stomach lately, accepting that the one thing Aaron needed my help with was the same thing that might take him away.

Cringe, I know. And if there was one place on that campus where I was fairly positive that I wouldn't run into a bunch of IV Boys, it was gonna be in the library. So I told him sure, that I'd come by after school.

He's standing at the security check-in when I get there—built like one of those tollbooths on the highway, except with gray stone. There's a man who sits inside with a gate lowered to block the cars, and you need an Iverson ID or to be escorted by someone with an Iverson ID before you can get past him during daylight hours.

Aaron flashes his ID card, and the guard waves me through.

Aaron's in his IV blazer, his Iverson sweater, the button-down underneath, and khakis. An Iverson navy blue beanie on but no coat. His hands are in his pockets, and his shoulders are scrunched up by his ears.

"Why?" I ask, tugging his sleeve, and he knows what I mean. That it makes *no sense* for him to be outside without a coat. "I yawned on the way over here, and my spit literally froze."

"We're gonna be fast," he says.

I stop walking and point up at the trees, just to slow us down. "Is that a white oak?"

"Oh no," he says, getting behind me, putting his hands on my shoulders. Guiding me forward. "Nope. Not today. We're hauling ass."

I laugh as we jog up the main steps.

Aaron pulls open the heavy wooden doors, and they close behind us with a quiet thud. It feels like an oven in here, warm enough to make me sleepy.

No, I just *am* sleepy.

The halls are empty, the blue-and-white tiled floor spotless even after a full day of classes. The lockers line both sides of the hallway, a deep blue that's chipping in the corners. Iverson is old. It's meant to be. In a classic, vintage way that families pay tens of thousands of dollars to claim as their own.

"How was battle today?" I ask.

Aaron stretches, pulls one arm across his chest using the other. "A little bruised, but I'm gonna make it." He keeps walking, and I follow his lead. I've been to the library twice before, both times because Nik needed to grab a book before we left, but we were so busy kissing, holding hands, planning where we'd go next that I don't remember the way at all.

Aaron hangs a left. "Thanks for coming by. I can't really show a whole bunch of people around here what I'm working on for Vandy."

"Always happy to help you keep your dirty little secrets," I tell him.

"Same. I still haven't told anyone where you put that body."

He pulls open the library door, and the room I remember stands before us. It's something like what I would imagine at Barnes. Rows and rows of books and distinguished wooden desks with little lamps to study at. A MacBook tethered to every one.

Aaron's stuff is piled in a chair at a table that seats three. He pulls my chair out with one hand and his out with the other. I shrug off my coat and reach across the table with gimme-fingers. "Let's see this one-way ticket you've crafted to get yourself out of here."

He slides me his laptop, already opened to his Google doc. Three paragraphs, single-spaced.

"Is there a prompt?" I ask.

"Oh, yeah, it's um . . ." He sits back in his seat and squints a little, trying to get the words right. "Challenge a popular belief and tell us why."

I nod and rest my chin in my hand as I start to read. All he's doing is waiting—not messing with his phone or digging through his backpack—and his patience makes me anxious. He's written about inertia—how an object at rest stays at rest unless an outside force acts upon it. But what *he's* saying is that sometimes, with humans, it's an inside force—not just what's happening around us but what's happening within.

"Challenging Newton is bold." I peer at him over his laptop.

He's still leaning back in his chair. He half smiles and shrugs. "Bro created those rules like four hundred years ago."

I bite back my laugh so I'm not the loud girl in the library and go back to reading.

But two sentences later, he asks, "Does Street U have an essay?"

I shake my head. "Just a transcript and a processing fee."

He nods. I start reading again. Then he says, "You know, maybe you can visit if I end up at Vandy. Like for a weekend or something. So you can get away for a little bit? Maybe you'd like it." His fingers pick at a sticker someone left on the leg of his chair.

It's nice to think that we're visit-each-other kind of friends, especially because I'm pretty sure he means it. But I smile and remind him, "How am I supposed to get all the way to Nashville?"

He makes a face. It's so reflexive that I'm sure he doesn't realize he's doing it. But suddenly the money he never talks about is just as present in this conversation as I am. "I can get you down to Nashville."

The library door swings open, a gust of air coming with it. Aaron's too busy looking at me to turn around, but I'm facing the door just by facing him, and I can't help but look.

Three IV Boys stand in the doorway—the one place on campus where they were never supposed to be. But here they are, and they step in like they're on a mission, their cold stares finding me in seconds. They're not carrying books, or backpacks, or laptops. They're hunting, and my knees start bouncing too fast to stop.

They sit down at a table nearby.

"Maybe," I tell Aaron in response to his unanswered invitation. I go back to his essay. But the words run together while I watch those Boys watching me from the corner of my eye.

"How was Thanksgiving at Nik's?" Aaron's voice pulls me back.

Does he see them over there? He's not acting like it. He's acting like it's just us, like we don't have an audience, like he doesn't notice my bouncing knees.

"Hendricks hates me." It comes out because I can't keep it in.

He smirks. "Well, you tried to drown him."

"It's more than that." I swallow as the Boy chewing gum balances on the back legs of his chair.

Aaron's smile fades, and he glances over his shoulder at whatever it is that has all my attention. The Boys' faces don't change when they notice him watching. They don't look away. They hardly even blink.

Aaron turns back to me. "What happened?"

I try to focus on him instead. His full lashes. His thick brows. This essay that seems really good so far, anti-physics and all. An argument in favor of the forces within us, but all I can feel is the crushing weight of their stares. "Can we leave?"

I push back from the table so hard that the front two legs of my chair lift off the floor and clatter back onto the tile. I speed-walk to the door. Their gazes follow. Aaron's chair legs screech against the floor.

He catches up to me before the door has a chance to close, and he steps with me into the hallway. The door shuts behind us both. Thank God for the emptiness—the *loneliness*—of being out here by ourselves.

"They look at me like they're freaking programmed!" My words quiver as they float down the hall. "Like they're possessed . . ."

"They look at me, too," Aaron says, not like that makes it okay, but he says it steadily, anyway—determined to be an anchor right now. "It's not just you."

"Yeah, but like . . ." And I don't have the words to explain it—how there's a moment when a look turns into something bigger, something that's meant to scare you to your core. "It's different now."

He nods. Steady. "I know."

I glance back at the library, where we left those three Boys, replicas of all the others. Their green and blue and hazel eyes. Staring with an obsession so deep and unwavering that I don't know how to believe it just now showed up. That it wasn't always there, hiding. "Why?"

He's doing the thing—where he looks into me instead of at me. He takes a deep breath, like he wishes he could make it make more sense. But all he says is, "The rumor."

My neck gets hot. My candies get hotter.

"What'd Hendricks do?" he pushes.

"He just . . ." I hug myself. I mean, what can I even say? "When I was at The Drive-In last night, a bunch of IVs started yelling out their windows. *Bitch. Slut. Cheater. Whore.* My dad had to like . . . take a flashlight and search the lot." Trying to tell the story is like swallowing glass. "*At The Drive-In.* Like . . . that's my home. And I don't know for a fact that Hendricks sent them. Or that they were talking to me. They never said, *Kady, Hendricks told us to tell you you're a slut.* But it just *felt* like that, you know? It just felt like . . . they wanted to crush me."

Aaron's hands are in his pockets, fingers fidgeting inside. "I didn't know that was going on last night." I'm sure he only says it because there's this unspoken truth that whatever one IV does, the rest protect.

"I know that," I promise.

He gnaws his bottom lip and looks down at the floor, and when he speaks, he only lifts his eyes. "*You can leave*, KD." It's like he's begging me to see it. "You're smart, you're good to people . . . you're even kind of funny sometimes. And this place . . . *it's not real*. Sometimes I feel like you know that—sometimes I feel like *you really fucking know that*—" He catches himself. His shoulders fall. "So why stay?"

That's when I almost do it—when I almost tell him everything about the candies and Spooks and Hendricks, too. What happened at Thanksgiving and the things Hendricks could have been doing to us all along. That's when I almost tell him that this stupid rumor is just a red herring—that it only exists so Hendricks can give the Boys a reason to come after me. And maybe—*just maybe*—Aaron's always felt weird around Hendricks because *it is* weird around Hendricks. Because he has the power to change everything in the palm of his hand. And I'd *love* to run away from all of that right now, from Hendricks's reigning power over *everything*. I'd love to visit Aaron in Nashville and ride a horse or whatever it is they do there. I'm gonna miss him so much it makes me mad just thinking about it. But the fact that things are so messed up is *why* I have to stay. Even if I wanted to go—*even if I could.* Because everyone I love is still here. I can't just save myself.

And if I tell him all that, and he just looks at me funny or thinks I've lost my mind or chooses Hendricks instead—then I'll take a candy and never say any of it at all.

He waits for me to answer, desperate to understand why I'd ever want to be here.

"Because the reasons to stay are big enough."

He shifts his gaze to the library door, off somewhere in his own thoughts while my hip tingles.

"I can't make them stop looking at you," he finally tells me. "The same way I can't make them stop looking at me. But I can tell you right now—they're not gonna do anything to you again. Alright?" He takes a step closer, eyebrows raised, making sure I hear. "They're not gonna say another word to you. And if anyone ever does—if anyone even tries to—you're gonna tell me. Like we talked about. Yeah?"

He means that conversation in his kitchen when we sat there eating pizza and he asked me to promise to tell him if the Boys got bad. But I never actually promised. Because, until now, magic seemed bigger. Stronger.

But I don't know what it is anymore.

I wrap my arms around his neck and squeeze. I know how much he means every word he just said, but he can't control anything that has Hendricks at the helm. And if it's hopeless, I don't want him to know.

I guess that's why I end up not telling him the truth.

It takes him a second to hug me back, to slide his arms around my waist with enough pressure to feel. And it hits me that I don't think we've ever done this before. Hugged—not for real. There was always space when Nik was here. Us together while Aaron was a few feet away. Now I see what his chest feels like for the first time. Thin but solid, even under all those clothes.

We let each other go.

"Lemme get my stuff and I'll walk you home," he says. "I'll get yours, too. You stay out here."

"I still need to finish reading your essay," I tell him. "So will you stay a little while? At my house?"

"Bet," he agrees, and goes back into the library. The door thuds softly behind him.

And now it's just me—for the first time ever—in one of Iverson's historic hallways.

I glance at the display cases filled with trophies, the achievement plaques, the giant *I* mosaic in the same font that they slap on T-shirts and sweats—followed by a bunch of affirmations:

am a leader.

am a scholar.

am a world-changer.

On and on until the final one:

I am Iverson.

Aaron
Tuesday, December 1

The sky. *Orange and purple and blue, swirled together like the color wheel in PowerPoint.*

The moon. *Faint, like someone erased it. Or just now started to draw it.*

The air. *Cold. And smells like car gas. A red pickup with a busted tailpipe rolls through the four-way stop and leaves a bunch of black smoke behind.*

KD was in a better mood now that we'd been walking away from Iverson for a while. Me too. That place had a weight to it, and I knew she felt it every time she was there. Me, not so much. Not anymore. I only felt it once I was gone, like how you don't realize you're clenching your teeth until you stop.

What I felt most right now was *her*. How she was better since we'd left but still not herself. How she would smile and even laugh, but not like she was happy.

I messed with my keys in my pocket, ran my thumb down the teeth on repeat. I used to know how to fix this stuff. When it was me and her and Nik, and Nik started getting on her nerves, my job was easy. A quick smirk. A dumb joke. They'd both laugh. But the balance was off now that it was just us. Or maybe it actually *was* balanced, and we just weren't used to that.

"You want to stop by The Spot?" I tried, but I knew it was wrong as soon as I said it.

"Not really," she answered, and peeked at the ground before looking up the road again. She'd taken a few of the braids on one side of her head and braided them into a bigger one. I liked it. It flowed from the bottom of her beanie with the rest of them. "I don't want to force you to be seen in public with me."

I held out my arms. Hopped a few steps ahead so I was walking backward in front of her instead. I smiled, like, *What's all this if it's not public?*

She smiled back, but something still wasn't right. I dipped my head a little, tried to catch her gaze and get her to look at me. But she wouldn't. "You probably think I'm such a loser," she said.

"I mean . . ." But she didn't start laughing. I squinted. "Wait, you're for real?"

That was when she finally looked at me, eyes filled to the brim with something different. But I couldn't grab it—not while the setting sun was glinting in her pupils and bouncing off her skin.

"You were just gonna act like it never happened?" she skeptically asked.

"Like *what* never happened?"

She hugged herself and reminded me. "The way Nik denied me while you played Uber last week."

"*You think I'm thinking about that?*" I fell into step next to her, shoved my hands back in my pockets and messed with my keys. But I watched her the whole time. "I'm not thinking about that at all." It was a lie, though. I'd thought about it a lot. When Nik and I talked about it on the way home. When Phil drove past her 'hood first on his way to drop me off after Warm Plates. When I texted her today, even, and asked her to meet up. But I wasn't thinking about it because I was trolling her. I was thinking about it because I was still buggin' about how that car ride had felt after Tipsy Crew. How quiet she was. And how her voice sounded when she did try to talk—like her vocal cords were pulled too tight. Like it *hurt*.

I nudged her, and she swayed way more than normal. No fight left to push me back. "But you still are." *Thinking about it,* I meant, and it made me want to go back to that car ride and do something. Toss Nik a bottle of water and tell him to sober up and say that she could come to the ball. Or at least tell her the real reason why she couldn't.

"It's just embarrassing." She took a breath and let it out. "Those guys look at me anyway. I want them to look at me at that ball. On his arm. In like"—she squinted at the world ahead of us—"a gorgeous gown and strappy heels and my hair done up in a princess bun. I want them to look at me like that, on Nik's arm, and try and tell me that they truly see the difference. Between me and them. That I still don't belong. After all these years. And that's when I'll know it's bullshit. For sure. If I can go to the ball, and look completely amazing, and exist for an entire night just like all the rest of them, and that *still* isn't good enough, then I'll know for sure it's bullshit."

It'd be bullshit.

I didn't say anything, though. I wanted to let her finish.

"You don't know what it's like . . ." She found a rock on the ground and kicked it. It skidded under a parked car. "Being on our side of Streetlight. Because, in some ways, we do belong. I mean, it's home. And we make it our home forever, just like they do. But it's like . . ." She chewed her lip, trying to figure out the way to explain it to someone like me: a Have-Lot in an old-money neighborhood. I was *that* guy. And it still felt weird as hell. "It's like, if Streetlight had a manual, and you read the small print, 'home' would have a bunch of provisions. For you guys, it's home because you own it. But for the rest of us, we're just a bunch of tenants."

"Hey." I stopped walking and waited for her to stop, too. "Listen to me, okay?" And she turned around, a few feet ahead of me. I was finally sure of what I'd seen in her eyes earlier. She was lost in this little-ass town. "I know I'm never gonna know what it feels like to be you in Streetlight. But I'm listening. It's valid. What you're talking about is real, and you're not wrong, okay? Don't let them gaslight you, because you're not wrong." I waited for her to give me anything—a nod, a confirmation, something to prove that that part had sunk in. Because she couldn't lose herself here—I couldn't let her.

She nodded.

I kept running my thumb over the teeth of my key. Three sharp points and a divot toward the base.

Three sharp points and a divot toward the base.

"If it's worth anything," I went on, "I know what you mean. Being a part of something but not really. I feel that way with the IVs all the time. And the Jack-Laurence thing? I mean, all of a sudden being associated with all that just because my pops got married? I'm never gonna feel like what's theirs is mine—no matter how many Christmases or Thanksgivings or vacations happen. And I know that's wack." I sucked my teeth, holding back the shame that came with it. The feeling that I had from the beginning—ever since Phil gave me his number, or Kat made apple pie for our first Thanksgiving and every one after that because she'd heard it was my favorite. The problem wasn't them; it was me.

KD blinked at me, looking at something she'd never seen before. Me, talking about them. Me, really talking about me.

"If I could change that for you?" I went on. "If I could give you that feeling of *belonging* somewhere? Just like, *Yo, this is me, this is my spot, these are my people*—I'd give that to you in a *heartbeat*." I squeezed my keys as I said it, hard enough to leave marks. "But I can promise you, the ball ain't it. That's not changing shit. So fuck the ball, fuck shit up, and get out of here. Streetlight doesn't have to be home forever."

After a second, she smiled. Finally. The first real time all afternoon. "Fuck the ball, fuck shit up, and get out of here," she said softly back.

I shrugged like it was nothing. "That easy."

She laughed, and that was when it hit me—how good it felt to make her smile.

"We should go on an adventure," she said.

"Damn, I left my compass in my other backpack."

"Good thing it's local."

"What are you trying to get me into, woman?" I accused.

Her lips curled. "Fairgrounds? And then your essay. Promise." She held out her pinkie at the very second that every lamppost on the block popped on. *Four on each side.*

I'd never met anyone who lingered in the dark and the cold as much as KD. But she was happy again. Seemed like it, anyway. So I agreed.

"Deal."

It was after five o'clock by the time we got there—it took twenty minutes to walk from where we were. We didn't say much while we went, but it wasn't the same kind of silence as before. This time it was just easy, coincidental. Maybe she was doing like me—listening for the sounds that weren't there. Trying to hold on to something when nothing existed. It was the quietest walk I'd ever taken, the hardest time I ever had trying to notice something worth noticing. Like walking through a movie that'd been muted.

Weird.

I kept on rubbing my keys.

"Why the fairgrounds?" I asked at one point, after the stars came out.

"Because it's not Spooks, and it's not Sparks," she answered. "Haven't you ever wondered what limbo looks like?"

Our feet crunched on the gravel as we veered off the road toward the metal fence. Sound again, finally. I stopped squeezing my keys so hard.

She slid her fingers through the chain links and peered onto the grounds. I'd never been here when it was empty. I only came for Spooks when the whole town came out. And that was the thing—it was even creepier now. Booths with no bright signs and stages with no curtains. A bunch of abandoned machines. Giant Santa faces stacked on the ground, smiling at nothing, and disassembled elves the size of human bodies. Floodlights beamed down on all that was undone. Wreckage. Like we'd survived an apocalypse no one else had.

Fence. *Rusted. Frozen. Something dusty on it that makes me want to rub my fingers together once I let go.*

"A valley of ashes," KD marveled. She peered through the fence like we were somewhere beautiful.

It sounded so familiar but it took me a minute to figure out why. "Gatsby," I realized.

"Em loves that movie." She bit back a smile. "Let's walk around."

She slipped through the gate. It was already open. Not all the way, but enough that she could step through without having to push it any farther. I followed her, three years of blood-brother conditioning kicking in.

"Do you like it here?" I asked, because my answer was *no*. I came because I had to—I couldn't skip Spooks—and I wouldn't miss it once I was gone. All the hype. All the obsession. All the time we spent that we could never get back.

"At the fairgrounds?" she asked. We were walking side by side, our steps on the gravel going off like bombs in the dead quiet. I nodded, and she said, "Yeah, I love it," like I was wrong if I didn't. "It's a totally different world. Where reason turns into nonsense, and you have no idea where you are anymore."

I watched her, her eyes darting around all the emptiness, awestruck. Or like she was looking for something. I couldn't tell. But I studied her as she gnawed her lip and her breath came out white, trying to figure out which it was.

She stopped walking, and then she called into the night, *"Hello!"* with her hands cupped around her mouth. But nothing answered back. Just her own voice, bouncing off the trees.

I told myself she just needed to yell for a second, go to the most magical place she knew and imagine what would happen if someone returned her call. Hoping someone would. Hoping in a hopeless town.

She dropped her hands from her mouth.

I pressed my lips together and gave her an extra second before I told her, "I think it's time to head back."

She was still looking around. Hoping. Waiting. "Yeah." She nodded. "Okay. I'm just gonna go to the bathroom. Will you hold my stuff?" She slid her backpack off and handed it to me, so she didn't have to leave it in the gravel.

"Yep."

She headed down the path to the portable bathrooms that were always at the fairgrounds. I stayed where she left me, holding her backpack against my chest while mine stayed on my back. And I looked at where I was. Imagined where all those Spooks attractions would be— in the same spots every year. How packed it always was, and alive. Swirling with all those secrets and stories. But tonight, she was right: it was just a valley full of ashes.

Her phone went off in a side pocket. It vibrated against my stomach.

I heard her before I saw her, steps crunching on the ground. She headed toward me, nothing else to look at but each other. That was why I stared—I couldn't help it. With the floodlights shining down like she was onstage and that smile that I was the only one around to see, there was nothing else to distract me. Nothing else worth remembering.

"You got a text," I told her once she was close enough that I didn't have to yell.

"From who?" she asked, taking her time.

I dug into her backpack pocket to check. "Nik."

"What'd he say?"

I smirked. "You can't come over here and read it yourself?"

She spread her arms and faced the sky. She spun in a circle instead.

I chuckled. "Code?"

"One nine two three four."

19234.

She kept spinning. My eyes shifted, looking closer at where we were.

On the right. *Four metal pipes, lying on the ground. One lying diagonal across the other three. Longer than one of me but not two.*

On the left. *A booth with a hammer resting on the surface. A pile of plywood on the ground in front of it. A box of black trash bags cast to the side.*

Straight ahead. *KD. Spinning. Carefree. Because maybe she doesn't know anything. Or maybe she knows everything.*

19234.

"What'd he do, write a novel?" she asked.

I shook myself out of it. I ran my fingers along one of the zippers on her bag instead and unlocked her phone with my free hand. I gnawed the inside of my cheek for a second, pushing the words into my brain, how they looked on her screen.

"He says, 'What are you doing at the fairgrounds?'"

Kady
Wednesday, December 2—
Friday, December 4

It's like their eyes have fingers, the way they tickle the back of my neck. The way they squeeze my chest until it's hard to take a deep breath. The way they cup my chin and turn my head so I'll notice.

But ever since Aaron and I left the library, it's only been their stares. They haven't said anything else to me, or *around* me, even though their voices at The Drive-In still torment my quiet mind. *Bitch. Slut. Whore. Cheater.* It plays on a loop like a melody.

But Aaron says it's over, that it's handled, even though I don't know what that means. All I know is that Nik called me late that night and told me that their words weren't for me. That they were just talking about the movie. "You know how that chick in *Inception* ruins everything," Nik said. But either way—he told me—he'd make it so I don't have to wonder anymore.

"That rumor," he said. "No one really believes it."

He's just talking, though. They believe it because Hendricks told them to. And Hendricks told them to because he needs me to know that as long as I have candies, his eyes will follow me everywhere.

It's the worst at night. When I'm in bed with the lights out. Alone, but it doesn't feel that way. Convinced I hear a whisper or feel fingers on my cheek. Constantly checking my phone for the time, to see if Hendricks changed it, even though—if he did—I wouldn't know. But I check my phone every minute, anyway. Until, one night, it hits me.

He's at Barnes.

And TK's rules . . . they weren't just about not going back to before Halloween night and using all my candies before the next one comes around. There was another one. About not using a candy outside of Streetlight. And Barnes is an hour away.

So when he's there, he *can't* use. The rules say so.

A chill snakes from my spine to my fingertips and toes. I sit up in bed, grab my bag of candies from my nightstand and hold it, glowing, in my palm. He wasn't in Streetlight today, so let's do today over. A few times.

I place a candy on my tongue and start to fall.

Kady
Saturday, December 5

Nineteen candies left.

I finally let it be Saturday. It's a good one, though. Bittersweet. They'd been calling for snow, so Nik stayed at Barnes this weekend. And I miss him so much. Before he graduated, we'd stay at his house forever on snow days, locked in his bedroom. We'd watch *Titanic* over and over—until he had it memorized and had to pretend not to love it as much as I do. He called it morbid—my obsession with watching a bunch of people freeze to death every time it snowed. But that's not what it was ever actually about. It's the fact that in this massive, unparalleled, devastating disaster, these two people who would have never met, and would have never belonged together, found a love that would last forever.

That's what it really is. A movie about a miracle.

It's my first snow day without Nik in years, and it's hard not to think about it. But as long as Nik is at Barnes, Hendricks probably is, too.

Besides. Today we need to get Em a Christmas tree.

Every day I repeated, she talked about the tree. The exact same way, just as excitedly. She wants it for the guys' apartment, to be the centerpiece for our anti-ball. She wants to dress it in fake pearls and white balls that she wraps in lace.

"An anti-ball is genius," Aaron tells her, as he drives us to the Christmas tree farm.

Em smiles from the passenger's side, twisted so her back is more against the door than the seat. "Yeah? You like it?"

Aaron's Jeep's tires crunch as we roll over the salted roads, passing all the parked cars on the curb that've been plowed in. It's warm enough in here that I unzipped my coat, and even though he's using the defroster, the corners of the windows are foggy enough to write on. He offered to take us today, since he has four-wheel drive and a car big enough to handle a tree strapped to the roof. Em's so grateful that she's already promised him a feast at The Spot after we finish.

"Hell yeah, that sounds dope," Aaron answers, slowing at a stop sign. "And you're gonna do it the same day as the ball, right?"

Em nods. "Same day, same time. Just infinitely better."

"I love it," Aaron insists. "A theme party. Fully decorated. *Catered?*" More like chips and however much we can carry from The Spot. "That's gonna be lit."

"Sounds like you're more into our party than yours." Shawn smirks from his seat next to me in the back.

"I mean . . . low key?" Aaron smiles and Shawn laughs. "I'm invited, right?"

"Of course you're—" Em starts.

But I cut her off. "You're going to the ball," I insist, leaving my fingerprint on my window. "You have to. It's okay."

Our glances brush in the rearview mirror, and as soon as they do, they lock. It'll permanently be the coolest thing ever that Aaron was willing to give up the ball all because he sucks at eating pizza, but I know he can't actually skip it. Not while there's already the Vanderbilt drama and the Boys won't stop staring. If they catch a whiff that he wasn't at their party because he was at ours, they'll watch us forever.

"Well, afterward," Aaron says, turning to Em. "Keep it going so I can swing by late-night, cool?" He offers her his fist.

She smiles and bumps his with hers. "Cool."

Oh Christmas Tree! is on the same farm where people pick apples in the summer and get pumpkins for Halloween. They have a general store where you can buy pie that they make from their own fruit. I feel like Luka would love it here, especially when the sun is setting and the trees cast shadows that dance in the corner of your eye. But Freeze Street is gonna be packed today. It's 50 percent off every time it snows enough to stick.

We climb out of Aaron's Jeep, and my boots sink into the snow, up to mid-calf. The trees stand before us in imperfect rows, now that people have been coming here for weeks, picking their favorites. When we know the one we want, one of the people in the bright red coats and reindeer antlers will come over and cut it down. Em will know when we've found the perfect one.

We start to wander, Em taking off one glove and holding her palm out so it brushes the needles of every tree that we might be interested in. Shawn tells her, "You're like the tree whisperer."

"You want one that tells you it wants you back," she says, continuing to lead the way.

Shawn frowns, but she moves on to the next tree before he can decide how genius that does or doesn't sound.

Aaron and I linger a few steps behind, the snow still fresh enough that it doesn't crunch as we walk. "You think trees have accents?" he asks, too softly for Shawn or Em to hear.

I smile. "Why would trees have accents?"

"Why *wouldn't* trees have accents?"

Fair. "Okay. What kind of accent do you think they'd have?"

He thinks about it. "Australian?"

"Zero chance."

His eyebrows come together like he's all taken aback. "The conviction."

I laugh. "Why would trees in Streetlight have Australian accents? When accents are just relative to the way you've heard language spoken? If no one around here has an Australian accent, why would the trees have an Australian accent?"

"So you think trees can hear."

Even though I'm looking straight ahead, at my friends wandering to trees that are almost right but not exactly, Aaron's smirky gaze is warming the side of my face. I bite back my smile. "I hate this conversation."

He shrugs. "Em started it."

I turn to him, his gray eyes the same color as the sky. "Yes," I decide. "I believe trees can hear. And I believe they can see, and I believe one is gonna choose Em, and that's the one we're gonna go home with."

"Well, crazier things happen here every day. So I'm with it."

I run my gloved fingers over the branches of a tree that Em just considered. I gather a handful of snow from its limbs. "Do you think trees get cold?"

"Depends on how cold it is."

"What if it's . . . this cold?" I press my snowball into his face, and for a second he just stands there, nodding to himself while my hand rubs it all over, and my neck gets hot with the laugh that I'm trying to keep in. I drop my hand, and we stand there, my snowball melting down his face, dripping into his collar.

"Run," he says.

I scream a little as I dart off, trying to avoid the trees while my boots slide through the snow.

When we reach a clearing, he snatches me around the waist and presses a snowball into my head. Chunks of it drip off my hat and down my ears, and the frigidness stops my heart.

Trying to get away from him, our boots slipping all over each other, I go spinning down into the snow. He catches himself before he falls flat on top of me, one hand landing on each side of my shoulders. I'm laughing so hard that there are tears in my eyes, and all he is is a blurry mess of colors. But in his voice, I hear him laughing, too. "You thought you were gonna get away with that shit? For real? Like in real life, you thought you were gonna get away with that shit?"

The tears run down my face, clearing my vision as I try to catch my breath. As his face crystalizes in my view. It's Aaron—the Boy who's been Nik's blood brother for years, who shrugs off his own jacket to make sure I'm warm, who's driven me around Streetlight on a hundred nights when Nik wasn't sober enough to drive himself. He's the same Boy I've been looking at since I was a freshman, but all of a sudden, it's different.

Through heavy breaths, he asks, "Truce?"

I nod. "Truce."

He rolls off me and sits in the snow instead.

I sit up, too, and cross my legs. My jeans are wet and my butt is freezing, but I can stand it for now. It feels good sitting here, where no one's watching.

Aaron nudges me. "So how come you don't want me at your anti-ball?"

"It's not that I don't *want* you there. It's just that I'm not gonna hold you to some stupid bet." I cock my head, reasoning with him. "We both know you have to go to the ball."

He wets his lips, and like he's telling the most unforgivable secret that will ever leave his mouth, he says, "It's really not all that great."

I hug my knees to my chest, lean in closer, and lower my voice. "What even happens there? Like, do you just do the Cupid Shuffle until someone turns the lights on?"

Please don't ice up and get all IV on me. Please tell me. Please choose me.

"Nah." He shakes his head. "It's worse. Speeches. Initiation stuff— the new guys get their pins. A bunch of OGs show up, guys who gradu- ated from Iverson years ago. Old. Like, *old* old. And everyone is super fucked up." He bends his legs and rests his wrists on his knees. "It sucks. Trust me. You're not missing anything."

I can't tell if he means it, or if he's just trying to make me feel better. But, either way, I'm appreciative.

"Well, you'll come by our better party when yours is done," I tell him.

"Oh, no doubt." And then he brings his eyes to mine. "You'll be there, right?"

It's like something blips when he says it. Like he's in my head and in front of me at the same time—at the *exact moment* when I have this crazy thought that I could just go to the ball myself, if I wanted. See what it's really like. Bring a bucket of balloons filled with red paint and launch an attack all over their dry-clean-only outfits. I could let Hendricks watch me *doing that*. I could let them stare at me *while they scream*. And then I could make it all go away.

"Where else would I be?" I ask.

He presses his hand into the snow, but he keeps watching me. After a second, he smiles. "Just asking."

Kady

Tuesday, December 8

When Nik tells me he's having a party at his apartment and wants me to be there, I ask him if he's just had a lobotomy.

But his jaw goes slack on FaceTime, and his brown eyes roll. *Don't be like that,* he says without saying so. Like it's been me, all this time—not his best friend or his school or his *brothers*—being some kind of way.

"So . . . what? You're just never gonna come to my apartment again?" Nik says, even though he doesn't really mean *again,* because I haven't been a first time yet.

"I just . . ." I sigh and lie back on my bed, leaving my phone face up on the pillow next to me.

"Kades, come on," he says. "Come back." He's officially annoyed, tired of this rift between his world and mine.

I pick my phone up and hold it in front of my face. "I don't know what to say."

"Well, maybe start by not asking me if someone drilled into my brain just because I asked you to come to my apartment."

"But it's not *your* apartment. It's the apartment you share with your asshole friend, who calls in favors with your Boys' club back home so they can tell me I'm a slut when he's not around to do it himself." I drop my phone back on the pillow next to me.

"Kades . . . Kady."

But I roll onto the side facing away from my phone and stare at the candies on my nightstand.

"Kady. *Kady*." He sighs, and for a little bit, he doesn't say anything. Neither do I. We just lie next to each other like he's here, but without the hug that I desperately need. "I'm gonna be in this apartment for the next four years," he finally says. "How's this supposed to work?"

My biggest fear is that I don't know. That it feels like we've finally reached that point that I've been dreading. It's getting harder, and he notices. I notice it, too. I can't just walk to his house, and we lock ourselves away from the world. He can't just invite me along for dinner with his friends. It's complicated now, and Nik's always hated complicated. He likes simple movies, won't play sudoku, and skips instructions whenever they're too long.

"I don't want it to be like this," Nik goes on. "I don't want you feeling weird around the guys or avoiding my apartment. I don't want to think about who's on an invite list before I decide whether I can hang out with my girlfriend that night. And I know it's not just you, I know Hendricks has kind of been on one lately, but . . . if you stop showing up, then what happens?"

It'd be easier right now to tell him about the candies. Not easy, but eas*ier*. I could tell him the truth about Hendricks—and about what I've been doing, too—so that he knows this isn't just about me skipping some party.

But I catch myself, as my candies' blue glow mixes with the yellow light from my lamp so it turns into something hazy and greenish. I'm completely fucked if the first thing he does is go into the living room and ask Hendricks what's going on.

"He wins, I guess," I answer.

"No one's competing, Kades. And even if you were, I'm crazy about you. That's why I don't want you to start bailing."

"I'm not bailing."

"So you'll come?" he asks.

My heart takes a sloppy beat. "Yeah."

I can feel his satisfaction through the phone. Softly, he adds, "I think you guys should talk when you get here."

Me and Hendricks, he means. And I actually feel like he's right. "I think so, too."

Now he's smiling. I can hear it in his voice. "Can I see your face?"

But I don't feel like rolling over.

Kady
Friday, December 11

I sit shotgun while Aaron drives me to Barnes, just the two of us. We play this game where whoever spots the next deer gets to choose the next song. Which is good, because it gives both of us a reason to be overly attentive to all the deer on this dark road. And my eyesight is infinitely better than Aaron's, so we've been listening to "Don't Stop Believin'" for the past twenty minutes.

Aaron grips the wheel like he's being tortured. "The rule was winner picks the next song, not the same song over and over again."

"Never said that," I tell him, and point out the windshield. "Deer."

He presses the brakes hard enough for me to slide forward in my seat. A deer and its baby stare right at us, headlights shining into their big black eyes. Aaron taps his horn to shake them from their trance. They walk easily to the thick trees on the other side of the road.

"No, no, take your time," Aaron tells them. "I'm just sitting here losing my mind, but it's fine. It's cool."

"Don't stop believin' . . . " I throw my head back and close my eyes.

"We get it, it's your all-time favorite song."

I laugh as he starts driving again. We haven't gone faster than thirty miles an hour since we turned onto this road, dark and windy with spots that could be icy.

"This was the graduation song last year," I tell him. "For Owen and Milo's class. I hadn't heard it before then."

"Yeah?" Aaron smiles. "So I guess you're just using this car ride to make up for seventeen years of lost time."

I rest my head on my seat and face him. "Can't you just see everything they're singing, though? These people in this town. Chasing everything and nothing. Keeping hope alive even when it feels dumb as hell?" I hug myself. "And it could be *so sad*. This could be such a sad song. But it's not. It's just these people's lives . . . and it's like they decided to be perfectly and completely okay with that."

"Deer," Aaron says.

I peer out the windshield just as he starts to hit the brakes, and I slide forward in my seat again. This one is a buck, with antlers that probably weigh as much as I do.

I hand him his phone as the buck steps to the side of the road. "Congratulations, you've saved yourself."

"God's real and he loves me," Aaron declares, and I laugh as he goes to Spotify.

We drive even slower while he messes with his phone, and I hug my knees to my chest and watch out the windshield to make sure we don't miss anything. GPS says we're twenty-four minutes away, and when we had forty-three minutes to go, I noticed something. Something small, at first, that our game and my incredible musical choice had distracted me from. But in the momentary silence, that small something has turned palpable. I can practically taste it in the air—sticky like cough syrup:

My candies, for the first time since I've had them, aren't warm.

Aaron chooses a song and sets his phone down in the space beneath his emergency brake. I wait for it to start, ready to give his choice just as much shit as he's given mine.

But "Don't Stop Believin'" starts playing again.

He's barely smiling as he watches the road. "Be cool or I'll change it."

The apartment complex is called The Pines.

That's what the black marble engraved sign says when we reach the gate. Aaron dials the number that Nik gave me: 9929. After a second, there's a buzz, and the gate slides open.

It's an entire little community with a pool, mini golf, and a gym. The apartment buildings all look the same—four stories tall and made of brick and white stone. It's easy to get lost, and that's why Nik told me to follow the signs to the pool and then turn right. Aaron does, and his building—number twelve—is on the left, just like Nik promised it'd be.

There's a keypad at the glass main door, and Aaron uses the same number that we used at the gate. Another buzz, and the door unlocks.

The lobby is tile with a penny fountain and a business center full of desktops. We take the elevator to the third floor and walk down the hall to apartment M. Art hangs on the walls, and there are seats positioned around tiny tables, in case you get tired on your walk home, I guess.

Aaron knocks twice, and Nik answers the door. Smiling big and slapping hands with Aaron before he picks me up and kisses my mouth. An attempt to make me happier to be here than I actually am. He moves from my lips to my neck, and I laugh and try to squeeze my shoulder to my cheek so that he'll stop.

For the few seconds I'm in the air, I get a glimpse of who's here. Some IV Boys. A bunch of people I don't recognize—new friends at Barnes, I guess. Saige is in the kitchen with a wineglass and a group of girls. Her hair is lying against the part, like it does when she gets drunk.

Nik sets me down. "You guys have a good drive?"

"Every time one of us saw a deer we got to pick the song we wanted to listen to next," I tell him, and it comes out like *yes*.

"Dude, the deer around here." Nik pushes his fingers through his hair. "It's fucking ridiculous."

"Yeah," Aaron agrees, but shrugs, so Nik knows it's cool. "I figure they were here first."

"Well, look," Nik says. "I've got Cokes in the fridge and some sparkling waters. You want something?" He raises his eyebrows and runs a thumb down my cheek. "Want some water?"

But before I can answer, the front door opens again. Hendricks—with his gelled hair and peacoat and knitted red scarf. He holds two six-packs and walks in like I don't even exist. It should be a relief, not being looked at, but he isn't just ignoring me—like I'm some housefly that isn't worth his time. There's this easy disregard about it—like he slapped me dead and didn't even pause to wipe the stain.

He smirks at Aaron and gives him a cordial nod. Aaron nods back, but he doesn't really smile. "What's up, man," he says, like he knows he has to. The way they do in *The Crown* because they have to acknowledge the Queen—no matter what she's done or how they feel.

Hendricks turns to Nik. "These are for girls only. Guys can go buy their own shit."

"Yep," Nik agrees. "Use the fridge in my room, people won't be in there."

Hendricks nods and turns to leave, and then his eyes get big like he's just now noticing me. Like I should speak up next time. And Mrs. Rios's voice is suddenly so clear it's like she's here.

You have to make them see you.

They ignore me, or they stare. I'd kill just to be seen.

Hendricks leans in close like he's about to kiss my cheek, and I tense into a statue. He smells like fruity gum and cigarette smoke as his lips slide past my face and hover centimeters from my ear. "Looking forward to chatting tonight," he says.

And then he slips away.

Nik gives me a tour of their apartment, but it doesn't take long, because it isn't very big. It's gorgeous, though—shiny hardwood floors that are so dark they're almost black. Floor to ceiling windows. A balcony. Nik is handing me the water he promised when a hand snakes onto my hip.

My candies.

I spin around and am face to face with Hendricks, his hand hovering in the space where my hip was a second ago. He smiles like it's a game of Whac-A-Mole and he wants to try again. "Jumpy tonight," he says, and then he raises his eyebrows. "Ready to talk?"

No. "Um—" I start.

"Go ahead," Nik tells me, kissing the top of my head from behind.

"We can talk out here," Hendricks tells me, and he doesn't wait to see if I'm following him before he starts walking through the crowd. I don't know what *out here* means, but I take my can and go with him to the front door. He opens it and then shuts it behind us. The hallway is already too quiet.

He goes to one of the seats placed flush against the wall, two of them positioned around a tiny table. So that's what they're for. Us.

I sit in the one across from him, and it instantly feels like I'm at Bianchi's again or Thanksgiving. Except now he's not even an arm's length away.

My mouth goes dry when he reaches into his pocket, but all he pulls out is a pack of cigarettes. He opens the little white box and taps one into his hand. Without lifting his chin, he raises his eyebrows at me. "You mind?"

My voice sounds the way sandpaper feels. "You can smoke out here?"

The corners of his lips tug upward, amused. "Why couldn't I?"

I squint. "Because it's Earth?"

He slides the cigarette into his mouth, and suddenly a lighter is in his hand, so quick that I don't even know where it came from. "Shitty planet Earth you live on."

The flame dances as he lights up. He exhales once, and everything is suddenly nicotine and tar.

"So." He sits back, crossing one ankle over the other. "Your boyfriend wants us to talk."

"Your best friend prefers it if we get along."

"You should, too." But he doesn't say it like it's nice to be happy and not have beef and all be friends. He says it like it's the worst idea ever to not be on his good side. "Didn't know you had moves like that, by the way."

At first, I have no clue what he's talking about, and then I remember how I put him on the ground outside Nik's house. It feels like forever ago. Maybe it was.

"Desperate times," I mutter.

"I'm sure it won't happen again." He takes a drag from his cigarette. "Kady, I'll be honest with you. I don't like to share. It's not really my thing."

I don't know what he doesn't feel like sharing right now. Whether it's his feelings or the candies or Nik. But what I do know is that he's an only child, and the Hendricks family has a full avenue named after them on the west side of Old Town. And one day, James Michael Hendricks IV, the Boy sitting across from me right now—smoking a cigarette in the middle of a hallway like it's a bar in some black-and-white movie—is probably going to inherit everything. The apartments. The bank. Have-Nots like me. And he won't have to share any of it with anyone.

"So, I don't love finding out someone else has something that used to only belong to me," he goes on. "I'm sure you understand." He ashes his cigarette on the beige carpet. "But since I'm a nice guy and all, I'm open to exploring your earlier proposal."

I squint. "Which was?"

"Finding a way to coexist." His eyes gleam, and his mouth twists. "We've gotta work on that memory of yours."

I gnaw the inside of my lip. He wouldn't have a change of heart this big unless he needed to. Unless it was good for *him*. "You don't use your candies when you're out here, do you?" I tell him. "Because there are rules. And you know it."

He smiles, watching the ember on his cigarette slowly eat its way closer to his hand. He doesn't answer me, but there's something about the way he takes his time and scoffs when I say *rules* that tells me what I've always known—that he isn't scared of getting burned.

"Tell me what you use your candies for," I go on, determined to get an answer from him. "And who you use your candies on. Or I'll keep you away from Streetlight. I'll stay in a day that you're not there so you can't come back at all, and you won't even realize I'm doing it."

"You'll run out of candies, sweetheart."

"Not anytime soon."

But I only have fourteen left, after using a few to fall asleep last night. Two weeks' worth, and that's only if I use just one a day. *One a day.* Like taking one deep breath a day.

"You sure about that?" He chuckles. "You know, if I was actually scared of you, I would have just swiped you after you surfed that night." He says it so easily, so knowingly.

"What are you talking about?" I whisper.

He flicks his ash on the table and watches the dust as it falls. "Surfed—*traveled with me*. Swiped—*erased your memories*. Because the second you surfed, all I had to do was take one more candy. Skip back five minutes earlier than I already did. You would have lost everything. You would have been fast asleep like everyone else, waiting for Thanksgiving morning." He takes another pull from his cigarette. "You think *you're* fucking with *me*? I've been doing this a long time, Kady." The smoke comes out his nostrils.

My mind spins. Is *that* how it works? If he has candies and so do I? We can each just half erase what the other knows until nothing even exists anymore? It hurts my head to process, to try to figure out all the permutations.

Why didn't I use TK when I had him? Why didn't I ask a million questions before I just accepted magic like it was a bag of Skittles? Or at least one question, before he disappeared:

Am I the only one tonight who's won?

"So how'd you get yours?" Hendricks peers at me.

"Spooks," I answer. I don't see a reason to lie.

He nods like he did, too. Like he's been going and playing that same game for years. But he was always smart enough to ask TK all the questions. "You know, we'd be more powerful together than apart. Why waste what we have fucking with each other? You and I get on the same page, we can make a good day last so much longer. A good night can go on forever. Any moment you want, it's yours. For twice as long. If we play nice." A single lock of hair dips into his eyes.

And there it is—the reason for the change of heart. And maybe, if I agree, the IVs stop staring. I won't have to worry about them calling me things—External Venture or worse. All the complicated stuff that Nik's been annoyed about lately goes away. It goes away for Aaron, too. Maybe I can even have the ball.

But I've been on this merry-go-round long enough to know how it always works. I play nice, I go to their bar nights, I let Aaron cater to me whenever they're watching—and then the rules change, and there's some new reason I'm not good enough. Or the same *real* reason, constantly. No matter what I do, because it's who I am.

So I hold the stare that's supposed to make me feel small and tell him, "No."

He puts a hand to his chest as if he just took a knife to the heart, but he smirks the whole time like it's my blood and not his. "Was it something I said?"

"It's *everything* you say. It's everything you *do*. You already have an army. You have *magic*. And you still want more."

He yawns. I want to stuff my can down his throat. "Look," he says. "You can either call me a partner, or I'll keep watching. People keep talking. And your boyfriend can't stop me." He slides his cigarette back between his lips. "He knows it, too."

I know it, too. But I'm not about to sit here and sell my soul just so Hendricks can change the rules again as soon as I give him what he wants. I'm not gonna help him create some plot where Streetlight only looks the way he wants it to. And if that really is my way in—if that's me being very smart and working very hard—I'd rather stay right where I am.

"Do it," I say dismissively, exhausted from years of trying to fight the inevitable. "Keep spreading that stupid rumor. Everyone who matters knows you're lying."

But his face changes, the first time I've ever seen it without that wisp of carelessness, the first time I've ever seen him completely serious about anything. "I'm not lying." His eyes shine like he's watching it happen right now—Aaron and me kissing, right in front of him. "It's not worth my time."

I swallow hard as I push back from the table, shoving my heart back down where it belongs. I'm done with this conversation, but he calls out before I make it back to the apartment.

"Think about it," he says.

His words hang between us. I've gotten so used to the poison he's been breathing into this hallway that I don't even smell it anymore. The bile in my stomach sways back and forth like I'm on a boat ready to capsize, and maybe this is the equivalent of drowning. But I don't care. I turn around and tell the back of his head, "No deal."

And I close the apartment door behind me before he can say anything else.

It's whiplash being back in here, the way it's exactly how we left it. A packed apartment where everyone's drinking and blissfully unaware.

I slip through the crowds of people. They dance and laugh and clink their glasses. They hug and lean into one another's ears just to yell. And when I make it to Nik's bedroom, it's like reaching the surface of the ocean just before my lungs explode.

I close the door behind me the second before I start to cry.

Aaron
Friday, December 11

"Can I grab you for a minute?" I slapped Nik on the shoulder.

His place was full of other IVs who drove out for the night, and ones who went to Barnes, and whoever those guys wanted to bring with them. A crew that looked a whole lot like Iverson, but it didn't *feel* the same. I hadn't been to a party like this with the guys ever. Where it was just drinks, no one getting fucked up. An apartment full of people who might actually remember what happened in the morning. An hour-long drive and it changed everything.

"Yeah, man, of course," he said. He finished reaching into the fridge, stood up holding a beer, and handed it to a girl standing on the other side of the peninsula.

Deep brown cabinets. White marble countertops. No veins.

"Thanks, Nik . . ." she said, tossing her hair. That drawn out voice girls use because it could lure you just about anywhere. I wondered if she knew about the IVs. If the dudes got to Barnes and whispered about how things were back in Streetlight. If she knew what it meant to get in good with a guy like Nik, and that's why she was being all sweet over a light beer.

"No problem," Nik said, and she smiled at him until she turned all the way around and walked back into the living room in a little sweater dress and knee-high boots. Nik watched her go.

He smirked. "College girls."

I'd noticed them, too. The way they walked different. Talked different. Like they were stronger out here. Or maybe we were just weaker. "Your girl's got 'em beat, though," I said, making sure he still thought so.

"Oh, hell yeah." He smiled. "That's eye candy, not steak."

I laughed, and he hung on my shoulders, laughing, too. "Some Pixy stick shit," I said.

"Just a little Kit Kat mess."

We stood in his kitchen, cracking up. We could have kept going, but I really did have to talk to him. "Step outside for a minute?" I said once I caught my breath.

He stood up straight again, like he'd just remembered that I'd come over here wanting to talk. "What kind of secrets we tellin'?"

He followed me through the crowd to the sliding back doors. They met in the middle and pushed out to the sides, and I only opened them wide enough for us to walk out. Nik slid them shut behind us.

The balcony was cement and a couple of feet wide. The railing was black iron and went up to my waist. It faced the lawn and a man-made pond. And the moon—almost full.

Neither one of us had coats, just me in a hoodie and Nik in a pullover. He shoved his hands into his pockets and pushed his shoulders up to his ears. "What's going on?" he asked.

I peered over the ledge for a second. I'd been thinking about it for days, but I still didn't know how to start. Pops always said lead with the facts, though. Agree on those and go from there.

"You know I'm down for you and KD." I looked back at him as I said it. "I'm your boy, and I think she's . . ." I couldn't think of a word that was big enough, that meant enough. I settled on, "Great. So, I'm not accusing you of anything, I'm just looking out."

Nik smiled, his chin still buried into his chest. "It's not getting any warmer out here, man."

I pushed my breath out through my lips. "Look, a couple days ago, she wasn't at her phone, and she asked me to read a message to her. So I asked for her code. And she told me it's one nine two three four." I decided to skip the part about where we'd been coming from and that the text was from him.

His smile faded. He was shivering, but, other than that, he was still. Straight-faced, all he said was, "Yeah."

Yeah. Like it was just some number. Not *the* number. The IV code number. The one that was buried in our crest, if you looked closely enough—past all the lions and swords and poppies. 1923—the year we were founded.

4—IV. *IV.* Us, in Roman numerals.

19234.

We hid everything behind that code. Meeting notes on Dropbox. The Zoom ID. Every secret we had. It was the code we whispered on our way into the ball, to prove everyone who was there was supposed to be. No one else. Just us and the people we'd chosen.

So it wasn't just *yeah*—that KD knew that number. It was proof. That maybe all these years that the guys had spent clowning him for dating her, all these years they'd spent looking at her funny and making sure she never came to the ball, all these years they spent worried she was getting a little too close—maybe they were right.

"Come on, man . . ." I wanted to shake him, remind him that no one was looking at us through those glass doors, no one was listening. "This is *me*." He hung his head, and I went on, "You know I'm gonna have your back no matter what. And you know I don't subscribe to all that secret high-society bullshit. But these guys have been on you for *years*. And you always said she didn't know anything. But she knows that number." The wind blew, and I let myself feel it, hold on to it. The way it broke through my skin like I didn't have any and went straight to my bones.

"Yeah," he said again, but it was different this time. Heavy. He was watching his shoes.

"I don't know how much she's talked to you about it . . ." I turned and faced the railing instead. Stared out at the pond. "But she's not having an easy time since you left. I know the guys have always been weird about her, but it's different. They look at her funny, and I know she notices."

"Who cares what they look at?" Nik muttered, like it was too dumb to worry about.

"*She does, man,*" I insisted, punching one of the bars on the railing on repeat. Not hard enough to hurt, just to feel. "She didn't sign up to be stared at. She shouldn't have to feel like these guys are looking at her sideways just because you're not around anymore. They know what they're doing. *That's why they do it.* And it feels like . . ." I shook my head. Tasted the air. Dry enough to give me cotton mouth. "It feels like you're carrying a million pounds."

I was still staring out at the pond, but I felt him shift next to me. His shoes scraped on the concrete. I glanced at them. They were pointing the same way mine were now.

"It's one thing if they're looking at her like that and they have no good reason to," I went on. "But it's another thing if it turns out that they do." I stopped punching the railing and cracked my knuckles instead. "I know you love her. I know you want her to be okay. I know

you guys did just about *everything* together for a really long time."
The blocks I'd been building in my own head over the past few days
started coming out of my mouth, one at a time. "I know the guys who
date Iverson girls get to keep it realer than you can. And I know that
probably sucks, because KD is cooler than all those girls. But I guess
it just seems like"—my knuckles popped, one after another—"it's not
safe for her to know too much if you're not gonna tell her everything."

I slid my hands into my pockets and slipped into noticing stuff
while I waited for him to answer. The water. *Black enough to be a
hole, except for the distorted reflection of the moon.* The edges. *Flat,
purposely imperfect rocks.* The silence. *Kind of nice, really.*

"So then why'd you tell her the code?" he said.

I turned to him, waiting for him to laugh it off or make it clear I'd
heard him wrong. But he just stared over the railing, out at the pond.
"I didn't tell her anything," I said, my glare glued to him, even though
he wouldn't look me in the eye.

"Well, neither did I," he said. "And you two have been hanging
out a whole lot lately. You could have told her just as easily as I could
have." He shrugged, like it was just one of those things. Like it was
some big shame that we'd never know for sure which one of us it was.

"Nik. *Come on.*" He had to be losing his entire mind. "You *know*
she doesn't randomly know that number. She has it for a reason. And she
chose to remember it because she knows it's important. And she knows
it's important because somebody told her. And that guy isn't me."

"Prove it," he said.

Nik had only turned on me one time before. End of sophomore year.
When I was telling him it'd never feel normal being the only Black kid
at Iverson. And back then he'd reminded me, "There's Tariq," like that
was supposed to fix it. Like the ability to name the only other Black

dude who existed—and who'd just graduated—didn't completely reinforce all there was to feel weird about.

I'd thought he was kidding. I'd smirked and said, "Cool, now name all the white ones."

And that was when it happened. When he turned. He said, "You talk about race a lot." And he said it like I should stop.

"I do?" I answered.

"Yeah," he said. "Like this. And when you said you feel weird walking around here. And when you asked if I knew what else 'Spooks' meant. And that time you wanted to know if I thought they made you and me blood brothers because neither one of us is white."

"I mean . . . you really think that was just some kind of coincidence?" Because it wasn't. I knew it wasn't. And every second until that one, I'd been glad it wasn't.

He said, "Look. People here aren't like that. I get that maybe Philly is different, but we don't notice race around here. So we don't have to talk about it all the time."

I waited for him to crack a smile. Prove he was joking. But he didn't. And because Pops always said to lead with the facts, I tried to. I told him, "But race is real . . ."

"Why?" he pushed. "Why do we have to be different just because some people want us to think we are?"

He'd been serious. He'd been *heated*. The same way he was right now. Ready to draw a line in the sand, throw this moment on a list of nonnegotiables in our relationship like I'd just called the world flat. But it was hitting me in that moment, while he stood there staring at the stars, that maybe his world was.

Because if he wanted to pretend like he wasn't the one who'd told KD the code, or act like race was just something I'd made up—he could. As long as he was willing to follow their rules, and call Street-light home, he could play make-believe whenever he wanted.

And that night, while he stood there not looking at me, vetoing our entire conversation—it wasn't just like he knew we were living in a goddamned fairy tale. It was like he loved it.

Kady

Friday, December 11

The big window in Nik's room looks out on a man-made pond. The lights are off in here, which is the entire reason why I can see the world and not just my reflection. It's a relief—I don't want to look at myself right now.

I pull my candies from my waistband. Even if it's a sign that I was never meant to have these, I still miss their pretty glow. Their comforting warmth. They were beautiful, and now they just look sad, like a dead phone that needs a charge. I feel like it's because I'm not supposed to use them here, but who knows?

Hendricks, probably.

I run my fingers over them as I hold the baggie in my palm. I bet these things can do so much more than I thought. How did that not even cross my mind until I was in that hallway with him? *Of course* there are tricks and shortcuts—an order of operations that makes them even better, even brighter.

It was stupid to tell Hendricks no so fast. I could have at least played nice until I knew as much as he did.

I peer back out at the pond, surrounded by a walking path and benches. The full moon is so bright that I'm sure Em's noticed it. Maybe Luka's somewhere right now, too, explaining to Shawn what those spots are on the surface. And imagining all of us watching the same moon at the same time feels, for a moment, like its own kind of magic. The good kind.

I look for so long that I start to see my eyes in the glass. And then, above my head, someone else's.

I spin around, and Nik's watching me. I didn't hear him come in. I didn't hear him walk over. I didn't even feel him there, close enough to kiss.

I almost rush to hide my candies, shove them back into my waistband, but it's pointless. He sees. He knows.

And then, voice so heavy that it crushes me, he says, "I thought we agreed to stop using."

Kady
THE PAST THREE YEARS

I was fourteen and he was fifteen, an almost-freshman and an almost-sophomore, at my very first IV Boys party. It was the first weekend in September, and Streetlight wasn't cold enough for coats, so the Boys had all the windows open, and there were people in the pool out back. They were drinking and I didn't want to, and Nik didn't try to make me. It was easy back then for him to protect me. I was so new that no one asked questions, no one cared. They didn't look at me. They didn't see me. They all assumed I wouldn't last.

We didn't care about them, either.

He had a beer bottle in his hand as we sat in the grass underneath the deck. Above us, people shouted about card games or thudded down the two flights of steps to the patio. But we were alone under there, in our own little world.

He kissed me for the first time, with beer-sticky lips. And everything inside me twisted into the tightest ball before it completely broke free and undid itself, and I was so light, I could have been floating.

"That was nice." I smiled.

"It was nice." He smirked into his lap, picking at the label on his bottle. "It was a good day."

It was our last day—of summer, at least. We'd spent all of it with each other, and every second had been amazing, but it was also sort of sad. How things happen and then they're gone.

Nik felt it, too—our last hours of freedom slipping away. He'd said it a few times as the time passed that day.

"Wanna do it again?" he asked, his face half shadow, half lit. There was a porch light shining through one of the slats above us.

I assumed he meant the kiss, and I leaned in close for another one.

But he stopped me and dug into his pocket instead. He pulled out a plastic baggie with two blue tablets inside.

Then he held my hand and put one in his mouth.

He said he'd found the magic at Spooks and made me promise to never tell a soul.

Every year, we went back. I lingered off to the side while he played his game and called his numbers and won his candies. And then we lost track of everything. The day, the month, ourselves. We skipped school to swim in the lake. We turned rainy days into rainy weeks so we could stay in his bed just a little bit longer. Once, we ran away for three days—we turned off our phones and just went. We'd stop at gas stations for jerky and at Cracker Barrel every time we passed one, and park at malls for the night and fall asleep in his back seat. We reached a beach at sunset and stood with our toes in the sand while the sun disappeared into the ocean. And when we got back to Streetlight, the second we passed the little welcome sign off the highway—before any of what we'd done could catch up with us—Nik pulled over, held me close, and erased it all.

Then this summer came. We held on to it for as long as we could. We relived so many moments I can't even remember which versions were real. It doesn't matter. All that mattered was that we were real, that every time we pinched ourselves, we felt it. This life wasn't a dream—it was ours. And we were determined to live it for as long as we could.

We were on his screened-in porch, hidden in blankets and pillows. Sweaty bodies and racing hearts. Dizzy from all the do-overs. He kissed my mouth, my neck, my ear. And then he laid his exhausted head on my chest.

I tried to catch my breath, tried to let my vision refocus. "Again," I insisted.

But he reached under him and held the empty baggie over my stomach, let it go, and it drifted down on top of me. Impossibly weightless.

"That's all I had," Nik told me.

And then we lay there and didn't say a word.

Kady
Friday, December 11

Nik glares at me in his dark room. "We said we were gonna stop when I left."

That's sort of how it went. Nik said that we *should* stop when he left. That we couldn't live like this forever. That we couldn't stay stuck where we were just because it felt good. Because that was a backward way of suggesting that we didn't believe it could get *better*. That our future was ill-fated. That we were living on borrowed time.

He was so convincing when he said it that I agreed. How could I believe in us if I never let us actually happen?

"I was going to," I promise, wiping my eyes. "But by the time Spooks came, I just missed you so much, and I thought that if I had the candies again, you wouldn't have to be gone so often. Or it wouldn't feel like it, at least. And I was *stunned* when it worked. You know I've never even tasted one of your candies, let alone played that game or heard all those rules before—TK *never* stopped to tell you rules; you were always in and out in two seconds. And I honestly thought I missed some crucial step and walked away with a penalty prize of poisoned Tic Tacs or something—that's how impossible it all seemed."

"But you won, so what now?" He squints. Disgusted. "You've been trapping me in Streetlight?"

"It's not a trap if it's where you want to be."

"*Kady!*" Nik grabs fistfuls of his hair and tugs, pacing in circles. "You can't decide where I'm gonna be. You can't choose where the hell I belong." He stops. He peers at me, and even though he's *right there*, he's never seemed so far away. "You have to stop."

"I can't—"

"*You have to—*"

"I *can't*—"

"I mean, are you out of your mind? What are you doing? Do you know what a fucking disaster this can be? I mean, shit, Kades—how long have you kept us spinning? Weeks? *Months?*"

"*Hendricks is using, too!*" It falls out of my mouth before I can stop it. Like a block of lead I swallowed and the weight is finally gone. Or it's between us, at least. For both of us to carry. "And I know how convinced you were that it was just us. That the odds of someone else guessing those numbers was impossible, and that that was the only way to win, and that maybe you and I got to have magic because we *are* magic. But I'm telling you, Hendricks is winning that game, and I don't know how, but he's been using for *years*. He knows tricks, and how to erase memories that were supposed to stick, and calls it *surfing* when you travel together—and that's why he hates me, by the way. Because he figured out that I got candies, too, and that fucks up everything. I mean, *two people with candies?*" I can see his head spinning like mine was in the hallway. "And I know that he's your friend, and that this sounds *completely unreal*, but you have to believe me. I would have told you so much sooner if I just thought you would have believed me."

The door opens, and the light flips on. Saige jumps when she sees us. "Oh shit." She takes a step backward. "Were you guys about to . . ."

I almost say yes just so that she'll leave. But Nik sighs and asks, "What's up, Saige?"

"I was gonna go to the bathroom." The words come out like *I'm sorry*.

"There's one in Hendricks's room," Nik tells her.

"His room is locked."

Nik rubs his hair and nods. She holds her hands in prayer position, and Nik still can't help but smile at her, even in the middle of everything that's happening.

The baggie in my hand sticks to my skin, wet from my sweating palm. And seeing her tipsily tiptoe to Nik's bathroom, I can't stop thinking about Thanksgiving. The way she pulled me aside and told me secret after secret. So I'd know who I was at dinner with. Who Streetlight is filled with.

"Hendricks isn't your friend." But it barely feels like that voice came from me.

Saige stops across the room, blinks at me from the bathroom doorway. "Sorry?"

I extend the palm holding my candies, my hand shaking. Nik's objecting, but it's background noise, like he's shouting at me from inside a car. "I know this is gonna sound completely impossible, but these candies . . . they can change things. They can change time—so you can go back and do stupid shit, over and over again, just because you want to. And Nik and I . . ." He won't even look at me. "We used to use them." I force myself to look at Saige instead, so it hurts less. "We thought it was only us. But Hendricks does, too. I saw it at Thanksgiving, that night you had déjà vu? *That's why.* And I wish I could prove it to you right now, but I can't. Not yet. But when we get back to Streetlight, if you'll let me, I'll show you. Okay?"

Her brown eyes blink at me under mascaraed lashes, bigger than they should be but beautiful, anyway, like all the deer that stared back at us tonight from the road. While the headlights reflected in their pupils, trusting that we'd stop. So unafraid when they shouldn't be.

"Nik, *come on*," I plead, but Saige is the one who answers.

Gently, softly. The voice I imagine one of those deer would have had. "Kady," she says. "We all use."

We all use. It seeps into the walls, the floor, the air. Me.

I turn to Nik, but he can breathe. His jaw is tight, his hair a mess from all the times he's grabbed it in the past few minutes. But he's okay. Not like someone just shined a giant spotlight on the world he thought he knew. Not like every single thing he's ever loved, or believed, has completely—*irreparably*—changed.

"My friends don't use." My voice shakes as I say it.

Saige cringes a little, like this is some kind of circle-of-life shit. Like she's the mom who has to figure out how to explain that my dog died or what sex is. She turns to Nik. "Help me out here."

He doesn't know what to say, either. "Kades," he starts, as he sits on the foot of his bed. But I can't be here anymore, with the two of them belonging and me floating in space. While they're grounded and know exactly what this is, exactly where they've always lived, and I drift untethered on my way to the moon.

I push my candies back into my waistband and sniff my tears back into my eyes.

"Kady, come on," Nik says as I turn.

But I rush out of his room before he can stop me.

Kady

Saturday, December 12

My phone vibrates again, glued between my thighs. I feel it but I don't, like being numbed at the dentist. I feel the pressure, the sensation, but not the meaning behind it. The pain and the damage and the trauma associated with it. It's just more buzzing.

Aaron and I haven't talked since he pulled out of the parking lot at the Pines. No games, no bets. He tried to play "Don't Stop Believin'" again, but I turned it off.

When I left Nik's bedroom, I left the apartment, too. I took the stairs down to the lobby, because I didn't want to risk him catching up with me while I waited for an elevator. I pulled out my phone as soon as I got outside, circled a lamppost while I waited for the ringing to start. Finally, Aaron's voice. "Hey," he said. "Get lost on your way to the kitchen?"

I told him that we had to leave right now. He asked me where I was. I told him I was by the parking lot, and, in a moment, he was there, too.

His eyes darted like lasers, scanning every inch of my face. "What happened?" he asked.

But I barely knew that answer myself. So I just watched him back, each of his blinks like a camera shutter closing before he took a new picture.

"We have to leave right now," I told him again.

He didn't push it, and before I could even fasten my seat belt, the calls from Nik started.

I stare out the window as the trees pass, and the faint outline of my reflection reminds me that I'm real. Whenever we slow down, I assume it's for another deer, but I don't look forward to check. The entire ride is just a compilation of accelerating and stopping, while my phone buzzes, and Aaron—any time I glance at him—watches straight ahead like I'm not even there.

We all use. Saige's voice in my head is a siren's melody. The sweet unaffectedness of it, the cold eeriness. I can't stop thinking about Em's wish to be haunted. To have spirits all around her that she can talk to and learn from. While we've been living in this horror story all along.

We all use.

Who's *we*?

When Aaron pulls up to my house, he puts his Jeep in park. He looks at me for the first time since we drove away from Barnes. "Will you talk to me?"

I pull my candies from the waistband of my pants, warmed again, recharged. They glow as I hold the baggie in the air between us, and Aaron looks at them like he's been hypnotized.

"Do you know what these are?" My voice cracks.

Maybe *we* is their little threesome that's been close forever—Saige, Hendricks, Nik. Maybe *we* is the kids who party—something to mix with their booze on Friday nights.

"What do you mean?" Aaron asks.

I swear he's buying time, but I swallow the accusation. "Yes or no, Aaron?"

We sit silently in the idle car, my candies twinkling in the dark. Until he finally tells me, "Yeah. I know what those are."

We.

I sniff back my tears and climb out of his car, while he unfastens himself and climbs out, too. While he calls after me as I walk up my lawn that we need to talk. That this is why he wants to leave. And, as I shut my front door behind me, he says:

"This is why I want you to leave, too."

Aaron
Saturday, December 12

KD played that song again the whole ride home and I pretended to hate it like that was the only thing wrong. But once she was inside, I drove slow on purpose. I was buggin' so hard that I wanted to slam the gas, but going slow was weirder. Easier to hold on to. To remember. So I forced myself to crawl down the street and notice everything I could. The stitching on the steering wheel—how it was a little bit thicker than the stitching on the gearshift. The way my joggers felt—nylon and smooth like butter now that they'd warmed up on the drive home. The way the heat coming through my vents made the air heavy—thick enough that I could swallow it and feel it all the way down.

I thought about how pissed Nik was out on his balcony, until I pretended to drop it. Played like I'd say I believed him, even if I didn't. I thought about how he smiled, wrapped an arm around my shoulders, called me his brother, and we walked back inside.

I needed to remember tonight, the truth about it, just like the IVs taught me to.

In the best times and the worst times, remember, we always said.

Because those were the nights that people liked to do over.

Kady
Sunday, December 13

---

6 DAYS BEFORE THE BALL

I don't know. Anything.

I don't know what time it is or what time it's ever been. I don't know who these people are or who I ever was in comparison. I don't know where I am, because this place that once was home just revealed itself as hell, and maybe that's why Em believes witches and elves clean our streets, and that sometimes the wind sounds like voices. Because it's not even the craziest thing.

I used to think that Nik and I were magic, but we're not.

We all use.

And we were never special.

My candies have stayed in my nightstand drawer since Aaron dropped me off. I feel them, but I'm scared to touch them, scared of all I don't know about them. How Nik and his friends have been using them. How much they do that the rest of us never remember. If it's always been that way. If Streetlight was made to be that way.

They already control everything. Why would our minds be the exception?

Kady
Monday, December 14

On Monday, we go to Sparks.

Shawn, Em, Luka, and me.

There's a preprogrammed part of me that keeps screaming that Nik and I promised we'd come here together this year, but I shove it down as deep as it'll go. The same way I've been doing with all my urges to answer his calls or listen to his voicemails or respond to his texts. We haven't spoken since I left his apartment.

But for a second, I forget about that, as we move with the swarm toward the main gates. It's stunning, prettier than I ever remembered as a little kid. A world where everything glitters and shines. Choreographed to make it look like menorahs are being lit and reindeer are taking off. And I know I'm still in Streetlight, but, for a second, I let myself believe that I'm not.

The giant sign at the gate twinkles, and it says:

Sparks!
Brightening Streetlight since 1968

"Do you feel that?" Luka asks as we walk the dusty gravel. Our steps are drowned out by a group of carolers dressed in bonnets and top hats singing "What Christmas Means to Me." "Like Pop Rocks, but in the air."

"Yes," Em says at the same time that Shawn says, "No." But he and Luka smile at each other as Luka takes his hand.

"You don't?" Luka asks. "Because it feels like this."

He starts pinching Shawn anywhere he isn't too bundled up to feel it. His cheeks, his neck, the back of his hands. Shawn laughs, pushing him away like he doesn't really want him gone.

"If that's what you feel, we're getting your brain scanned," Shawn says.

But I feel it, too. These tiny electric shocks in the air, little fireworks everywhere.

"Ooh, do you guys want caramel apples?" Em asks, noticing the booth.

"I'm actually gonna run to the bathroom," I tell her. "But I'll meet you at the caramel apples."

The attractions are different than they are at Spooks, but the paths are the same, and I walk the one that I have memorized. It takes me past face painting and a line to sit on Santa's lap. Until I eventually turn the bend to the bathrooms.

I hold my breath as I squeeze through the crowd, praying that when the sea of people parts, TK's booth will be there. And TK will be, too. But when I make it through the madness, there is no booth, and there is no man.

My heart knocks my chest, steady and hollow like a gong, while the needles in the air threaten to prick me until I bleed.

I don't know what I would have said to him, anyway.

I guess that's what makes it kind of okay, as I hug myself on my trek back to the caramel apples. For weeks, I've wanted to make sure it was alright that my candies were so warm—because Nik's never were—and see how bad it'd really be if I took us back to what I thought was a perfect summer. But all of that feels so irrelevant after Saturday night, and now I don't even know where I'd start.

My friends are almost at the front of the caramel apple line by the time I make it back to them. The guys are laughing, and Em's talking to them about the metaverse, some TikTok explanation she saw that explained it's pretty much just Sims for rich people.

I've been on the fence all weekend about whether or not I should tell them. But it's this moment that makes me sure that I can't. Because I'd do anything in the world to keep them happy.

I pout. "Mom just texted to see if I could come by The Drive-In tonight. Someone called in sick."

"*Oh no.*" Em pouts back.

"We'll get these apples and then go with you," Shawn says, and turns to Luka. "We can come back to Sparks on your next night off. It'll be here until New Year's."

"Perfect," Luka agrees.

"No way, you guys stay here," I insist. Shawn and Em look at me like I just tried to eat glue. "Seriously. It'll be fun. And we're playing *Jingle Jangle*—you know Em doesn't like to see *Jingle Jangle* until Christmas Eve." I point threateningly at each of them. "Tag me in anything you post, or I'll murder you."

"Are you sure you don't want us to come?" Em asks as I hug her goodbye.

"Positive." I hug Luka next. "Have so much fun."

"We'll miss you," he tells me.

"Miss you too." I hug Shawn last. "Don't forget to get the hot chocolate."

"Text me," Shawn says as I start to walk away.

A cold breeze stings my cheeks as I walk against the current of families heading into Sparks. Mom never texted me; I just know I need to leave. I'm not ready to exist like things are normal yet.

It's empty now that I've passed the main gates and I'm beyond the crowds. The buzz of it all is still behind me, but the street in front of me is quiet and dark. I take a deep breath and stand still for a minute.

But then I notice something—and I blink to make sure it's not just one of the big branches that hangs over the sidewalk in this part of town. It's not. It's a man, walking away from here, with a backpack slung over his shoulder and his hands in his coat pockets. He's not walking fast, but he's far enough down the way that I'd have to jog to catch up with him. So I do, just to try and get a better look.

The closer I get, the surer I am. "TK!" I call.

My voice moves slower in the ice-cold air. But he stops after a second and turns around. Those warm brown eyes and the scratchy beard. A wool flat cap on his salt-and-pepper hair. He smiles while he waits for me to catch up.

"Hi," I say as I stop in front of him. "I'm sorry. You probably don't remember me . . . I'm Kady."

"Of course I remember you," he tells me, his voice the exact smooth velvet that I remember. "How might I be helpin' you tonight, Kady?"

I can't believe he's actually here, standing in front of me. That I walked out of Sparks just in time to spot him before he vanished. I was so close to convincing myself that he was never real at all. That nothing I ever believed in was.

"I wanted to talk to you about the candies," I tell him.

His eyes don't change, and neither does his smile. But he gives me a little nod. "Absolutely."

I hug myself as the wind slips between us, a quiet guest excusing itself from our conversation. "Was I the only one who won your game that night?"

"Oh, well, everyone wins. No use in anybody leaving feeling bad about themselves."

"I mean . . . big winner. Like . . . did anybody else win your candies?"

"*Oh.*" TK nods to himself. "Well, that's another mighty good question, Kady. And yes—there were others."

Even though I already knew it, my throat burns now that I'm hearing it, now that it exists so simply in front of me. "My boyfriend used to go to you every year. And play your game. And win. He told me it was just us. And that's what I thought for years. Until I found out over the weekend that he was lying."

TK frowns, his eyes soft with empathy. "That's not a nice thing to find out."

"My boyfriend and his friends . . . they come from these really rich and powerful families. They own, like, everything in Streetlight. They have buildings and streets named after them. And I just have this feeling . . . this fear, you know? That they're the only ones who really know about this. That they're the only ones who win. And that the rest of us just . . . spin . . ."

TK nods, watching me so closely that it feels like he's seeing my words just as much as he's hearing them. With a sad smile, he tells me, "That's probably about right."

And hearing him say it, how easily he agrees, leaves goose bumps all over my body. I never thought anything could be so big—that something as essential as *time* could be inherited just like their names and their homes. Ingrained in who they are like new cars and fancy clothes and all the other pretty things they get to play with. If Nik uses, do his parents? When Mrs. Rios sat me down at Thanksgiving and told me to make myself seen, did she have a feeling Nik had shared the magic with me, too? And that's why she thought I was strong enough to work my way into their circle? Or did she challenge me to do it anyway? Prove myself by penetrating their magical world without any of the magic they'd always had?

I take a sharp breath. "Can you make them stop?"

His lips form a tight, sad line. "Unfortunately, I don't believe I can. Not really my place. But you all are more than welcome to stop yourselves, whenever you're ready."

The weight of the mere idea, of *me* having the power to stop theirs, flattens me into the pavement.

"Time is a funny thing, isn't it?" TK says, his warm eyes pulling me back up. "It's magic all on its own, really. It's fast, yet it's slow. It's never stopped existing and never will. It heals in ways that no medicine can." TK smiles to himself, like he's talking about an old friend. "It really is quite astounding. We don't have to help it much."

"I thought I understood these candies." My voice cracks. "I really tried to listen when you told me how they worked, because I've never gotten them on my own before and I didn't want to risk breaking anything. But I thought I was the only one. And now that it's . . . *who knows how many people* . . . I'm just scared that the rest of our lives become casualties. I mean, what if they're erasing some of the best days we've ever had? What if they're undoing the day that one of us wins the lottery or falls in love? What if they're breaking our fate on purpose, or worse—what if they don't even care?"

"It's a scary thing; I know it is. But I've been doing this for a long time now, Kady. And one thing I can promise you is this: Fate can't be undone. Not even my candies are strong enough for that." He gives me a wink that seals his promise like a spell.

I wipe my tears. It was beautiful all those nights ago at The Drive-In when Em talked about fate, and it's beautiful now. The possibility—maybe even the truth—that not even Have-Lots can steal what's meant to be mine.

"Can I tell you something?" he gently asks with a smile. "I have a feeling I can."

I smile back through my tears. "Yeah, you can."

He leans in closer and lowers his voice. "Someone wound time back a little too far."

"How do you mean?"

"To before this year's Halloween. A few days before, actually. It's the reason for that tingle in the air." He holds up his finger, raises his nose like he's catching a whiff. "Yep, that's it, alright. It's been picking up over the past couple days, too."

"But that's against the rules," I slowly insist.

"It is. And the people who are most familiar with the candies will be the most sensitive to it. Sniffing around for a cause. This feeling in their bones that something's off. But other people will notice it, too. The ones most attuned to the universe, the atmosphere—whatever it is you want to call it. The part of life that's bigger than all of us." He sighs, like it is what it is, even if what it is isn't all that great. "Anywho, it'll keep getting worse until you pass the day when the rule was broken. Then the air will slowly start to feel breathable again. And you'll all be able to carry on."

Reeks, doesn't it?

My stomach twists around the dinner I haven't had yet. "What was the day?"

"December nineteenth," TK answers, committed to memory like a birthday.

I count the days in my head. "That's Saturday."

That's the ball.

A car rolls past, the first one I've seen since we started talking. We let its taillights fade into the darkness.

"It is, isn't it?" He seems to be counting now, too. "Well, you all will be there in no time. Just a matter of days now."

But it gets worse before it gets better.

"Do you know who did it?" I ask. "Who broke the rule?"

"I do."

"Can I . . . know that, too?"

TK laughs into the night, a booming sound that squeezes my soul. "You do ask *fantastic* questions. But I'm afraid I should be on my way. I've got a long walk ahead of me tonight." He raises his eyebrows. "Will I be seeing you next year?"

I hug myself. It's cold out here without my candies, and even colder now that we're saying goodbye.

"I don't think so," I answer, swallowing the icy night air.

And he smiles at me like that's perfectly fine.

He hikes his backpack farther up on his shoulder and turns around to keep walking. His workman boots clunking down the sidewalk is the only sound for miles.

"TK?" I call, before he's too far to hear me.

He stops and turns back around. I push my braids out of my face as the wind tries to do the opposite.

"I feel like we could have been doing better. With your candies. I feel like—" I sniff and slide my hand under my eyes. "I just feel like we could have done better. And I'm sorry."

He gives me a sad smile. "The worst thing you can do with the time you have is worry about the time you've spent. You'll fix what needs fixing. No need for apologies."

He nods at me, his fingertips tipping the brim of his hat.

And this time, I let him disappear into the night.

Kady
Monday, December 14

I'm walking the opposite way that TK went. Not toward anything in particular, but in the direction of Something. He was heading toward the edge of town. A path that leads to the dump and then I'm not sure what comes after. A path toward Nothing.

I pull out my phone. Aaron's texted me seven times since Saturday night, and I haven't responded to any of them.

Can we talk when you wake up?

U up?

KD . . .

I'm sorry. Pls let's just talk

I'll tell u everything u want to know. For real, this isn't me trying to cover my ass. I'm sorry. Really. Call me?

Are u ok?

I kno it sounds like bullshit. But u can trust me still

I finally text him back:

Are you around?

The three dots are fading in and out on my screen as soon as I press send.

In a meeting. Almost out. Where can we meet?

An IV meeting. In the chapel on Iverson's campus. The last place I want to be, but I also refuse to run away from it tonight.

I text him back:

I'll come to you

I walk there slowly, up the middle of the street, under the watching stars. It's a sleepy night in Streetlight, while everyone who isn't working is probably at Sparks. I wonder what Shawn, Em, and Luka are up to, and I open Instagram to see if I've been tagged in anything. Not yet.

I step onto Iverson's campus, no guard to check in with now that it's after hours. The lights that dot the brick walkway are the only ones that exist besides the moon, and fortunately it's bright tonight. Bright enough for me to see the main building in the distance and the stone lions' eyes as I pass. I never noticed it before, but their mouths have a bend to them—like Cheshire cats.

Aaron is waiting on a bench by the chapel. I see him while I'm still a few yards away, only because he's looking at something on his phone, and the glow from his hands is like the North Star. He looks up—maybe he hears my steps on the frozen grass. He stands and faces me, like I'm someone who matters. And I stop in my tracks, because I have no idea who I am.

There's still a yard or two between us, the chapel dark and lifeless on my left. It's such a small space from the outside, like one of those tiny houses you can move across the country. It never made sense to me why Iverson built it in the first place when it couldn't even fit everyone who goes here inside, but Nik said it was because Iverson was meant to be its own little world. Self-sufficient like that.

And you can't have a world without a church, he said.

"Hey," Aaron tries after a second.

"Hey," I answer back.

He wets his lips but doesn't look away. "I'm sorry. About everything. And I'm sorry that I never told you."

I hug myself and peer at the chapel. Stained glass windows look almost like sad eyes in the dark. "Did you mean it?" I turn back to him. "When you said that this is why you want to leave?"

He lets out an exhausted half laugh, a tired smile on his mouth. "Hell yeah. This shit sucks." He kicks at the perfect lawn. "And I know leaving doesn't erase it. Someone pops a candy in Streetlight, and the whole world spins backward; they just never realize it. And I guess I'm hoping that if I'm far enough for long enough, I'll stop realizing it, too."

A town so tiny, we're hardly on the map. As easy to pass as a lamppost. And somehow, we're the axis of a world that doesn't even know we exist. It's too much, and I need to sit, so I go to the bench. Aaron sits next to me, and I curl one leg under the other as I turn to face him. He's facing me, too. "I want you to tell me everything. Every single detail. Okay?"

He nods. "Deal."

"But after I say this." I take a deep breath. "I just left Sparks, and I talked to TK. You know him, right?"

Straight-faced, Aaron tells me, "Yeah."

"Okay. Well, he told me that someone used a candy to go back to a few days *before* this Halloween. Which is against the rules. And that

people can like . . . *sense* it now. Especially if they already use candies—
like you guys do. And I think that's partly why Hendricks and your
friends have been *such dicks* lately. Because they have this like . . .
Spidey-sense thing going on. And TK says that it's gonna get worse
before it gets better, but it'll start getting better once we get past the
day when the rule was broken. Which is Saturday. *Which is the ball.*"

I blink. I wait. He looks into my eyes like only he can.

"Okay." I nudge him. "Go."

"Did he tell you who did it?"

I shake my head, and maybe it's his elusive gaze, or that it's time
for us to start being 100 percent honest with each other, but something
makes me promise, "It wasn't me."

"I know." He faces forward now, to where the chapel sits empty at
the end of the walkway. He rests his elbows on his knees and clasps his
hands in a fist. In the dark, it looks almost like he's praying.

And then he says, "It was me."

Aaron
Saturday, December 19

THE BALL

"Tick." *Snap*. "Tick." *Snap*.

On that old wooden stage, the IVs snapped our fingers and chanted on repeat. Like a spell that turned that whole room into a giant clock while the crowd silently stared. And you felt it—on your skin, in the air—as time took over. As it *transformed* into this thing you could touch and twist and change.

The Boys and I sat in rows based on rank. Sophomores in the back, juniors in the middle, seniors—like me—up front. And five chairs set up next to Perry's mic stand—where our pledges were.

"Tick." *Snap*. "Tick." *Snap*.

Our audience sat in the dark at their tables, under all the multicolored lights. Pinks and blues and purples reflected off their tuxes and gowns and those high ceilings. Flickering across the masks that covered our eyes, or went down to our cheeks, or sometimes hid our whole faces. We were just in that damn event hall. We passed that thing *every day*. But the ball turned it into something else. The walls fell away and this town fell away, until we were in space, on some star somewhere. Slowly dying and too fucked up to care.

"Tick." *Snap*. "Tick." *Snap*.

And while they sat at those tables, masked and waiting, they weren't captivated or transfixed or mesmerized. They were salivating.

"So, what do y'all think?" Perry leaned into the mic, in a tux and mask like the rest of us onstage—only his eyes covered so he was easier to hear. He was asking the audience but smiling at the pledges. "Shall we induct some new blood brothers tonight?"

We'd already done everything that comes before that. A table sweep to make sure no one was here who shouldn't be. A round of applause for the Hendricks family—three generations in the room that night. Perry had read the pledges' biographies off note cards, all the stuff their parents did and what they owned. All the reasons we should want them.

"Well, don't just sit there all pretty like it's your first rodeo," Perry told the crowd. "Link up."

They took each other's hands like clockwork, while me and the guys kept going:

"Tick." *Snap.* "Tick." *Snap.*

The pledges shared a glance.

A week ago, one of them—Joey—had asked me what was gonna happen tonight. He'd said, "You're not gonna, like, shit in our mouths, are you?" He was joking, so I smiled.

"Nah, man," I'd told him. "We're not gonna shit in your mouth."

We were gonna do worse.

"Brotherhood is trust." Perry's voice echoed through the room. "It's not a given. It's earned." He faced the pledges. "Every guy on this stage endured what you're about to in order to gain what only we have. Every one of them earned our trust. And, in turn, we earned theirs. *That's* what makes us so powerful—the way we choose. *Who* we choose. How we choose." He glanced back at the audience, their thick anticipation hot like a blanket I couldn't kick off fast enough.

He smiled. "You guys like that? Thought I'd try out a different script this year."

They cheered. They laughed. Dudes at tables in the back hooted, *"Let's goooo!"* But they never stopped holding hands.

"Brothers!" Perry called, and three sophomores, two juniors stood up and jogged with him behind the curtain on the far side of the stage. The five we'd voted to be the newest big brothers.

The rest of us kept going: "Tick." *Snap.* "Tick." *Snap.*

The guys came from backstage wheeling a cooler. They pushed it up to the mic and stood next to Perry. Their hands rubbed together like houseflies while they waited.

Perry took the lid off. "Tick." *Snap.*

And he set it down on the stage. "Tick." *Snap.*

The crowd held their breath for magic. "Tick." *Snap.*

And when he stood, he had the knife.

"Tick." *Snap.*

The blade was as long as his forearm. Iridescent under the lights. "We've talked a lot about the brotherhood," Perry said to the room. He peeled his eyes from his hands and peered back at the tables. "Guess it's time we get to the blood."

Our audience erupted. The guys on stage did, too. They'd been waiting a whole year for this.

But I kept chanting. Snapping. On my own now.

"Tick." *Snap.* "Tick." *Snap.*

Back when it was my turn, Nik wore a mask that covered his whole face. I didn't run—there was no point. It was all of them versus one of me, and I knew how bad those odds were, even then. How bad they still are now.

The night it was my turn, they'd made one of the pledges face the crowd. Shaking and sweating through his shirt. Mask off, so he couldn't hide. And when his blood brother dug the knife into his back, through his tux, while the other big brothers held him still, it was like he screamed in reverse. Like his lungs sucked the sound in instead of pushing it out. And he stared at that crowd like any sane person would, searching for someone to save him. But all they did was cheer. And all our brothers did was laugh.

The next pledge, on that night three years ago, had his arm sliced right up the middle. Another got his hand stabbed to the stage.

And when it was my turn, and I stood in front of Nik while he took that blade from Hendricks, and it dripped with the blood of the guys who'd gone before me, I told myself I wouldn't scream, no matter what. The more we hurt, the happier they got.

But it's scary as hell when someone holds a knife up to you and you can't even see their face. You have no idea what they're thinking. What they're planning. Just you and a mask that smiles back.

I held my breath when Nik pointed the tip of that knife at me. My heart thudded so hard it was like that clock the IVs had created with their snaps and their voices was inside me. Keeping time with the ticking seconds. Counting down the moments I had left.

And you know who I'd felt the worst for?

Charlotte.

Because I could smell how bad that crowd wanted my blood. I knew there were guys on that stage who wanted it to hurt ten times more for me. And that it would never matter how many books she donated or charities she supported or kids she treated like family. Because Streetlight would always have people like this, who saw her last name—even worse on someone like me—and would destroy it all if they knew they could get away with it.

Nik dragged the tip of that blade across my throat. Down my chest. Through the palm of my hand. Each time, too light to break the skin.

But when it was time to draw blood, his eyes stared into mine from behind that white mask, and his hand was steady.

He nicked my ear. Swift and clean. I barely felt it.

No one clapped.

And when he handed the knife back, I swore Hendricks was mad enough to come back over and stab me himself.

I didn't watch the new guys get sliced this year. I hadn't watched since it was my turn. I just stared out at the crowd until their bodies blurred and their shrieking laughs were nothing more than background noise. I tic-snapped until it wasn't just *like* I was on a star somewhere, but I actually was. Drifting in multicolored darkness.

"They bleed, ladies and gentlemen!" Perry declared.

It was over. Our five pledges stood in front of us, shaking, crying, bleeding through their tuxes. Standing, at least. Sometimes they couldn't. Year after I got here, they voted the O'Grady brothers to be blood brothers—Brady and Bobby. First time blood brothers were ever biological. And Brady shoved that blade so deep in Bobby's gut he just about died.

Until we saved him.

"Still trust us?" Perry grinned.

No one ever answered, though. Shock took over.

Perry turned to the rest of us and leaned into the mic. "How about we show them why they should? Link up, Boys."

We linked at our elbows while Perry set the bloodstained knife back into the cooler. When he stood up, he was holding a single blue candy. Stowed on ice with all the rest. We chilled them so they wouldn't glow, so they'd stop burning dudes when they got too lit about the binger they were on. Some guys were so addicted to the way they tasted right off the ice that they started keeping them on ice at home.

"Crowd linked to source?" Perry asked over the mic.

Vic, who'd been at the edge of my row onstage, was leaning over the edge, holding hands with a girl at the nearest table. "Crowd linked to source," he called back.

"Pledges linked to source?" Perry asked next.

And one by one, each blood brother—one hand on their pledge's trembling shoulder and the other hand holding one of ours—said, "Pledge linked to source."

"Pledge linked to source."

"Pledge linked to source."

"Pledge linked to source."

"Pledge linked to source."

"Beautiful," Perry said. "It's like you all know what you're doing or something." Everyone laughed. "Time check?"

Jeff was Perry's link, and he gave him a glimpse at his watch. From the stage, I could hear his answer: 9:07.

"Got it," Perry said, and stayed close enough to the mic for everyone else to hear the rest. "What do you say we do about ten minutes earlier? Eight fifty-seven p.m., December nineteenth?"

The crowd's suspense was as sharp as that knife.

Perry took a final look at our bleeding pledges. Tuxes heavy with stains that grew by the second. Trembling in pain. Pale enough to pass out. But standing in spite of their weak knees, because they'd lived here their whole lives, and they blindly believed something I knew I never could:

That anything is worth it to be IV.

"Thanks for trusting us," Perry told them, and put the candy on his tongue.

I watched the crowd as the brightness crept into the edges of my vision, until their dresses and tuxes distorted like I'd taken a picture with the flash too bright, and then everything was gone.

When I blinked, no one was linked anymore. Perry was at the mic with his note cards. The pledges were back in their seats, unmarked. Breathing heavy. Patting themselves down. Alive, with no idea how.

The crowd gave a standing ovation, like it was the finale of some incredible magic act. The night that—when it happened to me—made it impossible for me to fall asleep for months. The night that made me go home and google *witchcraft*. The night I knew it didn't matter what happened from that point on, Nik had my loyalty. Because he could have tried to kill me—they *wanted* him to try—and he'd barely made a scratch.

They clapped like all that was just fun and games. Like it deserved an encore.

Perry reached into the cooler and pulled out five bags of candies. He handed one to each of our pledges. And as he placed them into their shaking hands, he smiled. "You boys clean up real nice."

Then the rest of the guys jumped them. Congratulated them.

Welcome to the brotherhood.

Tomorrow, they'd be forced to join a meeting no matter how nauseous they were from their first night using (the ball was always rough on the new guys), and at that meeting, Perry would tell them the rest of the story. About that first Spooks, and how we'd played that game by accident and walked away with magic. How, back then, all you had to do was get five balls into five jars—there was no number calling until those guys decided they wanted an exclusive. So they talked to TK—or whoever it was back then—and made the game harder. Instead of just getting five balls into five jars, you'd also have to call five numbers—in the right order—before he'd give you candies.

19234.

But Perry wasn't gonna tell that story here. Because the IVs had to be a divine right. Everything fell to shit if people stopped believing that. If *we* stopped believing that. We had to be untouchable. We had to be impenetrable. We couldn't just be *lucky*.

We were chosen.

Perry turned back to the mic and waited until everyone quieted down to remind us of the rules. He took this part seriously, because it was. And everyone was silent while he warned the crowd what to never do:

First, never use a candy to go back to a moment earlier than when the ball officially begins. An IV rule. For us, we could use from one Halloween to the next—but for anyone who was gonna get candies for the first time tonight, we changed the start date. Inventory tracking.

Second, never use a candy outside Streetlight. A TK rule. One of the terms we had to agree to if we wanted him to grant us exclusivity.

Perry told them, if they broke the rules, we'd know. We'd find them. They'd never see the ball or another good day again. It was always enough. No one wanted to fall out with The IV Boys.

And once we'd made it through the fine print, it was time for the next phase of the night. To satisfy the last rule that TK gave us before he agreed to change his game and make it harder for anyone besides us to win: He said we had to figure out a way to share.

So we did.

For a price, of course.

Perry took the mic off its stand and crooned, "Now, who's ready for an auction?"

They rushed the stage like we were famous. Grabbed for us and begged to be the next bidder. They screamed out their offers, and Perry asked us what we thought. Guys held up fingers depending on how much they felt like a bid was worth. Two candies. Four candies.

Sometimes, none. When Saige Alexander offered one of us a night with her, it took a while to decide how many candies that was worth. Some guys said eight. Some said nine.

I drifted back out to my star after not too long. Stayed there until the auction was over.

"On behalf of myself and all your favorite Boys," Perry finally said into the mic, and the girls in the crowd howled when he did, "we'd like to thank you yet again for participating in another IV auction. For welcoming our new blood. For respecting our rules. And for being a truly beautiful group of people. And with that—" He gave the room a sweeping wave. "Let the ball begin!"

Applause. Music. A few of the guys went to lock the cooler, still full of at least half our candies, in a storage closet backstage. Hendricks intercepted Perry as soon as he was back on the floor, probably to give him notes on how to do better next year.

Nik intercepted me.

"That was sick, man," he said. "The Boys did good."

I smirked. "Don't tell your friend."

Nik chuckled, and we both glanced at Hendricks and Perry's conversation; Hendricks in his ear while Perry nodded. "Hey." Nik nudged me, and I turned back to him. A green mask that went down past his nose. "Try to have fun tonight, alright?" He said the same thing to me every year.

"I hear you, man."

"Good." He started to back away. "And hey, you better surf with me later. At least once."

"Bet."

People were already using. *Getting fucked up,* we called it. The smart ones would save at least a few candies to go home with, but some of them got so hooked on the feeling that they couldn't help it. Sometimes their candies were gone before the beer was. Especially once we wheeled out the One Night Only crates, stuffed with a little bit of everything—needles, lighters, peppers hotter than the sun, crystal bowls that shattered like a splash. It's unreal how many people want to try something dumb as shit, just once. Just to see how it feels and erase the consequences.

It was the one night when I'd let my guard down. We all would. We didn't try to stuff the truth into our heads. And we didn't try to make sense of what the hell we did or why. Our masks protected us, and the energy took over, traveled through the air, and wrapped around our limbs. This out-of-body surge that made it feel like you could do something wild—be at the edge of a cliff and shove the person next to you.

Joey was swaying when I eventually bumped into him. I clapped his back. "So, we didn't shit in your mouth."

"Dude!" He gripped my shoulders. "You guys made me *a god*. Shit in my mouth all you want if I get to be *God*!"

I leaned into his ear. "Sometimes it helps to get outside. Get a little fresh air. Stare at something that doesn't move—like a tree."

"Oh, I'm good, dude, don't worry about me. Hey—brothers for life!"

He stumbled back into the crowd.

I wasn't using, but I felt it. There were too many candies happening at once to not notice the tilt, like I was leaning just a little bit, no matter how straight I stood. I'd bet cash that the new guys were gonna throw up.

Fresh air did sound good.

"Hello, sir. Leaving? Shall I get your coat?"

I didn't even realize I'd gotten that close to the door until the coat check guy stopped me. Gray hair and tuxed-up like the rest of us. Those damn dots on his bowtie slid around my vision like Pac-Man.

"Nah, I'm good. I'll be back in a minute."

I passed a group standing on the sidelines, talking low. They nodded and I did, too. Retired IVs, probably. They liked to sit back all proud at these things. The dads, and the uncles, and the businessmen, and the mayor. Taking in everything they'd helped create.

I reached the doors to the hallway and pushed.

And there you were, sitting on the floor.

Your back was against the wall like someone had thrown you there. I was convinced we'd been spinning so hard that now I was hallucinating. But you looked at me, and I knew that was real. Those tears in your eyes and how bad they made me want to disappear.

"What the fuck, Aaron?" you whispered like it took all the breath you had.

"*What are you doing here?*" I didn't know what to do with you besides get close. I knelt and held your face in my hands. I think a part of me was trying to be a shield. Shield you from them and them from you. "Are those balloons?" I peered into the paper bag you had with you.

"Fuck the ball, fuck shit up, and get out of here, right?" you said. And then, like a gut punch: "*What the hell are you guys doing?*"

I slid my hands under your arms and pulled you to your feet. And I searched your eyes for something—*anything*—that would tell me what you thought you'd seen.

"Michael, too?" you choked.

"Who the fuck is Michael?"

"*Who the fuck is Michael?*"

"KD—" We didn't have time for that—time to talk, or figure shit out, or go through the guest list. "We gotta get out of here." But it was like talking to a zombie. You didn't hear me. You weren't even looking at me. You were looking past. "Wherever you want to go, we'll go. Okay? But we gotta go. You can't stay here."

They would have destroyed you.

"Oh, fuck off," you said. Your voice was shaking, and you weren't talking to me. I glanced over my shoulder, and there was Hendricks. Leaning against the opposite wall, mask pushed to the top of his head, too focused to be a jackass. That was how I knew how bad it was—because he wasn't smirking; he wasn't thinking; he was glaring. Pupils darting. He didn't even answer you. He just watched while his fingers rubbed up and down the brick wall, forming the memory.

All I wanted to do was protect you.

So I pulled a candy out of my jacket and put it in my mouth, fast. And I kissed you even though I didn't make sure it was okay—of course, it wasn't okay—but I had to give Hendricks's mind something else. Something huge. It wasn't foolproof, but it worked that way, sometimes. The bigger the memory—the heavier it was—the more likely it was to stick. There was nothing else I could think of that might be heavier for him than seeing you in that hallway, besides—maybe—if he saw me kissing you.

The candy dissolved while my mouth was on yours. Thank God you didn't pull away.

I took us back to the day before. You'd been at my house, helping me study. And when we looked at each other across my island, you were terrified. You started crying the second you saw me.

"Let me explain," I said.

I was gonna tell you. I really was—I was ready for you to know *everything*. And I wanted you to trust me enough to tell me everything, too. What you knew, and how long you'd known, and who'd told you—or *showed* you.

But before I could calm you down and talk you through it, and apologize a thousand times—you were grabbing for your hip.

The only reason my candy beat yours was because you dropped it. You were shaking, and it rolled across the floor. And you dove for it faster than I could dive for you, and I couldn't let you swipe me—I couldn't let you do all this on your own.

So I grabbed another one of mine as fast as I could. If I went back to a few days before Spooks, that would throw Hendricks off, too. Maybe enough to forget he ever saw you at the ball at all. And then I could go to Spooks *with* you this time. See if you got your candies there or found them somewhere else, or maybe Nik was your supplier—I didn't know. I didn't have time to think about it. You were half a second from ruining your life.

So I swiped you instead.

Kady
Monday, December 14

---

5 DAYS BEFORE THE BALL

Everything collides so hard it explodes. My nightmare. The blood. My vague recollection of how sick I felt as I sank to the floor. The disappointment of walking into that event hall for the first time and realizing it was no fancier than our cafeteria. The blip in the snow at Oh Christmas Tree! and how hung up Aaron was on me going to our anti-ball. Those words that feel so familiar: "Fuck the ball, fuck shit up, and get out of here."

The images fly through my mind too fast to know what's really mine or just imagined. A boy onstage bleeding from the chest. A knife slow-sliding down his middle like a zipper.

"They torture you," I whisper.

Aaron is still facing the chapel—it's easier that way. For him, maybe. For me, definitely. "We torture each other," he corrects, head hanging.

"At least you hate it. Everyone else is laughing and loving it—I mean, *the mayor*?" How can anything be that big? And I be *so small*? "That's like Roman Empire shit . . ."

"Honestly?" He looks up from the ground. "If I'm the only one who doesn't get it, maybe I'm the problem. Dudes feel like they've been straight-up resurrected at the end. Invincible, you know?" His breath comes out like fog.

I try to catch my own. "Nik told me it was just him and me who used." It hurts so bad, admitting it to Aaron. "Like it was our secret superpower. And that's why I could never tell anyone else."

He nods and rests his forearms on his knees. "Nik's a good guy. I stand by that. He's just a liar." He cracks his knuckles. "We all are."

He lets me sit with it for a minute—everything he's said and the life I never knew. But I feel like a sponge trying to suck up the ocean, destined to drown and drift away.

"And that means these past few weeks . . . it's your second time doing them . . ."

His gray eyes are grayer under the moonlight. "Yeah. As far as I know, at least. You can't really know for sure, when a bunch of people are using at once." He scratches his head through his navy blue beanie. "We call them cycles. When you're consciously reliving a timeline. But the thing is, unless you're the one cycling . . ." He twirls his pointer next to his ear like he's winding a clock. "You pretty much just do the same stuff each time. Like . . . if you didn't know we already had this conversation, *why would* you say anything different than you would the first time? And if I *did* know we've done this before, why *wouldn't* I say something different? Even just to see what happens when I do? So the only person who really changes at all, cycle to cycle, is the person who's doing the cycling. Everyone else is just . . . doing the same thing, over and over." He clears his throat and assures me, "We haven't had this conversation before, by the way. At least, not as far as I know."

I hold my head in my hands to try to slow it all down. "Okay."

He sadly mumbles, "You're like, *What the hell is going on?*"

"*No,*" I promise. "Well, yes. But I get what you're saying. I get the cycle stuff."

Aaron wets his lips, scoots a little closer. "That's what I've been so scared about. That, as far as you knew, you were doing all this for the first time. And I couldn't let you crash that ball again, KD. There's a part of Hendricks that already knows you were there. And if he saw you again . . . if it clicked like that . . . it would have been a death sentence."

I study him. "That's why you made that bet with me."

"That's why I lost that bet," Aaron corrects. "You really think I can't eat more pizza than you?" He sucks his teeth. "Get outta here, you're wylin'."

"Yeah, okay."

"Without a doubt I would've ate more," Aaron assures himself, soft enough that I'm not supposed to hear.

I roll my eyes.

"You know, this cycle was a weird one, though." He leans back and traces the grooves in the bench with his finger. "Because after I broke the rule, a lot of the guys weren't doing what they were doing the first time. Like, there was no rumor in the first cycle. Hendricks wasn't on one like he has been lately. They were still looking at you, but it was more about being pricks now that Nik wasn't around, not this creepy accusatory shit that's been going down lately. And the anti-ball idea? *Legendary.* You guys didn't do that last cycle." He looks back up from the lines he's been tracing, and his eyes look so, so tired. Have they been like that all this time? "Please don't show up at the ball again. I'm begging you."

"I won't." For him. A breeze tickles the back of my neck. He exhales like he's been holding his breath for years. "How long have you guys been doing this?" I whisper.

"Too long," he admits. "In my first cycle, I had this talk with Phil. Jack-Laurence." I've never heard him referenced so casually. He's only ever been *Phil Jack-Laurence who just bought some soccer team* or *Phil Jack-Laurence who just invested in that new tech startup that*

CNN has been talking about. "He was driving me home from one of their charity events, and I asked him why he hates the IVs so much. Because he really does. Talks about them like they're a bunch of little bitches." He smiles at the thought. "But yeah. He told me his dad was in the IVs, dude named Greg. That he bailed because he was tired of being part of a group that was powerful enough to really make a difference and they still didn't want to change a damn thing." He shrugs. "Jack-Laurences haven't been down with the IVs ever since.

"And after I talked to him, I had this thing in my head I couldn't shake. So I talked to some of the guys. Asked them when we first got the candies. 1968. Same year Greg left." He brings his gaze back to me. "So I kind of think that's what Greg meant, you know? When he was talking about power. I feel like he meant it literally. I mean . . ." He squints. "Why the hell do we have *time* in the palm of our hands and all we ever wanna do with it is throw a weeklong party?"

It makes me nauseous. "Have parties really been weeks long?"

"You don't even want to know how long."

He's probably right.

"You don't use, do you?" I ask. It's the way he's talking about it all, the way I'm finally noticing how much it looks like he needs sleep. This hasn't been bliss for him but a burden, the kind that weighs so much your bones start to crack.

"I tried it at first. And I mean, I still have candies." He pats his side, and I guess that's where they are. Tucked away like a wallet or keys. "Because we all do. I just don't use mine. Couldn't get into it." He shakes his head. "I was always thinking about all these people stuck in these cycles that they have no idea they're even living. And maybe they could have started their own business by now. Or gotten a degree by now. Or stopped being sad over their dead dog by now. Or *just gotten the hell out of here by now*—if we'd just let them live their lives." He rubs his eyes. "That's what it feels like to me, sometimes. Like we're stealing your life."

"Your lives, too."

He cracks a sad smile. "Yeah, but we love our lives."

We're quiet for a moment—what even *is* a moment anymore?—and I hug my knees to my chest. I've never been on campus when it's dark like this, and the trees without their leaves are like claws grabbing the sky.

"Did I change?" I finally ask. "From the first cycle to this one?" He looks at me, and I go on. "You said the guys did. But did I?"

For a second, he doesn't answer, almost like he's not sure if he should. But then he nods. "Yeah. You did. Not huge stuff—it just felt like you had a shorter fuse. Probably because of how the guys were acting this go-round. Like, you never threw that drink at Hendricks the first time. And when Nik told you you weren't coming to the ball on that car ride home from Tipsy Crew, the first time you were just sad about it—got real quiet and asked me to take you home. It wasn't like that huge fight you guys had this time—screaming and getting mean with each other. And you know what else? In my first cycle, you actually took me to the fairgrounds. Before Sparks was set up, so it was a junkyard. And you got this text from Nik that you wanted me to check for you, so you gave me your code, and I'm pretty sure that's when I knew. That you had an idea about what goes on around here, I mean. But I didn't wanna believe it. And sometimes I wonder what would have happened if I just talked to you then. If maybe I could have spared you from going to that ball at all. And I should have. I should have tried. You deserved at least that much."

I close my eyes and hope that the soft breeze can blow the pictures back into my mind like Polaroids in the wind. I take a deep breath, but nothing comes. And the failure is so heavy my shoulders sink.

"I don't remember," I finally say.

"You're not supposed to." His voice is a guilt-filled apology. After a moment, he asks, "You know when we were looking at my notebooks? And I told you about how I remember stuff? Well." He takes a breath. "That's how all the guys remember stuff. Not for tests and shit they don't care about, but for life here. So that we notice it more when something feels familiar. So we can recognize when it feels like we're doing it again. TK—" He shakes his head a little. "Or someone like him . . . whoever gave us the candies to begin with—they taught us that. How to make memories stickier. So that if any of the guys ever did try to use a candy to go back earlier than that year's Halloween, we'd be the first ones to feel it."

"But why Halloween? Why does it even matter?"

"The first guys did it to protect themselves—to make sure one of them didn't swipe everyone else, and rewind time, just to hit up that first Spooks and strike a deal with TK that kept the rest of them out of it. But after a few years of training—like, learning how to remember stuff—the guys would have felt it right away if someone tried to pull that. So these days? I think we stick to the Halloween thing in part for the tradition of it all. And because it keeps us focused on the short term, the here and now. Stops the renegades from having any wild ideas about saving the world. And then there's the auction—if candies are only good for a year, then people always have to come back for more. Makes them need us." He nods to himself, this mix between knowing how smart it all is and how much it sucks.

"We have this whole meeting and everything, right after Spooks each year," he continues. "We huddle in that chapel, and drop our candies on ice, and go around in a circle recording every little thing any one of us remembered from that night. And then we play it for ourselves over and over . . . I'm telling you, if you see one of us wearing headphones the first two weeks after Spooks, that's what we're listening to. Until it's so drilled into our minds, it's like a stamp.

"And when I sat in that chapel with those dudes a second time, talking about that same Spooks all over again . . . man, it was instant. It was like the second we got in there, they smelled smoke. And I knew it'd be like that—*of course I knew*." He frowns at the darkness that he's watching now instead of me. "But it just didn't matter anymore . . . not to me." He squints like he can see the whole thing all over again, a projector flashing the scenes on the prickly air. "I know the guys have been giving you shit—and I hate that, KD, I really do—but trust me. They've been giving me shit, too."

"You risked your entire world just to try and save mine." My voice is almost too soft to hear.

His cheek twitches like he'd never thought of it that way before. "I guess so."

"You're an idiot," I declare, but I mean the opposite.

He chuckles.

"And I guess . . ." I trip over the words, so I swallow hard and try them again. "I guess that means . . . that rumor about us really wasn't a rumor after all."

And Hendricks—every time he stared at me and told me exactly what I'd done—was right.

"Yeah." Aaron swallows, too. "I'm sorry—"

"Don't be sorry—"

"No, I am. Really." His entire face means it. "Nik's my boy, and I respect you a lot, KD. Like . . . *big*. So, I know I probably shouldn't have done it, I just . . . I wanted things to be right."

I almost tell him that just because everything else isn't right, it doesn't mean that kissing me was wrong. I can't, though. It's just how crazy this night has already been. It's making me crazy, too.

"I traveled—*surfed*—with Hendricks." It feels like he should know, but I hug my legs tighter so it's easier to say. "On Thanksgiving. At Nik's house. And maybe I did it the first cycle, too, or maybe I didn't—I don't know. But he cornered me outside and was gonna make me forget, so I grabbed him. He knows I have candies. And Nik knows. And Saige knows. And maybe everyone by now. That's why I wanted to leave Nik's party early."

When I was eight and Owen was ten, the iron fell on my leg when our parents weren't home. I can't remember why we'd turned it on, but I do remember how it felt—like nothing and then like everything, a fire burning its way from my shin all the way up my left side. I was sobbing, and I knew it was bad, and Owen knew it was bad, too. But he looked at me like Aaron is now. Like it was better if I believed that it wasn't.

"Okay." He nods. He swallows. He breathes. "We'll figure it out."

He turns back to the chapel, and I don't bother to ask him how.

Instead, I stay quiet and exactly where I am. It's supposed to be in the twenties tonight, but I don't feel it. It doesn't matter when you have no idea what time it is. When some IV Boy could be on the other side of Streetlight right now, keeping us here for days and we wouldn't even know it. Or when we could make the choice ourselves—take one of Aaron's candies and have this convo inside instead. I'm not actually cold, and I'm not actually on Iverson's campus, and my stomach isn't actually as empty as it feels. Because if anything can be undone, what's real?

"Who's Michael?" Aaron asks, his voice somewhere far away. Like in the time we've spent not speaking, he's been recounting everything else, detail by detail, until he reached one that didn't make sense.

I rest my ear on my knees and face him. "He was at Nik's Thanksgiving, too. Manning the front door. I guess you guys also hire him for the ball."

"And you remembered *him*?"

He opened the door for me. Spelled my name the right way. I'm sure now that his was the voice in my nightmare—the moment I knew I was somewhere else. But, to Aaron, I say, "He took my coat." It comes out like *of course*.

He nods, thinking, but I'm not sure about what. Wondering, maybe. How he can count the number of birds in the sky and scratch surfaces until their textures are etched in his mind, but he never saw a man who was standing right in front of him.

My phone vibrates and I jump. I forgot I was even holding it, and when I check to see what the message is, Nik's name shines back at me.

My thumb unlocks my phone on reflex; the same instinct that makes me blink or breathe.

What are you doing at Iverson?

I put my phone to silent.

"What day did you take us—I mean, yourself . . ." I take a breath and try again. "What day did you end up going back to?"

"October twenty-fifth." He sighs. "No reason, really. I just had to think fast, and it was on my mind 'cause I'd been studying. Purple notebook, bent corners, Avengers stickers. The day we invaded Grenada."

The day that was imprinted in my mind, too. For far less historically significant reasons but life-changing ones for me. When I knew what it was to feel watched for the first time—the way everything speeds up and slows down at once. And, for a second, I wondered if I was as pretty as the leaves were—pretty enough to be dying. But then Nik's arms slid around me, and I knew I was safe and that I'd do anything to make him stay.

It was the day when the ball finally felt close enough to graze with my fingertips. The day I walked home with a bag full of Tupperware because Hendricks didn't want me, and I didn't know why, but it didn't matter, because I was almost who I'd always wanted to be. And while I walked down the middle of the road, with Em on the phone and those giant homes on either side of me, I finally believed that all I had to do was push up on tiptoes and really, truly reach—and I'd get there. It was *possible*.

And it was amazing.

I wonder if it felt that good the first time.

Kady
Tuesday, December 15

Nik's Range Rover is waiting outside my house when I walk out the front door to go to school. The windows are too tinted to see him, but the white smoke billowing from the exhaust tells me it's on and that he's inside.

Ignore it. But I can't. Not answering him over the past couple of days has already gone against every natural urge that I have. Before Nik left for Barnes, we used to sit somewhere and hold hands whenever we were really, really mad at each other. Until one of us cracked and started laughing about how ridiculous it was, and the other one pounced on them victoriously because they'd won the fight.

We've never had a fight too big for hand-holding.

He rolls down the window as I walk up to the driver's side. "Don't you have class or finals or something?"

There are bags under his eyes. I guess no one sleeps anymore. "This is more important," he tells me.

Up the street, all the kids who go to my school are walking in droves. Not together, but still as one. In puffy coats and backpacks. They're the same ones who went to elementary school with me, and middle school with me, and will end up at Street U with me if they don't start a job instead. Nik's seen them a thousand times, but he doesn't know it. Doesn't smile or nod as they pass. Strangers in a town too small to even have a community pool.

"It's seven a.m.," I say.

"I don't care if it's seven a.m. or three a.m. You gotta let me talk to you, Kades."

"Shawn and Em are gonna be waiting."

"I'll give them a ride."

"No." I hug myself and glance at the intersection, at the tree with the roots that are pushing up the pavement, where I meet them every day before we keep walking. "I'll text them."

I send my text as I walk around the front of the car—tell them that Nik surprised me with breakfast and I'll see them at school. Then I climb inside and yank the door shut behind me. The whole car shakes. But when it stops, we're so still that I feel it when he breathes.

He's in an Iverson hoodie and Iverson sweats, and his hair has tufts shooting in different directions—bed head that's always looked so good on him and somehow, even now, still does.

But I'm scared. I didn't know it before, but I know it now. I'm scared of who this person is, how he could smile at me the way he did and love me the way he has, while he lied to me about absolutely everything. I'm scared of the world that he invented, or at least was complicit in, and of the illusion he created that I'd be safe there. And I'm scared of what that all means—for what we were and what we can't be anymore.

"Why were you at Iverson last night?" he asks. It's the same question he texted me, still sitting unanswered on my phone.

"Just walking by." I pick at my nails. It's a lie, and we both know it, but what's one more?

"Kades, I—" His words stop like someone cut off his air supply. "I never wanted this to happen. I didn't know Hendricks was gonna talk to you about the candies—I didn't even know you had candies. He said he talked to me about it the day after Thanksgiving—asked me what you knew—but when I swore I had no idea what he was talking about, he swiped the conversation." Nik shrugs, like *What can you do?* Like Hendricks stealing his memories is no bigger deal than someone changing the TV channel while you're in the bathroom. "And when you and I were in my room, and Saige walked in . . . stuff just spiraled too fast to stop it. But you know—come on." He shifts in his seat and takes my hand. "You know I never wanted you to find out like that."

I pull my hand back and bring my knees to my chest, the heels of my shoes digging into the leather of this seat. "Then why didn't you just undo it?" I mean it as much as I don't.

"Because when I said I was gonna stop using, I did."

"You seriously want me to believe you haven't used once since this summer? Just quit cold turkey while your friends kept going?"

He frowns. He shrugs. "I told you we were gonna stop," as if that means anything at all.

"Well, I'm sure Saige would have lent you one. Or Hendricks." I won't look away so he won't either. "Who else could have lent you one?"

And even though Aaron already told me everything, I so badly want to hear it from Nik. I *need* to hear it from him. Because it's here now. We're in it—the choice that'll blow all other choices out of the water. The choice that's a million times bigger than leaving Bianchi's or defending me in an alley or even taking me to the ball. This is the choice that defines who we are. Not to each other, but as people. Is he someone who lies? Am I someone who lets him?

"It's complicated," he answers, and my heart goes into a slow, cold hibernation.

"I thought the magic was just for us," I hiss. "That we were special, and you wanted me to have it because *I* was special. To you."

"I *had* to make you think that." Nik rests his back against his door. "So that it just stayed between us. I wanted you there with me—I *did*, Kades—but I couldn't risk you finding out about anyone else because I couldn't risk anyone else finding out about you."

I squint at him through wet eyes. "What the *fuck*, Nik?"

He pushes his hand through his messy hair and soft-bangs his head against the window. "Look, Hendricks told me about the offer he made you. And I know he can be a real dick sometimes, but I really do feel like that was coming from a good place, Kades. It can't be you on your own with these candies. The people who use . . . it's like a club. It's like . . . a mini society."

It's the IVs.

"And if this gets out, it's gonna be bad. But if you can just . . . *stay quiet*. And work with them and not against them . . . I can protect you. They'll all protect you."

"But who's gonna protect Em?" My throat is on fire as my tears stream, but I can't lose my voice, not now. "Who's gonna protect Shawn? And Luka? And Owen and Milo? Who's gonna protect my parents? Or theirs?"

"No one's worried about them—trust me. They're fine. They're not using, so they're fine."

"They're not fine, Nik!" I kick the glove compartment. "They are spinning. They are swirling in this messed-up blender that you guys created while it pulverizes our lives. They don't know they're not moving forward. They don't know they're living the same days over, and over, and over again—"

"So why was it okay when we were the ones doing it?"

"What?"

"They didn't know then. When we were in that blender together for all that time. Why was it cool when it was us?"

He's right. It slams me in the chest, but he is. I've been playing this game, too. Lying to my friends, putting everyone's lives on pause just so I could kiss my boyfriend a little longer. At least, that's how it used to be, until I stopped believing in candies for fun and started using them for survival. Each one of mine fed into the same tornado that I've been sick about for days. And maybe that's the real reason why Nik always loved me, why he noticed me that night at The Drive-In, why he decided I was different from those other Have-Not girls. Not because we're electric together and laugh so hard we cry. But because he saw it in me—the ability to be a monster, just like them.

"It wasn't okay when it was us, either." My hot tears drip onto my knees.

"Kades . . . this has been going on in Streetlight forever. *And you've been happy. We've* been happy. Em, Shawn, Owen—they're not hurting. They're good. And using . . . it's just fun. You know that." He takes my hand again and holds it to his mouth. I'm too tired to pull it away. "It's just a couple months every year after Spooks leaves town. Almost everyone's used all their candies by January. And if you just let me fix this, I can. So they can keep using. You and me can start up again, too, yeah? Let's take a whole month—we'll go wherever you want and get rid of it once we get back. Okay?"

But, suddenly, all I can imagine is him with a knife, in a mask, on that stage. How he didn't try to hurt Aaron, but he still drew blood. And maybe, to Aaron, that's the most admirable thing a person can do. Maybe it *is*. But I can't stop wondering what he would have done if it had been me. If he would have cut me, too. And if making me bleed—but not that much—warranted my undying devotion or nothing at all.

I don't trust him, and I don't forgive him. But I also don't want to ruin him.

So I let myself out of the car and grab my backpack as I tell him we'll talk later. He says he can stick around today, pick me up after school. But I tell him I'll just call him. I promise I will.

"Hey, Kades?" he says before I can close the door. His arm is on the center console as he leans onto the passenger side. "All those rules he gave you when you got the candies . . . you're following them, right?"

Nik holds his breath like this is the most important part. Not us. Not the people on this side of Streetlight. Just the rules.

"Right," I mutter.

He smiles. "Good. And hey—I love you."

But I don't say it back as I shut the door. And when I start walking up the street with everyone else, I go to Find My and stop sharing my location.

Kady
Thursday, December 17

Tonight, we're walking to Freeze Street—Shawn, Em, and I—under the white-bright stars. Every storefront laced with lights, every lamppost dressed with garland. There's mistletoe over the door at Bianchi's, and three different twosomes play along in the time it takes us to walk past. An IV Boy I recognize with a girl I don't. A man carrying a toddler; he kisses her cheek while she squeals. Mr. and Mrs. Hollingsworth—they're both on the school board—kiss on their way out the door. It's standing room only at the front of the restaurant—people adorned in pearls and cashmere, smiling and laughing with tiny gift bags and boxes that are made to hold things that glitter and cost a fortune.

As we pass the giant front window, with *Bianchi's* in gold cursive across the middle, I face straight ahead and try to listen to Em instead, chatting happily about our anti-ball. I imagine her words written on the air in front of me, rolling into the sky like a teleprompter. Because it's easier that way to ignore the eyes. The stares. The way the heads in Bianchi's snap toward the window like they're under a spell, blankly watching as I pass. Candy users, young and old, or maybe past and present, or maybe both. Sensing the rule-break, the outsider, the violation. The electricity in the air. It has gotten worse, like TK promised it would.

Two more days.

The huge Christmas tree shines with lights and balls as people hold hands and skate loops around it. The star that dazzles at the top is ten pounds and has been used on the Streetlight Evergreen since 1954—a fact they taught us all in our third grade Streetlight Pride lessons. They say if you watch closely enough on Christmas Eve, you'll see Santa's sleigh fly past it.

"What do you think the difference is between haunted and enchanted?" I ask, cutting Em off. Shawn glances up from his phone—he's been caught up with some BuzzFeed article about the Kennedys for two blocks now—but he doesn't try to answer. This is an Em kind of question.

"Hmmm." She gives it a second, our shoes scraping on the cobblestones. "I don't know," she admits. "I feel like I know it when I see it—like Sparks would be enchanted, but Spooks would be haunted. I just don't know why." Her eyes brighten. "Maybe it's that people feel like enchanted is more mystical and haunted is more scary?" She frowns. "But you know I don't subscribe to that. Because Snow White was in an enchanted forest, and that sucked for her. And Casper haunted that mansion, and I've never wanted to live anywhere more."

"I have a theory." Shawn slides his phone into his pocket.

Em and I look at him, surprised. Skeptical.

"I think they're exactly the same." He shrugs. "Just depends which side of the magic you're on."

He pulls open the door to Freeze Street, and the warm air sucks us inside. Luka is behind the counter in his T-shirt and backward visor, taking an order. He smiles when he sees us, but he can't talk yet, and that's when Em tells Shawn, unequivocally, "You're right."

"Genius." I pinch his cheek so it all seems normal. But his answer wraps around me and won't let go.

"Hey!" Luka calls, and we head up to the counter now that he's done. He hugs Shawn first. Then me. Then Em. He holds her by the shoulders before their embrace ends. "We got in this peanut butter pistachio ice cream today, which sounds not okay, I know. But it's actually *so good*. And if you like it, I bet I can bring some on Saturday." To the anti-ball, he means. "We've got tons more of it in the back."

Em's eyes get big. "Ooh, samples, please."

Luka dips three tasting spoons in the vat that they have next to all the other flavors, behind the glass display. He hands one to each of us and waits hesitantly for reactions. Which is fair, honestly, after the way Shawn deemed him a sociopath when he found out he's into mint chip.

Em's smile makes me smile, the way it forms in spite of the hunk of ice cream in her mouth. "This is ridiculous," she declares.

The salty sweetness melts on my tongue, rich and smooth like chocolate. The stickiness of the peanut butter lingers on the roof of my mouth, and it sounds like it as I say, "This is like what your parents get you when you're little and you do something outrageously good. Like resuscitate an old person."

"It kind of tastes like an old person," Shawn says, holding out his hand for an extra taste.

Luka laughs as he hands more to each of us. "*What?* Eat the rich, not the old . . ."

"Not old people but old times," Shawn corrects, holding back his own laugh as he eats his second sample. "Like something they would have really eaten in *Gatsby*. Like banana pudding and shrimp cocktail."

Em scrunches her nose, trying to remember. "Is that what they ate?"

"I don't know." Shawn tosses his sample spoons in the trash. "But I think this'll be great at your party."

And now Em picks up where I cut her off outside, updating us on how many people from our school said that they're coming, and the decorations for the night, and the menu. It's her favorite thing to talk about and my favorite thing to listen to her talk about, because it helps me see the good stuff, the stuff that's so easy to forget lately. Like Luka and Shawn—how amazing they are together, how much they smile and laugh and *fit*. And maybe that makes it okay that they're spinning, because they get to live their good days again and again.

When I think about it like that, it almost makes me forget that I soft-blocked Nik after I stopped sharing my location. I haven't talked to him since I got out of the car Tuesday morning. And I almost stop wondering how much time I have left before Hendricks sends his army after me because I'm officially an enemy.

That stuff doesn't matter the same way while Em is sitting here planning, and Shawn and Luka are exactly where they should be. Because we're in this moment, and, even if we're spinning and there's nothing we can do about it, at least my friends are happy while we're here.

"So, we were watching this documentary on black holes," Luka says.

I'm not sure when we switched topics, but I glance at Shawn, because he does *not* watch documentaries on black holes.

He rolls his eyes and tells me, "We finished *The Crown*."

"And there's this *mind-blowing* Hawking theory," Luka goes on. "That's way too big for me to ever fully claim I understand but basically says that everything that gets sucked into a black hole may stay exactly the same as it was outside of the black hole. Like it doesn't blow up, or obliterate, or get flattened. It could actually just be existing—but inside of a black hole instead." He rests his hands on the counter and leans forward. "So here's the million dollar question."

Shawn nudges Em. "You warmed up?"

"Are *we* living inside of a black hole?" Luka slaps the counter and folds his arms.

"And the answer is obviously not," Shawn says, catching us up on a conversation that they've clearly already had.

"Why is it *obviously* not?!" Luka insists. "*I* don't think it has to be obviously not."

"Was Stephen Hawking, like . . . *in* the documentary?" I genuinely ask Luka. "Or was it more like a logo-slap—like those fake *Shark Tank* ads on Instagram?"

Shawn snickers.

"If we lived in a black hole . . ." Em says, already ready to accept it as a possibility. "And everything that gets sucked in stays exactly how it was on the outside . . ." Her voice comes out slowly, like she's working through a word problem. "Does it stay that way forever, or does time get sucked in, too? Like, are we aging, and stuff?"

I gnaw my lip as she thinks, her eyes squinted and strands from her bun framing her face. For a second, everyone's quiet, because nobody knows.

"Black holes can't suck up time," Shawn finally decides. "Because you can't suck up something that doesn't exist."

"*What do you mean 'time doesn't exist'?*" Luka cries. "It's literally everything! It's like . . . *the only thing.*"

"Okay, yes." Shawn allows. "But black holes are just these giant pits of excessive gravity, right? And gravity works on every*thing*, but it still needs a *thing* to latch on to. And time is a concept, which isn't tangible. It's not . . ." He shapes his hands around an imaginary ball, searching for a word. "*Physical.* You can't grab it and throw it across the room, or in the trash, *or into a black hole.*"

Again, we're quiet. Thinking. Em's dark eyes imagining the impossible.

"Would you like it?" I ask, hugging myself. "If we were in some hypothetical black hole where time isn't real? Or maybe it is real but not the way we thought it was. Do you think you'd be happy?"

They study me, trying to decide while I do, too. And the air—it's like hot rubber bands snapping my skin. Luka rubs his cheek. Maybe it's a coincidence.

"Is it all I've ever known?" Em asks.

"Yeah, it is."

She nods to herself. "Then I think I'd be okay."

The bell rings over the door, and two middle-aged women walk in. We step out of the way, and Luka builds their orders, scoop by scoop. Em rubs her neck. It's a little bit red.

Coincidence. Maybe.

The women move down to Luka's colleague to pay, and Shawn, Em, and I step back up to the counter.

"You know why I'm actually obsessed with black holes now, though?" Luka says, leaning in close. "Because they literally do *whatever* they want. They don't care at all about what physics says—they don't care what *Stephen Hawking says*. And that's so incredibly bad-ass. To just exist, you know? And defy everything. To break every rule there is, and that's what makes you real."

I blink at him, and if there was a moment since Saturday when I wished my candies weren't stuffed in my nightstand, it's now. So I can hear him say what he just said again, so I can commit the words, exactly how they came, to memory.

Because they give me an idea—*finally*—for how we might be able to stop ourselves.

Kady
Saturday, December 19

In the Iverson event hall, there's a ball full of monsters wearing masks—but this time, I'm not there.

The guys' apartment looks incredible, with shimmering tassels hanging in the corners, and fake disco balls that we taped to the ceiling, and a floor full of balloons that Shawn spent the whole afternoon blowing up. There's food from The Spot and the pistachio peanut butter ice cream that Luka brought over. The Christmas tree that we decorated a couple of weeks ago is a little Charlie Brown–ish, but it's ours, and everyone who's here brought a gift and left it under the branches—so we can each grab one before we go home.

There are people here from Street U and others from our school. Probably forty or so, in all. It's not the rager that Dexter threw, but we also promised Owen and Milo that it wouldn't be. They have a security deposit to think about.

It's the perfect group. None of them are glaring at me vacantly like dolls. None of them are whispering about me and hoping I'll hear. Everyone dressed to the theme, like we've left this town, *left this century*, and are in the pages of a book somewhere. A book sucked into a black hole where time doesn't exist.

"Thank you." I wrap my arms around Em's neck and close my eyes as I squeeze. Her draped "pearls" tangle with the frills dangling from my dress.

"Aw." She laughs into my ear. "Are you happy? You deserve to be so happy it hurts."

"It does hurt," I tell her, and squeeze a little longer.

Aaron is on his way, and that's why my heart is pumping so hard that I wonder if she feels it. When he gets here, we'll leave and say it's to go pick up pizza for everyone. And if we still can—after we go through with our plan—I'm sure we will.

I let Em go, and she's smiling, in bright red lipstick and hair that she pinned under so it looks short and bob-ish. Her white strapless dress is all sequins, and she's more blinding than sunshine on melting snow. "*Good,*" she says.

I've been hugging a lot tonight, but there's enough beer and cheap champagne that no one seems to think it's weird. I've hugged Luka. I've hugged Shawn—three times. I hugged Milo in the kitchen and Owen for the first time that I can even remember. He always has me in a head-lock, or I'm shoving him away, but we're never *hugging*. I'm surprised he let me.

"No, you can't have another party here next week," he said while we held each other.

I laughed. "Fine."

He's the DJ for the night, and right now "Primetime" by Janelle Monáe and Miguel is playing. People are dancing in the living room, and Shawn and Luka are two of them. Shawn in a silk bathrobe and pajama pants with velvet slippers and a pipe. Luka in Nik's hooded IV sweatshirt that I let him borrow, underneath a suit jacket and pants, with a bow tie and top hat. He wanted to be an IV Boy tonight.

They sing the words dramatically to each other, holding fake mics and laughing. Em twirls me under her arm and drags me over to join them.

This is better than the ball; I know it is. Even if I don't remember it, I know it so completely that I feel stupid for ever wanting that ball so bad in the first place. For pushing for it year after year, and not letting go. TK's promise warms me from the inside out. *Fate can't be undone*—and this night has always been mine. The hugs. Singing in this circle with my best friends. And whatever happens to Aaron and me once we leave.

All of it, unavoidably, written in the stars.

The apartment door opens, and he's here, looking around the room for faces he recognizes. I lean into Em's ear. "Aaron's here and we're gonna pick everyone up pizza!"

Em clutches her heart. *"Heroic."*

"What's happening?" Shawn asks, leaning in close.

"Kady and Aaron are gonna pick up pizza for everyone."

Shawn raises his eyebrows. "Need extra hands?"

"No, we've got it." And then I hug them both again. Every time feels so good. I squeeze Luka's hand and tell him, "I'll be back."

"Missss youuuu," he croons, and keeps on dancing.

I slide through the crowd, and Aaron spots me when I'm halfway there. He smiles, still in his tux. His bow tie is dangling around his neck.

"KD . . ." He sounds impressed, eyeing me from my flapper headband to my purple dress to my patent leather heels. "I see you."

I hold my arm out to the room. "Doesn't our party look better than yours?"

"Oh, no doubt." He looks around the apartment, nods at someone—probably Em or Shawn. "Do you wanna stay a little while, or should we go?"

"We can go," I tell him. Staying longer will just make it harder to leave.

We walk down the dark hallway to the elevator, and it's waiting for us when Aaron presses the button. We take it down to the lobby, and I immediately flash back to the lobby at the Pines. The penny fountains and shining tile floors. The rent has to be five times what people are paying here, but it's not better. I'd rather be here forever, if I ever have to choose.

Aaron pulls open the door, and the cold air slams me like I just fell through thin ice. My coat's upstairs, but it's not worth going back for it. Besides. *It's not real.* None of this is, as long as there are candies everywhere.

"Use mine when we get back out," Aaron says, as he unlocks the doors to his Jeep. "It's in the back."

We climb inside, and he starts blasting the heat. I point my vents toward me. "How was the ball?"

"You should know." He watches over his shoulder as he backs out of his spot. We pass under a lamppost, and there's a half smile on his face. "It's not like you've never been."

"You know, funnily enough . . ." I tap my chin. "I can't seem to remember much."

"Really?" He shifts gears, and we start moving forward. "Well, it would've been a wasted memory, anyway."

I still want it, though. All of it—not just the crumbs I've been left with. That's the thing. I don't wish I was there instead of here, and I don't yearn for an invitation like I used to, but I still feel like that memory belongs to me, that stealing it doesn't make it any less true. I want to know if I walked through the main doors or snuck through a window. I want to know what I had planned for those balloons. If they were really filled with red paint. If I showed up to stain a bunch of IVs the same way my nightmare stained me. But I'll never really know. And crumbs aren't good enough—they'll never fill me up. So lately, I wish that I didn't even have them. And that swiping . . . I don't know. That swiping could work just a little bit better.

We're driving now.

I peer out my window; I don't know where we're going. Aaron said he'd figure it out after I called him Thursday night when I got home from Freeze Street. Luka's newfound love for black holes had sucked me in. And that thing he had said about breaking the rules— how breaking all the rules was the reason they were *real*.

So I called Aaron, and I said, "What if we break the candy rules?"

"Did that, remember?" he said at the time.

"But that was an IV rule, right? That's what you said when you told me the story about the ball—you said IVs were the ones who gave the candies an expiration date. But TK made the rule about Streetlight— the one that says we can never use a candy if we're not in town. What if we break TK's rule instead?"

And now, here we are.

Maybe nothing happens, and we pick up pizza and go back to the anti-ball, accepting defeat. Or maybe everything happens—maybe the black hole collapses and we're free. Or it collapses and takes us with it. All I know is I've been following Streetlight's rules forever, and all that's done is kept me trapped where I've always been.

I hug myself.

"Nik asked about you tonight," Aaron says after a little bit. "If I've talked to you at all."

I turn to him. "What'd you say?"

" 'Not recently.' " He waits a second and adds, "He doesn't know about our conversation, or that you crashed the ball in my first cycle, or that I kissed you . . . he doesn't need to know any of that."

My already racing heart skips a beat. That's another memory that I want. The kiss.

"Doesn't it piss you off?" I glare out the windshield, and my cheeks get warm when he glances at me. "How much you can't remember? Because it got stolen?"

"Sometimes," he admits, his voice rough. "But I listen to people really closely. And I look at them really hard." His thumb scratches the steering wheel. "I don't think I forget as much as they think I do."

All the twitching, all the fidgeting, the way he looks at me like no one else can. Were those memories? Him fighting to hold on to what was happening, just in case? He keeps his eyes on the road, and it hits me all of a sudden how much he must have seen, how much he might've suffered. If he recognized some of the times when he was spinning in someone else's cycles. The hell of living in a constant state of déjà vu.

"When I used with Nik—" I swallow past the lump in my throat. "We would relive weeks at a time just to be together longer. And I never thought twice about it until I realized it was happening to me." I gnaw my lip. "I've stolen probably *thousands* of memories from you. That's a lifetime. And I'm so, so sorry."

It feels like it's been minutes before he finally says something.

"Sometimes I think about the difference between forever and never," he admits. "How many times something has to happen before it's like it's not even happening at all. The point where it's easy to turn a blind eye or tell yourself that's just the way it is. And I was *convinced* forever had reached the point of never in Streetlight. Like we'd just been doing this shit for so long there was no saving us. And then you said fuck it and crashed the ball." He smiles to himself, and I wipe my eyes. "Don't be sorry, KD. I've been needing something like you from the second I got here."

He turns on the radio, so there's noise, at least. Something more than just our breaths and anxious hearts. "Do you know where we're going?" I ask, sitting on my hands now that they're sweating.

"Yep," he tells me.

"Are we close?"

"Yep." He rests one hand on the wheel and taps along to a song I'm barely listening to. "Hey, you wanna know something else that was different about cycle one?"

Dark trees pass outside his window. "I'm assuming that's rhetorical."

He chuckles, but his teeth grab his bottom lip and hold it. "There was no Luka."

I blink. "What?"

"At least, you never mentioned him. And I feel like you would've." He frowns the same way he does when he's studying. "Right?"

"But why wouldn't we meet Luka?"

"Maybe since I didn't go to Spooks with you all the first time." He says it like there could be a million explanations, but that's the one he believes the most. "So you got there a little earlier than you did with me, or a little later, or played the shootout game a little earlier, or a little later. And Luka was in the bathroom or on a break the first time." He keeps on tapping the steering wheel. "It doesn't take much to change a lot."

There's a knot in my stomach. The kind that twists in the center of your gut when you're in a car that just barely avoids a crash. This tight little ball that holds all the scary what-ifs. How different things could have been. How different they almost were.

But as the world beyond the windshield gets less and less familiar, that knot inside me slowly unravels. And my thoughts start to swirl, not like a tornado but a Ferris wheel—bright with a beautiful view. Because if the candies are the reason why Shawn smiles like that now, and Em has someone to talk numerology with, and I met a space-loving boy who crawled into my mind and planted the idea that might actually save us, then maybe the candies—in all their hell and chaos—really were part of our fate all along.

And yeah, it sucks to think that we almost didn't meet Luka. But maybe the point is that *we did*. All because Aaron used a candy to choose me instead.

"Thank you for choosing me." My voice cracks as it hits me that that's exactly what's happened. It wasn't Nik, but it was someone. Finally.

He watches the road, while his fingers tap the steering wheel, and he takes us to wherever it is we're going. "Any time."

One song later, he turns off the main road into a stunning neighborhood. Sprawling mansions immaculately decorated for the holidays, sitting on knolls and in valleys.

Aaron slows to a stop in front of a white-brick estate with black trim. There's a wreath in every window, and there are *dozens* of windows.

"Where are we?" I ask.

He puts his car in park. "The Jack-Laurence house." He glances at the home up on the hill. "And exactly seventeen miles outside of Streetlight."

I stare at it, recounting all the stories about this family that Saige whispered to me at Thanksgiving. Some of them silly. Some almost sinister. But there's been too much else to think about since then.

"I can't go in the Jack-Laurence house dressed like a flapper!"

Aaron smiles. "Relax. We're not going in." Then his smile fades, and he reaches into his pocket. He pulls out his baggie of candies—dull and lifeless. He rolls the bag around in his hand for a second, watching it as he does. Then his gaze meets mine. "I don't want you to do this with me."

"Aaron—"

"No, for real. I've been thinking about it for two days. And I don't know what's gonna happen when we do this, but I know the guys are gonna be out for blood if it works. And I don't want you anywhere near that. I don't want you remembering any of this shit. If Hendricks, or Nik, or anyone comes to you—I want you to honestly be able to say you have no idea what they're talking about. Okay?" He's turned his whole body to face me. He's the same serious he gets when he makes me take his coat or won't let me walk home alone, and I know I can't change his mind.

"Okay."

He nods, a silent thank-you for not arguing. He opens his car door.

"Wait—" I blurt.

He shuts it again.

"You're not gonna like . . . combust or anything, right?" My adrenaline could fuel a rocket ship. "Like it's not like . . . something's gonna happen to *you* for breaking the rules, right?"

He laughs, but it's forced. He's just trying to make me feel better. "I don't think I'll combust. But I'm gonna do it out here, just in case." He shrugs a little. "Fresh whip and all."

I laugh even though none of this is funny.

He cuts the engine and climbs out of the car. I do, too. I don't bother grabbing his coat, and he's too distracted to remind me. He walks a few steps ahead until he's perfectly beneath the beam of a lamppost.

He turns to face me, but I never stopped facing him. *What the hell are we doing?* Trying, I guess. Hoping a different Streetlight will be a better one. Trusting that it's worth it, even if it's a world we've never known.

Hot tears sting my eyes as the cold chills my bones. And I focus on the way they feel, streaking down my cheeks. I notice the way his silver vest has the top button undone. I run my fingertips along the raised hairs on my arm and feel the way they tickle. I try to imprint this moment in my mind in the ways that he does and claim it permanently as mine.

Aaron chokes when he speaks across the distance between us. "As much as I don't want you to remember *this*, I still hope you somehow remember all the reasons you should want to leave this place. And know that you can. Because you really can, KD. This doesn't have to be a life sentence for you."

"I'll try," I tell him. I can't stand the thought of him worrying about me right now.

"Okay."

Then he takes a deep breath and glances around one last time. At the Jack-Laurence house. At the baggie in his hands. At me. Creating a memory, too, I think. Just in case.

He reaches into his baggie and pulls out a candy, just as a gust blows by. It whips my braids into my face, and I hurry to tame them so I don't lose sight of him. His lips move, but it's not for me to hear—it's the date he's requesting of the candies, the moment we'll all go back to, sucked into the black hole. Or maybe not.

He looks at only me, and then the candy's on his tongue.

And that's when I run, as fast as I can, right into his illuminated body, glowing under this lamppost and the moon. I knew I was doing this with him from the moment I said that I wouldn't—and maybe this is exactly what he meant when he wrote that essay about inertia. Maybe I'm living proof. Because nothing's pushing me, or pulling me, but it's everything *inside* me that's the reason why I'm moving faster than I ever have in my life.

I grip his cheeks and press my mouth against his. The kiss that was always ours, finally existing again.

"No, no, no—KD, what are you doing?" He holds my face, rushing through the seconds we have left. "You have to stay . . . you can't come with me. What's the matter with you, huh? What are you thinking?"

I'm trembling and so is he, but neither one of us lets go as we stare into each other's anxious gazes. His breath smells like nothing but magic.

"Fuck shit up and get out of here, right?" The whisper leaves my lips just in time.

And then the ground falls out from beneath our feet, and we're gone.

TOMORROW

Can't repeat the past? . . . Why, of course you can!
—F. SCOTT FITZGERALD, *THE GREAT GATSBY*

TK the Timekeeper

Streetlight's not all that different from the other towns I've been. It has families that work hard to put food on the table and ones that were born with a silver spoon. It has people who never want to leave and others who can't wait to be anywhere else. They certainly love to tell stories and sure do know how to keep secrets. Just a whole bunch of folks who spend a whole bunch of time seeing what's different about them instead of all the stuff they have in common.

But as far as I've seen, it's a little like that everywhere.

Now, I know how funny this whole thing might sound. *Time travel, TK?* The skeptics always want to say, *If time travel's real, then why don't we be seeing time travelers?* But that's the thing. *We do.* They just aren't leaping hundreds of years; they're leaping hundreds of seconds, hundreds of minutes. Fixing the little things. Giving themselves another chance. Going back to their happiest times. That's what human nature is, what just about everyone really wants, after all. To rewind a few days, a few weeks, so they can have the best things just a little bit longer or do the worst things just a little bit differently.

And I'm happy to help. It's an honor, really. Grateful every day that I've been blessed with the ability to change lives in this way, just like my daddy was blessed before me. It's the family business, you see. We've been at this for generations.

Now, I had no idea how popular I was gonna be when I got to

Streetlight. But the way that boy's eyes shined when he won my biggest prize . . . *whew*. I knew I was in for something. James Michael Hendricks II, that was his name. I never forget a name.

Lord, I thought they'd have me here forever. But unfortunately, I can't tolerate my rules being broken. Bad for business.

It's a bittersweet thing, leaving a place that kept me around for so long. But all the places I've ever been—and that's a little bit of everywhere—always let me go eventually. Once they realize their best days are still ahead of them.

And me? Oh, I'll be alright. You can play with time, but you can't stop it—you can trust me on that. It marches on, and so will I, until I find the next town where the people are as good to me as they were in Streetlight.

CREDITS

DUTTON BOOKS AND PENGUIN YOUNG READERS GROUP

ART AND DESIGN
Anna Booth
Kristin Boyle

CONTRACTS
Anton Abrahamsen

**COPYEDITORS AND
PROOFREADERS**
Rob Farren
Kat Keating
Brian Luster

EDITOR
Andrew Karre

MANAGING EDITORS
Madison Penico
Natalie Vielkind
Rye White
Jayne Ziemba

MARKETING
James Akinaka
Christina Colangelo

Alex Garber
Brianna Lockhart
Danielle Presley
Shannon Spann
Felicity Vallence

PRODUCTION MANAGER
Vanessa Robles

PUBLICITY
Karter Powell

PUBLISHER
Julie Strauss-Gabel

SALES
Raven Andrus
Jill Bailey
Andrea Baird
Maggie Brennan
Dandy Conway
Colleen Conway Ramos
Nichole Cousins
Stephanie Davey
Nicole Davies

Sara Grochowski
Lauren Mackey
Mary McGrath
Carol Monteiro
Jennifer Ridgway
Amy Rockwell
Devin Rutland
Michele Sadler
Judy Samuels
Kate Sullivan
Nicole White
Dawn Zahorik

**SCHOOL AND LIBRARY
MARKETING AND
PROMOTION**
Venessa Carson
Judith Huerta
Carmela Iaria
Trevor Ingerson
Summer Ogata
Gaby Paez

SUBSIDIARY RIGHTS
Micah Hecht

LISTENING LIBRARY

Diane McKiernan
Rebecca Waugh

THE TOBIAS LITERARY AGENCY

Ann Rose